ALICE AND THE IMPOSSIBLE GAME

ANNA FOXKIRK

FLOCK PRESS

OTHER TITLES

Passport to Love series:
Holly Ever After
The Worst Noelle
Be My Valerie
Alice in Wanderlust
Alice and the Impossible Game

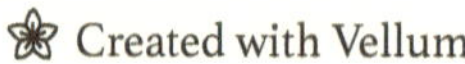 Created with Vellum

Dear reader,

'Alice and the Impossible Game' is dedicated to my petrol-head husband, Steve. We've now got a few miles on the clock together, and I'm never happier than when I'm traveling with him at my side. I'm so very grateful for his unwavering support. He never stops believing in me and my writing, no matter how badly I whinge about losing my way and messing it all up!

Steve has a fair bit of Irish in him (must be all the 'black stuff' he's sunk over the years!), and I'm rather fond of this Irish blessing which I send to you, dear reader, with my sincere best wishes wherever your road ahead may lead:

May the road rise to meet you. May the wind be always at your back. May the sunshine always warm your face, the rain fall soft upon your fields, and until we meet again, may God hold you in the palm of his hand.

Happy reading!
Anna

The only way to achieve the impossible
is to believe it is possible.
Lewis Carroll,
Alice Through the Looking Glass

AUSTRALIA

1

ALICE

Attempting to walk like you're sober as a nun while feeling giddy with lust is quite frankly impossible. I steal a sideways glance, forget to breathe altogether, and stumble over my own two feet.

Stifling a laugh, Guy steadies me with a hand on my arm and a grin on his face.

"Hold on." I pause to take off my heels.

We've known each other for less than a week and yet every time our eyes meet, it's pandemonium beneath my ribcage. I'm sober enough to realize I'm a hot mess, but not sober enough to care. I've just had the best night of my entire life singing with Guy's band, Riff-Raff, at a charity event on board a luxury yacht raising money for Australia's unsung heroes, and I feel like a ruddy champion myself. Normally I'd run a mile before stepping on stage and putting myself under the spotlight, but singing with Guy, I forgot my nerves. Now I'm feeling on top of the world. Anything is possible! It's the first hour of the first day of a brand-new year and—shoes in hand—I'm feeling properly footloose and fancy-free for the first time in my hitherto woefully uneventful existence.

On impulse, I turn to Guy. "Can I ask you a question?"

His lips quirk. "That was a question."

"Okay, smart-ass."

His dimples flash. "Ask away."

I resist the temptation to roll my eyes. "What do you think of me? I mean, my singing. How did I fare compared to Tilly? Be honest."

He laughs. "I think that's a loaded question." The way his eyes settle on mine, as if he could bore a hole direct to my core threatens to melt me into a hot puddle on the sidewalk. "But . . . you were extraordinary!"

"R-really?"

It's impossible to ignore the effect he has on me or his obvious physical assets—he's a heady cocktail of imposing height, broad shoulders, expressive eyebrows, fencepost jawline, soft eyes, and beguiling mouth. The whole damn package. I know he's got the reputation for being a tormented musician with the morals of an alley cat, and his voice makes every woman within earshot want to rip her clothes off—myself included—but there's more to Guy than that. He's no fool. I enjoy the verbal tussling. I'm in awe of his musical talent. And, believe it or not, it could just be that he's genuinely an awesome human being . . . and then some. Quite possibly a different species.

I clamp down on my mounting excitement. To be honest, I've had more than a couple of glasses of champagne and that, coupled with his come-hither eyes, probably go some way to explaining my light-headedness. Or maybe it's just blood not getting where it needs to— like my brain.

Tonight feels for all the world like I've stepped into an old Holly-wood movie, all sepia tones and fuzzy focus, the backdrop, distant music, laughter and fireworks. Sydney at showtime. Magical and mysterious. Windowpanes silvered, the breeze a warm caress, the whiff of danger and smoke from the earlier fireworks lacing the air.

"Out of interest, what d'you think of *us*?" he asks.

Beneath my bare feet, the pavement shifts from dark to amber with every streetlight. Guy and I separate like streams diverging either side of a lamppost, before coming together again.

"Us?" I repeat stupidly. He obviously means *us*, the band, RiffRaff.

The back of his hand brushes mine and heat surges up my arm as if I've been hot-wired.

"Um . . . I'd say . . . uh . . . RiffRaff's magic."

"Magic?" Smiling, he mimics my Yorkshire accent and hooks his fingertips beneath mine, drawing me close. My breath hitches as he holds my hand against his hard chest. "No, what about *us*, us . . . ?"

Us, us? There's some weird voodoo zapping through the streets tonight. No wonder I'm unraveling. "Us, we're . . . when it comes to singing . . . I think we're very compatible," I say, desperately clinging onto the vestiges of my propriety.

A chuckle rumbles in his chest vibrating through my fingertips. Heat courses through my veins and spreads like a flash fire. "Flattery will get you everywhere," he murmurs.

"Ha, ha. That's the idea. My ticket to travel." I lick my lips. His lips are so close and yet so far.

"And what about you and me?" he asks, his voice dropping a register.

I cannot breathe. Twister, my identical twin sister, who's so well-versed in all things to do with men and relationships, would tell me to play it cool. "I have no idea what you mean. I think you're exceptionally talented and I've enjoyed singing with the band, but I'm not about to become a gropey . . . *groupie!*"

He laughs.

I squirm and step away to give myself some breathing space. *Holy crap, my clodhopping tongue!* Could I be any more awkward and inept and out of my depth?

We stroll on some more, me torturing myself for making a hash of every potential relationship, while the devil on my shoulder keeps telling me I shouldn't be here in the first place. I'm an imposter. This should be Twister here, not me.

"You okay? You've gone very quiet," he says.

I'm quiet because I'm probably reading this situation all wrong.

I'm quiet because I'm burning up, caught in the bushfire between desire and desperation, and the certainty I'm going to mess this up before it's even got started. "Oh, I'm fine," I squeak, failing abysmally at sounding indifferent.

My mind strays again to Twister. Why the hell has she left? What was the situation between her and Guy? Should I ask him? Should I mention my sister is back in the UK?

"Is your place much farther?" I ask.

"Not far. Not getting cold feet, are you?"

"Dirty feet, more like."

His appreciative laugh reassures me. I can do this. God, I'm bloody hilarious! Tonight, I could give Twister a run for her money. In my head at least.

"Dirty, I approve of," says Guy, reeling me back into his arms. He pauses to cup my face between his palms before kissing me.

And.

Dear.

God.

This isn't some tonsil-tackling wrangle behind the bike sheds at school. Guy's kiss is startling and languid in equal measure. He's assured. Confident. Overwhelming. Everything I'm not.

I latch on to him limpet-fashion while Twister's advice —*Play it cool* — repeats like a persistent ringtone in my head.

Play it cool. Play it cool. Play it cool.

Cool is not possible when my brain is overheating and my heart sloshing around crotch-level. Kissing Guy is hitting every sweet spot. While my insides slide south, my hands clutch at fistfuls of his shirt, breathing in his laughter as he walks me steadily backward toward a brick wall.

Wedged between the wall and Guy, a voice whines in my head like a damn mosquito. *Oh, come on, Alice, you cannot be serious. Not here. Not like this.*

But I want this. I want *exactly* this. For once in my life, I want to be totally reckless. Guy is not only the best aphrodisiac, he's the best analgesic. No more sensible, strait-laced Alice. No more, Alice, Tilly's awkward sister. No more Alice McMalice.

Not tonight.

I swat romance-sabotaging Alice McMalice thoughts aside. If Twister can abandon me and jump on a plane back to England without apology or explanation, I'm sure I can abandon my inhibitions for one evening . . .

Classy! says the voice in my head. *So, you're going to shag him up against a brick wall next to some garbage reeking of rotten cabbage? How romantic. I suppose it'll be memorable if nothing else.*

I tear my lips from Guy's. "Not here!"

The back of Guy's fingers brush my cheek making me shiver. "Sorry, you're just so irresistible."

Me? Irresistible? I bite my lip. If the world is my oyster, I desperately want to be its shiny pearl. In front of me is my very own rock star, guitar slung across his back, his smile a magnetic force, waiting . . . So why can't I simply throw caution to the wind, dance down the street and twirl around lampposts like Twister undoubtedly would?

"Come on." Taking hold of my hand, Guy pulls me along in his wake, racing us both along the street.

"Slow down!" I gasp, gurgling with laughter as I try to match his long strides.

"My place is just around the corner. Keep up!" He grins back at me, slowing only a fraction.

This is like coasting on water or surfing a wave that's carrying me onwards and upwards. I want to shout out and yell. Tonight is the first night of the rest of my life and I *deserve* to be reckless. Tonight I'm finally stepping out of Twister's twilight and becoming my best myself. Tonight, I can be anyone I want to be: sexy diva, sex goddess, sex kitten, sex—

"Ow! Shit! Ow! Ow! Stop!" I hop about on one foot. "My bloody foot!" I wobble, still clinging on to Guy's hand trying to inspect the sole of my foot—not easy when the street lighting is so dim.

"What've you done?" Guy bends over inspecting my foot, black with grime.

"Bleedin' heck! My f-fornicating foot!"

Guy snorts. "Your fornicating foot?"

It's the *vicar's daughter* coming out in me. "Okay, fuck, my *fucking* foot!" How's that for reckless?

Unexpectedly, out of nowhere, Guys scoops me up in his arms.

Is he for real? "Don't be soft! Put me down!" I giggle.

Or maybe don't. Being carried is a novelty I could get used to. Looping my arms around his neck, I bury my face in his hair and inhale. Deeply. Good God, he smells delicious. Like the ocean and fireworks and leather and spice. A scent capsule containing this whole incredible evening that I don't want to ever end.

"How far d'you think you can carry me like this?" I ask.

"S'not that far . . . just around . . . the corner." He staggers bravely on a few more steps before putting me down and opening a gate; I sympathize with its protesting hinges. But the terraced house in front of us is a good distraction. It's enchanting. Brilliant pink bougainvillea trailing along the wall, a bijou front garden and wooden front porch, above which is a wrought-iron balustrade on the second floor. I'm already visualizing a scene from Romeo and Juliet.

"You live here? But it's so . . . so gorgeous!"

He smiles. "What were you expecting? A dump?"

"Ha, no! I don't know. Not this. I love it!" I can't keep the joy from my voice. The image of the two of us in fifty years' time sitting on those deck chairs on the front terrace, champagne flutes in hand, watching the world go by, flashes through my head before being quickly dispelled by his arm around my waist, helping me up the garden path to his front door.

"How am I meant to resist you? You're so damn gorgeous," he growls in my ear, as he props me up against the door and unlocks it.

My breath hitches as he trails kisses down my neck to my shoulder.

Me? Gorgeous? I'll take that. *Tonight, I'm the goddess of gorgeous.* I clutch his broad shoulders as the door swings open behind me. Laughing, Guy gathers me up in his arms again and lifts me over the threshold.

Ding! Dong! Church bells chime in my head. "I didn't have you pegged as a romantic."

"Ah, but you don't know me very well. Yet."

Aye, but if I have my way, I will soon. Every sexy inch of him.

Still carrying me, Guy staggers along the hallway, flicking on a light switch with his elbow while I send a football flying from the hall table with my foot. It bounces noisily across the floorboards as we pinball together along the passageway, down a couple of steps into a kitchen where Guy sets me down on a cluttered counter. He removes his guitar from his back and leans it up against the wall.

So this room is more like what I was expecting. There's crap everywhere: a mountain of clothes, an avalanche of letters, a teetering book stack and a whole lot of junk—a half-eaten apple, a squashed hat, an unwashed mug, an empty bottle of red wine, another guitar with strings draped like spaghetti over the back of a stool . . .

I take a deep breath. Okay, so it's not quite as charming in here as it was outside, but I can be cool with bohemian. Especially his brand of bohemian. I'm open to being more—

Big hands wrap around my ankles, as Guy swivels me around on the counter. I try not to be derailed by the fact he puts my filthy foot in his kitchen sink.

"What now?" I ask, leaning back, attempting to blot out thoughts of E.coli and focus on my best sex-kitten impression.

"Now I take care of you," he says.

I have to bite my lip to stop myself from purring.

My eyes track his every move as he fills the sink with water, peers at my grubby foot and pulls a face to confirm just how unsexy it is. Wetting a dishcloth and wringing it out, he lifts my foot and gently begins to wipe.

I yelp, sitting up abruptly.

"Stop being a baby, it's just a scratch."

Nervous laughter bubbles out of me. "I know that. I'm just very sensitive."

"Are you now?"

Oh hell, Alice. Remember casual? Confident? Sassy? I attempt to recapture my former sexy-diva vibe.

Guy slowly and deliberately pushes the hem of my dress up my thigh. "Wouldn't want it getting wet," he murmurs. Guy lowers my injured foot into the warm water, which swirls gray.

Hot damn. My whole core is clenched tight. I don't give a shit about getting any of me wet. He can give me a flannel wash . . . with his *tongue*—

I writhe like a cut snake as he carefully washes away more grime.

"What is this? Do you have a foot fetish?" I snap.

"Not that I know of, but I could be persuaded." His lips curve into a wicked grin. All sorts of images flash through my head. Guy's mouth tenderly kissing my instep, my ankle, then slowly trailing up the inside of my leg. Guy peeling off my clothes and taking me right here on the kitchen counter, although I'm not quite sure how the logistics of that would work. Would I need to turn sideways? Or would I—

"Ouch!"

Still holding onto my foot, Guy frowns. "I think you may have a piece of glass in there."

"It's *nowt!*"

"What?"

"It's nothing! I'm all good." Well, maybe not quite so *good* anymore. Maybe tonight I'll be a tad *bad*. "You really don't need to worry about it. It'll be fine." Although I sound like I've inhaled the contents of a helium balloon.

Guy studies my foot some more, his dark hair veiling his eyes. I couldn't care less about my damn foot. Right now, I would happily have it amputated. I just want to get back to the kissing part. My body is a cocktail of pleasure and pain. *Sex kitten, sex kitten, sex kitten!*

"Don't move." He strides from the room.

What?

Where's he gone now? I brace myself on my hands, trying out a series of poses. It's not easy, perched up here. I suck in my stomach and lean back a bit further . . . until my arms begin to shake. Bloody hell. I'm not sure I'm cut out to be a sex kitten.

I barely have chance to rearrange my hair and gather my wits before Guy comes striding back in, towel slung over one shoulder, brandishing a red plastic first-aid kit. "Found it!" He lifts my foot from the water and gently dries it.

"You're going to ruin your towel," I say. Good one, Alice. Oh, so sexy.

"Hmmm." Guy inspects the sole of my foot, dries it and then with tweezers, removes a tiny shard of glass and holds it aloft for me to inspect.

"What man owns tweezers?"

"This one, and aren't you glad I do?" He laughs as he discards the glass in the bin. Then he applies a plaster to my foot.

Eyes fixed on my face, he lifts my foot to his mouth and, staring into my eyes, kisses my instep. "Better?"

"Argggh!" I'm very ticklish. I attempt to jerk my leg away, but he holds it fast in his grip.

Despite being lean, he's strong, his forearms corded with muscle. "Not so fast. Give me your other foot."

"You've got to be kidding. My other foot is fine!"

"It needs washing."

"I thought you said you approved of dirty."

"That rather depends on what we're referring to." Smiling, he runs clean water into the sink.

Enough already. "You're a sadist!"

His dimples reappear. He eases my good foot into the sink, then gently begins to massage it with the warm, soapy water.

"Oh . . . oh! Oh! That's . . . ah . . . *Mee-ooow!*" There's no stopping the mewling, but that's about as far as my sex-kitten impression goes.

His wicked smile broadens as I crumple, throwing my arms around his shoulders. "Guy, please!" With Guy between my legs, my red silk evening dress rucked up around my hips, my damaged foot dangling behind him and my other foot in his very capable hands, I'm ready for anything. Wet hands trace two fiery lines from my ankles, along my calves and up my inner thighs. He draws me closer still, wrapping my legs around his hips.

"Ready?" he asks.

"Yes!" I croak. "I've never been readier!" I can barely get the words out, let alone speak coherent English. Just as I think I'm going to start growling, his hands encase my backside, and he carries me across the room. I am in awe of this man's strength.

"I'm putting you down." I'm also in awe that he doesn't just dump me; he lowers me carefully to my feet. "Okay?"

I nod, unable to find the words, happy for him to take the lead.

He steps behind me, hooks his fingers beneath the straps of my dress, and slides them off my shoulders. "You're so damn beautiful."

Me, beautiful.

Slowly, he unzips my dress.

I shiver as the satin slithers to the floor. I'm in danger of doing the same myself, but with one hand pressed against my stomach, he holds me against him while he kisses the nape of my neck. Heat spreads everywhere.

Oh. Good. God.

His breath is hot in my ear. "Christ, I want you so much Tilly."

Oh.

God.

What the actual fuck!

It's like stubbing my toe.

Fuck, seriously just fuck! Like slamming my fingers in a door slammed. Like being stabbed between the ribs with a knife. The pain is so sharp I'm unable to breathe. Unable to speak. Unable to believe what he just called me.

And then, thankfully, my brain takes control. I wrench myself from his hands, spinning around to face him, inadvertently stepping on my injured heel—"Ow!"—before shoving him off me. "What the hell did you just call me?"

His face pales. His smile slides from his face. His lips tighten. We both know very well. "I'm not sure. I wasn't—"

"You called me Tilly!" I grit my teeth. If I were a sex kitten for real,

I'd be claws out, back arched and fur standing on end, hissing. Most times I don't mind people mistaking me for Twister, but tonight is not one of those nights. Not when I had such high hopes . . . and Guy at my fingertips.

"I'm sorry, I—"

"You're sorry? Shit! Shitting, fucking, Mcfuckery!" I cannot believe the language coming out of my mouth: Twister would be impressed; my parents would be horribly disappointed. I blink like a maniac to keep the unshed tears from spilling. I've got to get the hell out of here before I start ugly sobbing.

And hissing and spitting.

"I'm not Tilly, you moron, I'm Alice!

Tonight is not going to be *the night*, after all. It's going to be another one of *those* nights.

"Dammit, I know you're Alice. I don't know what I was thinking." Guy smacks the heel of his hand against his forehead.

I think it's pretty clear what he was thinking, or at least *who* he was thinking about. Tilly. Twister. My dear beloved sister. Perhaps he'd like *me* to smack his head for him. I'd do it a damn sight harder. Maybe smack some sense into his thick Neanderthal skull. And mine. What an idiot. What a fool. What a loser.

A nervous laugh escapes him. "Tilly's name just slipped out. I'm sorry." He shrugs. "Honest, Alice. I just know Tilly better than you. I'm used to spending time with her. It just came out."

Just how well does he know her? How much time does he spend with my sister? He could have lied to me about the whole thing.

"I'm sorry," he says, lips compressed into a tight line.

I should have listened to Alice McMalice after all. "Not half as sorry as I am," I say, fumbling blindly for my dress. "And for the record, I'm not interested in your apologies!"

"It was a simple mistake," he says.

"Damn right it was. This whole evening was a mistake." Alice, the sexy diva, has well and truly been put back in her rightful place. Any magical whimsy has fled along with the sex kitten out through some invisible cat flap. Breathing noisily through my nose, biting my lower lip, refusing to howl at the unfairness of it all, I scramble into my dress, only to hear an audible rip as I yank it upward.

Fan-bloody-tastic. Wouldn't you know it?

"It was a simple slip of the tongue, Alice. Nothing more. Alice? Forgive me, Alice. Alice!" He repeats my name like a mantra, like if he says it enough times, he'll convince me he's genuine. Or perhaps remember who he's trying to screw.

"Calling me Tilly might've been a slip of the tongue but kissing me was clearly a slip of your limited brain cells into your gonads. You're right, *this* means nothing. *This*,"—I gesture wildly between us —"is not happening. Not in a million years. I've no idea what the hell I'm even doing here. I must be mad. I'm not some consolation prize for you not having Tilly. It was bad enough pretending to be her tonight singing with RiffRaff, but you know what my worst mistake in all of this is?"

Guy has gone pale, his shoulders hunched, and his hands tucked into his jean pockets.

"Thinking for one moment you might actually like *me*." A sob escapes me. I'm utterly pathetic. And desperate to get the hell out of here before I fall apart entirely. But I'm struggling to fasten my bloody zip which appears to have snagged. God, I can't even manage to do *angry* properly.

"Here, let me," mumbles Guy.

Wretchedly I turn my back on him and tears slide from my eyes.

"I do really like you," he says. Then the jerk places his hands on my shoulders.

I shoot forward as if he's jabbed me with a pitchfork. "Don't you dare touch me! You . . . you . . ." I limp over to the kitchen counter to retrieve my bag, knocking a sheaf of papers to the floor in the process. "You manky bastard! You need to sort out your life. Tidy your shit up! You're a health hazard! You only like me because I look like Tilly, but once you got to know the real me, let me tell you, you'd be sorely disappointed. The real me is nothing like my sister. I don't need this shit. Or you!"

The vision of Twister's miserable expression the last time I'd seen her flashes before my eyes. She must have been upset because of Guy. That must be why she wouldn't open the door to him.

"Answer me one thing, and tell me the truth for a change because I've had it up to here with your bullshit. You and Tilly were an item, weren't you?"

A muscle pulses in his jaw. "An item as in we sing together, yes, but not like you're implying."

"So what, you just use each other for sex? Friends with benefits and all that bullshit. You self-centered, egotistical . . . *bastard!* I'm not in the least bit surprised she's done a runner back to the UK—"

"Hold on, what? Tilly's in the UK?"

A snort escapes me. "You mean she didn't tell you? Too bad. Guess she's just not that into you. But believe me, if I find out *you're* the reason she's left the country, I'll come back here and bloody string you up. Men like you don't care how many lives you screw up, do you? Flippin' heck, I need my head examined, and you"—I poke him in the chest for good measure—"*you* need castrating!"

In case it's escaped anyone's notice, the first day of the new year is turning out to be the worst day of my life.

2
____

GUY

I'm sure there are worse ways to start the year than in the company of a thumping hangover and plagued by the knowledge I've fucked up big time, but right now, staring at the news headline that's popped up on my email feed, I can only see the black downhill slide.

I groan. There are a few blurry photos of me with my arm around Alice's shoulders. To be honest, it could be a photo of me and any girl, taken in any damn place, but it's hardly what I want to see right now, and I don't want to even begin to think how Alice will react.

Grabbing another beer, I collapse on the couch and flick through the socials. Crap, the same story is running on numerous media accounts. Where are my mates when I need to bellyache? I share the house with Brum, Fin and Scooter, but right now, even though it's like two in the morning, they're out raising hell elsewhere.

"Fuck!"

Perhaps I should be flattered I've made the news at all, but it would be nice if the gossip was about the music and not this sort of trash.

My mouth twists into a grimace. And then, a rueful smile. I've got to hand it to Alice, the girl gave me a right royal roasting. Is it bad to be both crucified and simultaneously turned on by the memory of how hot she looked when she was angry? Yup. I'm undoubtedly an asshole. But she was undoubtedly undeniably *hot*. HOT in a cruise missile do-not-touch-me-or-I-will-annihilate-your-ass-to-oblivion kind of way. Imagine her reaction if she sees these photos.

Holy crap. Shaking my head, I can't help chuckling. Why I am finding this situation remotely entertaining is beyond me, but it's like my life has become a runaway train ever since Tilly joined the band and all I can do now is hang on for the ride.

Absentmindedly, I scratch my stomach. There's one bloody bugbear bugging the hell out of me. Why has Tilly pissed off back to England without mentioning it? To any of us? That sucks. That's seriously flaky. I'm pissed she's left without any explanation or warning, but also concerned. It takes a hell of a lot to rattle Tilly, and I fucking hate admitting how integral she's become to RiffRaff's growing popularity. Somehow, she made the band feel complete. Somehow, since she joined, our popularity seemed to be on the up . . . If only she wasn't quite so un-fucking-reliable.

I probably should wait until I've had some decent sleep and I'm feeling sober, but Tilly needs to provide some answers. It's the least she can do.

Surprise, surprise, she doesn't answer her phone, so I leave a voice message.

"Hey Tills, what's this about you being back in the UK? What happened? When were you going to tell me at any point? Also, in case it slipped your mind, we're meant to be playing at my brother's wedding in less than a week . . ." I pause. I've been more curt than tactful, but the longer I chew on this, the madder it makes me. What if she doesn't come back at all? Do I replace her? She's already on all our posters for gigs this year. I've written her into the music scores. Having no female band member changes the whole dynamic of Riff-Raff. "Tills, maybe you'd be kind enough to call me and let me know when you're coming back." Damn. I can't keep the aggro out of my voice. "Please."

There's no response. But perhaps I shouldn't be surprised. I haven't exactly been at my most charming, but I'm not feeling too sympathetic at present. If I want to get any sort of response out of Tilly, I suspect there's a better way to get her attention.

"Oh, yeah, you're probably wondering how I know you're in the UK and that wasn't you I was singing with tonight. Alice let slip when I kind of hooked up with her . . . I know it's against our *band-mates-are-not-fuck-mates* rule but given I'd figured out she was an imposter, I thought, you know, fair cop. She's not really in the band and—"

My phone lights up with an incoming call.

"You bloody didn't!" says Tilly when I connect. "I don't believe it." There's a hard edge to her voice she normally reserves for assholes in the audience.

"Which part? That my brother is getting married or I hooked up with Alice?"

"Alice wouldn't . . . Alice wouldn't get involved with the likes of you!"

"Why thank you."

"You're welcome, dipshit. What the hell, Guy? Are you serious? You messed with my sister?"

I sigh. "No. Keep your hair on. I only kissed her. Besides, accidentally calling her Tilly threw a spanner in any romantic notions I may have had."

She snorts. "Ha! Like you have a romantic bone in your body. How did she react?"

"Madder than a cut snake."

"Can't say I blame her."

I hold the phone away from my ear as Tilly starts on a rant. She's normally pretty laid back and this pissy-sounding Tilly is an actual earache. "God. Stop busting my balls. We only kissed."

"You sure?"

I clear my throat. "Okay, I may have removed her dress."

"Don't joke about this, you jerk. And don't tell me to calm down. This is my sister we're talking about."

"Yeah, I gathered. I'm intrigued to know why you didn't mention before now that you had an identical twin."

There's a pause. "I forgot."

I snort. "Of course, you did. So easy to forget one has a sibling who looks identical to you—"

"We lead very separate lives and maybe I wanted to protect her. She's not equipped to deal with dickheads like you. I'm amazed she let you anywhere near her."

"Harsh." Very harsh. Tilly is not usually this uptight, but I guess this is her sister we're talking about.

"Your scoresheet with women is not exactly brief."

"Yeah, so, maybe I like to share myself around being the hot lead singer of the hottest band in town an' all."

"Get over yourself! You and RiffRaff are tepid at best. And Alice has more refined tastes. She'd never fall for your brand of bad boy."

"Oh really. So what if she did?"

She sighs theatrically. "Let's not even go there. You'd better fill me in. What actually happened?"

I give her a brief, somewhat edited, run down of our singing rehearsals, the awesome New Year's Eve event on the luxury yacht, and Alice's performance. Just thinking about singing with her brings a smile to my lips. There's a quality to her voice that Tilly doesn't have. Where Tilly exudes raw sex appeal, Alice's voice is . . . pure. Almost celestial. Definitely pearly-gates-of-heaven and out-of-reach angelic. But I brush over it. I need Tilly back without any sibling rivalry getting in the way. I don't want her thinking I have the hots for her sister. I give her an honest, if somewhat edited, rundown of New Year's Eve. I even mention it may have been my fault Alice dropped her phone overboard. The wreck I made of the situation back at our house is heavily edited because I'd really prefer the reason for Tilly's return not just to be to string me up by the balls.

Her silence on the other end of the line when I've finished filling her in on the whole Alice balls-up is unnerving.

"Look, you have my word. If you get your ass back out here pronto I even promise not to go near her again. RiffRaff isn't the same without you," I add grudgingly.

"Awww! As flattering as that is, I can' t . . . Not for the foreseeable future, anyhow."

"What the fuck, Tilly?! Why?" I demand.

"Can you stop asking so many questions? It's private, okay."

Not okay, I groan. This conversation is not exactly reassuring me any. "This isn't fair to RiffRaff. Or Alice."

"Life isn't fair." There's silence for a while. "How did you leave things with her?" asks Tilly.

"She more or less slammed the door in my face and told me I was Satan, but apart from that, yeah great."

She scoffs. "God. You are such a douche."

"Thanks again."

"Damn it, Guy! You have literally FUBARed this whole situation. Now, she'll probably want to get on the first plane home. I was kind of hoping she might stay and sing with RiffRaff in my place for a while."

"What? And you thought we wouldn't notice the difference?"

"Hmm. I wasn't thinking straight, but it's not too late to rectify the situation."

"You think?" I'm not convinced. "You wouldn't prefer just to tell her you'll be on the next flight back here?" There is no answer. "You are coming back, aren't you? Even if you're not here in time for my brother's wedding, we have a full list of gigs this summer." *I fucking hate how needy I sound.*

"Sorry, I really can't make any promises . . ."

"Great! What am I supposed to tell the guys?"

"Shit happens? I was not expecting . . ." Her voice quavers, which is very unlike the tough-as-tits girl I know. "I just can't be there right now. Don't get mad at me, please, but I can't give you details."

"Are you okay? You're not dying or anything are you? Because if you are I take back all that nasty shit I said to you."

Her laugh sounds a bit broken. "I'm fine."

"Well, if you're fine, fucking hell. This is shit! I thought we had a deal. We've just got to the point when the band is gaining traction, and this bullshit is going to put us back to square one!"

"Oh, quit catastrophizing! I'll sort it."

I fail to see how, but I grit my teeth and say nothing.

"Look, I'm really sorry," she says. "I was kind of hoping Alice might enjoy being part of the band. I was then going to talk to her about taking my place. It'd have done us all a favor and no-one would have needed be any the wiser. Alice needs to have some fun. Loosen up. Enjoy herself. Show the world how incredibly talented she is."

I can't argue with that. "So, what do you suggest, smart-ass?"

Tilly clears her throat. "There may be a way to twist her arm . . . I have an idea that might work . . . If you could do me a bit of a favor and play along. I think between the two of us we could persuade Alice to hold the fort for a while."

Why don't I like the sound of this already? I haven't even heard her out yet, but Tilly's mind is a rabbit warren. She can be as kind, as she can be cruel. As unpredictable, as she is unreliable. But despite her hard-ass attitude, she's also totally balls-on-the-line supportive whenever we've needed her.

And I'm all out of ideas myself.

"I don't see how you're going to persuade your sister to come within five feet of me, let alone sing with the band again. From that last look she tossed at me, I imagine she'd probably rather eat strychnine."

"Leave it with me," says Tilly, unperturbed. "Alice owes me. And she has a forgiving nature. With a little coaxing, I'm sure she'll come round."

"I doubt even coaxing with a cattle prod will make her come round."

"Have a little faith. Believe in the impossible."

"Says the woman who just destroyed my life."

"No, I haven't. Look, first off, go and buy her a replacement phone. I'll transfer you the money for it. And go to see her in person. Tell her, the phone's from you. That'll be a step toward mending bridges. I have a feeling this is all going to work out just fine."

I also have a feeling my next few weeks are joining the sewage on a one-way trip to Shitsville.

"Fine," I say, too knackered to keep arguing.

"And tell Alice to ring me as soon as possible. Tell her it's urgent. And can you also give me another call afterward to let me know how she's *really* doing?"

"Anything else, ma'am?" I snap.

"Try to be nice if that's in your wheelhouse. I'm about to put her through hell."

3

ALICE

1st January

I am Down Under in Hell. Seriously, Twister has left me in Sydney without any sort of explanation and I've just made a total tit of myself over a guy. It's the first day of the new year and instead of feeling excited and full of hope, I feel like total CRAP! I can't believe I fell for his utter bullshit. I can't even call Twister to talk about it because I haven't got a phone. And I can't help but worry I may have unknowingly screwed her over. Again. I'm not sure she's forgiven me for Colin yet, so God knows how she'll react when she finds out about me kissing Guy.

My New Year's resolutions:

1. Do NOT even think about GB. He is not worth the time of day.

2. Find out what's going on with Twister and do whatever it takes to fix this situation.

3. Do NOT look at another man while I am traveling . . . let alone men Twister has shown a passing interest in.

4. Stick to my resolutions for more than five minutes!

I n the gray hours before dawn, lying on the lumpy futon in our shoebox apartment in Paddington, I chew over the events of the last couple of days like they're gristle.

Twister pleaded with me to pretend to be her and sing with Guy and his band, RiffRaff, for a New Year's Eve event for heroes on board a luxury yacht. As we're identical and I've been studying her my whole life, it was pretty easy to imitate her. And I almost got away with it too. RiffRaff's performance had gone well. I'd stepped outside my comfort zone and survived. Almost. If only I hadn't got swept up in the aftermath and stupidly believed what I felt for Guy was in any way reciprocated. Thinking about him makes my throat tighten and my eyes prick. God, I've made such a fool of myself, and for what? A guy who, in the heat of the moment, couldn't even remember my name. A guy who may or may not have been screwing my sister. A guy who may have the body of an Adonis and be an incredibly talented musician to boot but plays hard and fast with women's feelings. Talent is certainly no excuse for me having practically thrown myself at him.

The walled-in sensation of panic presses heavily on my chest. What if this gives Twister an excuse to bring up Colin again? What if this time she doesn't forgive me? What if she never trusts me again? Never wants to speak to me?

It sounds pathetic, but I cannot imagine life without my sister. I'm nothing without her. Yin without yang. Bread without butter. Living without purpose. Or something like that.

The thing is, with Twister, her reaction could go any which way.

Hence her nickname. She's the human equivalent of a tornado. She could shrug this off… or she could make my life a living hell.

Switching on the kettle, I flop on the couch and stare at the flaky ceiling. The ceiling could be a metaphor for my life: hopes, dreams, travel plans all delaminating. I have to talk to Twister and soon, but my guts are knotted worse than a pretzel.

Returning to the journal she gave me for Christmas, I chew the end of my pen. My mind keeps bolting. Trying so hard not to think of Guy makes my head spin … or it could be that I'm hungover. Putting pen to paper, I finally start writing:

> *Tbh, it pisses me off that Twister's buggered off back home without any warning or explanation when we're supposed to be traveling together and after we've been saving up for what feels like forever! But it pisses me off even more that Guy turned out to be such a wanker. Ugh! And I've potentially managed to be thoughtless and selfish and hurt Twister in the process. Again.*
>
> *This year was meant to be so good. It was meant to be the two of us seeing the world and finding ourselves, and not being distracted by assholes like Guy and Colin and Axel… Needless to say, I'm having a super sucky time and it's a very unhappy start to the year!*

'Sometimes you win and sometimes you learn,' Mum would say, but she's not here to jolly me along, is she? Honest to God, sometimes, I only feel like I'm a high achiever when it comes to failing at life … and men.

> *Sometimes it is so damn hard to be positive and grateful. I suppose if I spill my worst fears onto the page, at least it'll keep me from spilling my guts to anyone else. Not that there is anyone else to spill to …*

I groan out loud and scribble with a flourish,

I hate writing this sodding journal!

—before throwing my pen down.

Writing solves nothing. I need to take *action*. Get the next flight back home and sort things out with Twister. I need to do whatever it takes to make this right. Being hungover isn't helping matters any. My head pulses like a troll having a rave in my skull. In the bathroom, I stare at myself in the mirror: I'm a pasty shade of green.

Housework has always proven a failsafe technique to soothe my tortured soul in the past so, despite feeling shaky and sick, I sweep and mop the floor, clean out the fridge—easily done, as it's very bare and everything is already sparkling white—do a half-load of laundry, plump cushions, dust where there is no dust—

Until someone raps on the front door.

4

GUY

I've rehearsed what I'm going to say, but I still feel like a douche standing outside Alice's apartment trying to inveigle my way back into her good books. I don't do this sort of shit—go cap in hand to ask a woman for forgiveness. Not ever. It's not like I'm asking her to be my girlfriend, but this situation feels ominously like I might be about to deliberately step on chewing gum. I've a hunch at some point in the not-too-distant future getting unstuck is going to be a messy fucking business. But I have my music, my band and my career to consider . . .

As well as feeling embarrassed about coming cap in hand, I have some serious doubts about Tilly's mad plan, the details of which are still somewhat obscure, possibly even to her. *Just play along,* she says. *Be your most charming self,* she says. *Unless you have any better ideas, if you want her to replace me until I return, you'd better get with the program,* she says.

So here I am, getting with Tilly's whacked program. Needs must. I have RiffRaff's future to think about, and it's not like I'm planning to do Alice any actual harm. Tilly assured me this would actually help Alice. I'm here to help. Fuck, I'm practically a good Samaritan.

I hammer on the door, but there's no response.

"Alice? Alice, you in there?" I knock again.

The muffled sound of footsteps. "If that's who I think it is, get lost!"

Right. Promising start. But I can't be deterred at the first hurdle even if this does feel kind of stalker-ish.

It sounds like she's pacing back and forth on the other side of the door.

"Please, Alice. At least give me the chance to apologize." I pause and put my ear to the door. Now it sounds like she's dragging something. Maybe she's boarding up the door with furniture as a precaution to keep me out? "Alice, I just wanted to tell you how sorry I am. I know I've been a fucking idiot, and I wanted to let you know I talked to Tilly and she—"

"You what?"

The door is flung open, and I stumble forward, almost crushing Alice underfoot.

"Get out!" she shouts, shoving me out the door again.

"Sorry. I'm really sorry," I say, holding up my hands. I don't want Alice thinking I'm trying to overstep any boundaries.

Discreetly, I inhale. The apartment smells distinctly of cleaning products, and Alice, clad in an apron and yellow latex gloves, is armed with a bottle of Ajax and a blue cloth. It does strange things to my insides. All things considered, despite her hair looking like a bird nested in there last night, Alice with bedhead and wearing an apron is strangely disconcerting. I'm tempted to brush the stray hair out of her eyes, but I suspect she'd be likely to squirt bleach in my face if I tried, so I shove my hands in my pockets instead and do my best to look harmless.

I can't help but notice the packed rucksack propped against the wall. Far out! Tilly was right about Alice getting the first plane home, but I thought she was exaggerating.

Alice dumps the cloth and Ajax bottle on the counter (which I consider a bit of a win as at least she's no longer armed), before folding her arms across her chest and scowling. No mistaking that body language: *Fuck off and never darken my doorstep again!*

My heart patters for no good reason—probably because this is awkward as fuck. Or maybe because she's even scarier than Tilly when she's in fight mode. What is it with these Havoc women? Clearly, she's upset, and I want to tell her I feel bad about that, but—

"What did she say?" she demands without preamble.

"Oh. Um. Yeah. Lots." Why am I stumbling over my words like a teenager?

"How is she?" asks Alice.

"Yeah. Um. Good." What is not good is the wayward images that keep striking out of the blue destroying any rational clear thinking— If Alice were to bend over and scrub the floor wearing just that apron —Yeah, like that's ever going to happen. Perhaps I should ask her to clean up the filthy mess that is my brain.

"So? You spoke to her? What did she say?"

This feels like a trick question. "Oh . . . um . . . yeah . . . lots." Bloody aye! I am already on a back foot sounding like a brainless teenager.

"How is she?" Alice rolls her eyes.

"Fine." Actually, I forgot to ask. My whole brain has been fed into a mincer.

"Did she tell you why she left?"

"Um . . . no. Not really." Again, I think I may have asked, but she deflected. I think. Damn, why didn't I get to the bottom of things while I had Tilly on the phone?

Alice sighs with exasperation and pushes a lock of hair out of her eyes with the back of her hand. She looks as if she's trying to summon up the appropriate energy just to laser me with her eyes. "So? Why are you here?" she asks like I'm some sort of religious zealot trying to sell her a bible.

I scratch the back of my neck, my brain now vacuum-sealed and prepped for a gentle *sous vide*.

Tilly hasn't told me specifically that I can't tell Alice that she wants to know how Alice is doing and then report back to her. But I'm not the total moron Alice obviously thinks I am. At least I hope not. Although I am acting like it. Probably best not to let her know Tilly wants me to keep an eye on her though. "She was concerned about you . . . obviously," I blather, "and she asked me to ask you to ring her."

"And how am I supposed to do that without a phone?" she snaps, grabbing hold of the door.

"Well, that's why I bought you this. I feel like it was kind of my fault you dropped your phone last night," I say, as she attempts to slam the door on my arm.

"Get your arm out of my bloody door! I don't want anything from the likes of you."

Ouch! I wedge my shoulder between the door and the doorframe. "For God's sake, just take it!" Honestly, the things I've done for the sake of RiffRaff: I should probably be sainted.

"Give me three good reasons I should even give you the time of day."

Whoever thought giving someone a free phone would be quite so challenging. "Okay! One, it was my fault you dropped your phone. Two, I said I'd get you a replacement. And . . . oh yeah, three, Tilly asked me to tell you it's urgent, and she needs to speak to you as soon as possible." I feel every bit as choked as I sound because the funny bone of my elbow is fizzing in a very unfunny way where the door caught it.

She chews her lower lip. Exactly like Tilly. Only when Alice does it, it ignites something uncomfortable and hot in my chest.

"Please. Take it. I'm not selling you crack, I'm just asking you to call your sister." I squeeze the plastic bag through the gap in the door and hope she doesn't amputate my fingers.

She snatches it, I snatch my hand back and the door slams. I hear the lock click and lean my head up against the wood. I rub my elbow. I feel like the biggest jerk on the planet right now. I just want to get out of here. But before I do, I go . . . Dear God. It sounds like she might be crying. I didn't think it was possible to feel worse than when I arrived.

"I'm sorry, Alice. Sincerely. You and Tilly are just so . . . similar." *Gah*, talk about stating the bleeding obvious. "I mean, I know you're not her and you're you . . . and you're both equally talented in your own way. And very lovely." Tilly was right—I am such a dipshit. "I like you, Alice, but she's . . . um . . . I need Tilly." Fuck, I may as well stuff both feet in my mouth. "I'm sorry. Okay? That's all I came to say. I'm sorry!"

"You and me both. Now leave me alone," Alice says through the door.

After a minute of huffing and blowing and wanting to punch something, I push away from the door and manage to walk back to the elevator without hurling myself over the balustrade.

For some reason, seeing Alice again in the sober light of day has made this much worse. It is not easy leaving knowing she thinks I'm scum. I shouldn't care what she thinks. But I do.

Perhaps I can vent some of that in a new song.

A Song for Alice.

Won't that be joyful. A real palate cleanser.

And Jeez Louise, I need to get the image of Alice in that apron out of my head.

And I also need to call Tilly again and receive another ear bashing.

And, "Bloody Havoc women!" I mutter, startling an elderly lady at the bus stop.

"Havoc? It's not our fault!" she snaps. "Bloody men have a lot to answer for!"

"Right. Of course, we do. Sorry." I place my hand on my chest and back away.

"Bloody larrikin!" she mutters. "Nearly gave me a heart attack."

Which is when the slight skid of my flipflop tells me I stepped in dog turd.

"You get your just desserts in life!" The elderly woman cackles.

Way to go. So the year is off to a cracking start.

Last night, on New Year's Eve, I had such high hopes. This morning, my hopes are literal turds.

My New Year's resolution should be a no brainer: avoid stepping in any more shit.

5

———

ALICE

Inside the bag is a brand-new iPhone and a handwritten note from Guy with my name on it.

Dear Alice,

I could not be more sorry that I hurt you and screwed up so badly.

I think you're incredible and not because you remind me of Tilly. You sing like an angel. You're so very talented. It was a privilege to share the stage with you last night.

There's no excuse for my clanger afterwards other than to say my mind was officially blown. By you. It still is. Words fail me, but I really hope you can come to forgive me.

Please accept this phone by way of an apology.

Guy

. . .

As far as letters go, it's short but packs a punch. But it doesn't change a thing. However, I do need a replacement phone and beggars can't be choosers. I unwrap it and put it on charge. While waiting, I write some notes in my journal, so I don't mess up what I need to say to Tilly.

Hi Tilly, I understand you've spoken to Guy. First, whatever he's told you, I want to make clear he means nothing to me. I enjoyed singing with RiffRaff, but I could never replace you and what's really important to me is our relationship. You know I'd do anything for you. I miss you.

I tear up reading my words. They don't come close to how I really feel about Twister, but the second she answers the call, my best intentions are derailed:

"Hi Twister, it's—"

"Well, Mother of Pearl, Hail Mary and Hallelujah! Anyone would think you'd been avoiding me!" she says. Her voice sounds upbeat, if a little manic, and it brings a premature smile to my lips.

"I wanted to call you, but I expect you heard I dropped my phone in the sea."

"I heard you dropped more than that," she says.

"What? I . . . Can you turn on your camera?"

Tilly's lips are pressed together in a tight line. Her blinking green eyes are tinged red. Which makes me feel terrible. She gnaws her bottom lip. God, what have I done? I know every telltale tic of her face because I've seen them so often in the mirror. We are two sides of the same coin. Being an identical twin is sometimes a marriage of inconvenience: we're stuck with one another, for better or worse. Right now, it's definitely feeling worse.

"Oh, Twister! I'm so sorry! Are you, um, okay?" I ask, my voice cracking. "What—"

"Oh, aye, I'm skipping around Ye Olde Vicarage, totally joyous, Malice. You?" She doesn't sound angry so much as flat. I was expecting a drama, but this is somehow so much worse.

The Old Vicarage is our family home back in Yorkshire, England. Our father is the vicar of the village of Little Pickering and a number of other small hamlet and village churches skirting the old market town of Burtonbridge. As far as backwaters go, it's right at the back of yonder.

"I'm doing okay," I say, "but I wish you were here. What's going on?"

She sniffs. "Nothing."

Of course, nothing. Nothing ever happens in Little Pickering.

"Are you going to tell me why you left? Why you're back home? I know we've had our disagreements, but leaving without warning me seems a little . . . extra."

"Extra? Yeah, well, you'd know all about *extra*." Her eyes narrow.

Twister never normally keeps anything from me. I shouldn't even have to ask what's going on, but it's like I can sense more than just the geographical distance opening up between us. It's like she's distancing herself emotionally as well. Mentally building a brick wall faster than I can dismantle it.

"How about you tell me what's happened with you first? Fill me in on your performance with Guy . . . on and off stage."

My mouth goes dry. Outside the apartment, an ambulance siren caterwauls. "It wasn't like that . . ." I rub my eyebrow. "I had no idea you and Guy were together. I thought you said you and Axel—"

"Hah! Axel and I didn't last five minutes." Axel owned the night-club she worked at.

"Oh. I could've sworn . . . when you were here, you said you were going to see him."

"Obviously not, seeing as I was on my way to the airport. Now, spill the tea on New Year's Eve. I want to hear everything. How'd it go?"

I take a deep breath. "The singing with RiffRaff went okay, I think. No-one suspected I wasn't you." Except for Roger, my boss, but the less said about him, the better. I am *so* handing in my notice today. "I did my best."

"Did you enjoy it?"

"Honestly? Yeah. It was fun."

"So you're telling me everyone genuinely bought your act? Even Guy."

Oh shit, here we go. "Um . . . not Guy, no." Even though she's not in the room with me, we know instinctively when the other is lying. It's another gift of being her twin—and also an impediment. I know better than to try to cover anything up with Twister. My internal alarm bells are firing Code Red. And yet, she's still not come clean. She hasn't disclosed her reasons for bailing on me. *And* she more or less press-ganged me into pretending to be her, singing with Guy. If it weren't for her, I wouldn't have met him or been in this predicament in the first place.

Not that I'm blaming her, but also . . . she's not entirely blameless.

"I survived. That's the important thing," I say, sounding lame even to my own ears.

"Is it?" She huffs. "I understand your performance was quite something. No, hang on, *sensational* was the word Guy used. I hear you took being *me* to a whole new level." There's a pause. It sucks that I've no idea what Guy's told her. I should have grilled him for more information. "Anything else you want to confess?"

Confess? "I just did what you asked me to," I say.

"I don't recall asking you to stick your tongue down Guy's throat."

"I didn't! I mean I didn't mean to! I admit I kissed him, and that was a big mistake, huge, but as soon as I realized—"

"Sorry, but how the hell do you kiss someone by mistake?"

I try to laugh it off and fail. "You know me and alcohol. Cheap date. Not that it was a date. But I'd had a couple of drinks, and you know what a lightweight I am, I guess I got wrapped up in the whole drama of the evening, the boat, the fireworks . . ."

"Guy."

"But as soon as I realized there was something going on between the pair of you, I stopped immediately."

She bites her lip. "Am I meant to thank you for that?"

"No, of course not. I'm really sorry. I honestly never thought—"

"For the *scholarship* girl, you really have no clue when it comes to life, do you?"

That hurts, but I guess not. I press my lips together and blink back tears.

"I'm . . . I'm so . . ." She smothers the camera on her phone.

Oh, God, that sounds like her crying, muffling her sobs. I feel wretched. I've done that to her. Because I've been such a shit sister. It kills me that I'm not there with her. "Tilly, please let me help. Whatever's going on, I want to understand. And I'm sorry. The thing with Guy . . . it meant nothing to either of us. It was thoughtless and stupid and—"

"Shut. Up." Grabbing a tissue, she blows her nose, drowning me out.

After sorting herself out, she comes back on the phone. "You'd better tell me exactly what happened with Guy and don't skimp on the details."

I stop myself from groaning. This is excruciating. "Really? You want more. You wouldn't rather we talk about—"

"Yes, really. Get on with it."

I take a deep breath. "Okay. I went back to Guy's house after the gig on the boat. I took my shoes off because your heels were killing me. On route, I trod on something sharp and cut my foot . . . Guy carried me back to his place. He washed my foot and gave me a Band-aid—"

"And a lot more besides—"

"One kiss. That was it."

She sucks through her teeth. "*And* you removed your dress."

Wow, Guy really had come clean. "Yeah, though technically, he removed..."

Her mouth twists from side to side.

"Okay, that too," I croak.

"Do you like him?"

I can't look her in the face. "No. I mean he's a good-looking guy, but we're like worlds apart."

"Totally. I suppose you think what you did is A-okay because, hey, we're twins, we share everything," she says.

"No, I know it's not okay. And it wasn't like that. Like I said, I'm very sorry!"

"So why don't you sound it?" she says.

"What do you want from me? Blood? If you'd told me what was going on between you—"

"This isn't about me. Don't try to turn this round on me! And don't you dare start preaching to me after all you said to Colin!" Her voice wobbles and goosebumps skitter down my back.

I'm still not sure Twister knows the whole ugly truth about Colin, and I don't want to go there. Colin was something of a heartthrob at school. Something of a legend in his own lunchbox. He was also Twister's boyfriend and a total knob. After I found out he was cheating on Twister, pretending to be her I'd told him exactly what I thought of him in front of everyone in the White Swan (or the Mucky Duck as most of us locals call the village pub), his coat of many colors may finally have faded a shade or two.

Although at the time I thought I'd done the village, nay the county, possibly the whole country, a public service, I felt good about myself for all of five minutes. The landlord pulled me aside and fired my ass (fired Twister's ass). Colin ghosted her.

Then some generous 'friend' showed Twister the video of me throwing a pint over Colin's head and shouting, "*I don't want you slobbering all over me. Not now. Not ever! You are a terrible kisser. I'd rather tongue a snake. The only thing incredible about you is your incredibly over-inflated opinion of yourself. You're without doubt the biggest bore and the worst shag I've ever had to suffer in my entire life. I wouldn't deign to wipe my gumboots on your pimply ass . . ."* before Colin stormed out of the pub.

Twister obviously knew it wasn't her, and I could hardly deny the video evidence.

I spent days —days!— begging her forgiveness for not only losing Twister her boyfriend, but also her job. She refused to speak to me for a month. I don't know how messy the situation with Colin got because Twister refused to confide in me, but I gather there may have been some begging on her part and some reciprocal vindictive public humiliation on his.

But they never got back together. I sincerely hope we've scared the two-timing jerk away permanently, but I can't help but be concerned now she's back within striking distance of him.

In the aftermath of their break-up, Harry, my brother, and I got to work convincing Twister there were plenty more attractive fish in the sea, absence makes the heart grow fonder, the world was her oyster and Colin a mere pipi in the ocean . . . and all that. I persuaded her to come to Australia with me and to her credit, Twister threw herself one hundred percent into the job of getting over Colin. She was always a party girl, but she jacked up her party act to a whole new level I couldn't —and didn't want to — keep up with.

Have we been ideal travel partners? Not really. *Not easy when your sister is square* (Twister's words) and when our traveling seemed to stall the minute we touched down in Sydney . . .

"Please just tell me this isn't about Colon," I say.

She flashes me an irritated glare, hating the nickname I use for Colin. She chews on a fingernail, a habit I thought she'd given up several years ago. "What do you care? If you cared even an atom about me, you would've waited to find out about Guy for certain, but, oh no, you couldn't even wait a couple of hours—"

"Of course, I care about you. You know I do. More than anyone on this planet. Look, I'll get the next flight home. I—"

"No! You will *not* get the first flight back home. You need to rewire that brain of yours. Stop worrying about me and worry about your-self. Take a long hard look in the mirror."

"I know I'm not perfect, but—"

"You wanted an adventure and you're going to have one, whether you like it or not!"

"Erm . . . ?" This is a worrying twist in the conversation.

"Your big travel plans don't need to stop just because I'm no longer there. Our happiness is not dependent upon one another. I can live vicariously while you have yourself your grand adventure."

I scratch my neck. "Erm . . . I don't think—"

"It's time you found out who you really are. You'll never become the person you need to be unless you stop worrying about doing the right thing all the time."

"I don't worry about doing the right thing all the time—"

"You are so lost you don't even realize it. It's about time we gave you a reboot."

I laugh. "A reboot? I'm not a computer." Cold waves prickle down my spine. I can smell last night's booze oozing from my pores and it's possible I may vomit into the phone. My gut roils. I suspect I know where this may be going . . .

"You still there?" asks Twister.

"Yerp." And I'm not too desperate to beg. "Please, Twister. You know I'd do anything to make this right. If I come home, we can sort this mess out."

A crooked smile pulls the corner of her upper lip. "I have a better plan." Her voice sounds strangely dismembered. "You really want to know why I left?"

I gulp. "Yes! Of course, I do."

"And you want my forgiveness?"

"Yes! I want things between us to go back to how they were . . ." This is going to need some *Pretty Woman*-level groveling. "I'll do whatever you ask. We should be traveling around Australia together, not rowing thousands of miles apart."

Twister's face is gray with determination, a sheen of perspiration on her forehead. "Okay, then. I say, we officially reinstate the Six Impossible Things Game, only this time round, I'm the one calling the shots."

I sag in my seat. My mouth opens and closes several times before I manage to say, "You can't be serious."

She scoffs. "Oh, I'm deadly serious."

The IT Game, or the Six Impossible Things Before Breakfast Game to give it its full title, originated from one of our favorite bedtime stories, *Alice's Adventures in Wonderland* and *Alice Through the Looking Glass* (okay, *my* favorite bedtime stories) When we were little, Tilly and I would come up with all sorts of Impossible Things to believe before breakfast. We created a whole world of make-believe and role-play, an imaginary world of fantastical friends and creatures. But in our teenage years it somehow graduated to a game of truth and dares, actually attempting to *do* Impossible Things. The IT challenges got us (well, mainly Twister) in no end of trouble, but as I got older, I became increasingly risk averse. Her expulsion from school brought our previous IT game to an abrupt halt, and we'd sworn we'd never revisit the IT Game again. When it didn't come up after the Colin incident, I kind of hoped she'd forgotten all about it.

"—like a robot. You never listen." Clearly not as I've no idea what she's harping on about now. "You need to reconnect with your feelings. Learn to believe in yourself. And if not in yourself, at least believe in the impossible." Her voice quivers with excitement.

I quiver with fear and close my eyes.

God. No.

This cannot be happening.

"This is . . ." The perfect way for her to get her revenge. Maybe she's been waiting all this time to make sure I was on my own in an unfamiliar country before wreaking *Havoc*. "I don't understand. Why would you do this?"

Twister blows out a breath. "I'll tell you just as soon as you've achieved six Impossibles. Right now, I don't feel ready to trust you. And if you want to win my trust back, you have to earn it."

I feel like I've been gut-punched.

She's not going to let this go.

I resign myself to whatever horrors she has in store for me. It means for the next six days or so, my life is going to be utter hell.

"So, a few matters of administration," she says brusquely. "While you've been avoiding my calls today, I cleaned out your bank account—"

"You what? I didn't avoid your calls. I lost my phone. In the sea! You can't do this! You've no right to touch my money!"

"So, eat me! Call it an additional level of assurance that you'll go along with my IT Game plan. You're stuck Down Under until you can either earn enough to get out of the hole you've dug yourself or you complete my six ITs. Think of it as a kickstart to your grand adventure."

My fists bunch at my sides. I bite my lip to stop myself from yelling at her. It will only make the situation worse. Sometimes I want to murder my twin. "Oh, come on! This is bull. Give me my money or I'll . . . I'll—"

"I'll tell Mum and Dad you're going off the grid for a while, so don't bother calling them," she says calmly. "I'll say you're in the outback traveling. Don't bother trying to contact them to ask for help, because I'll know. If you break your word, that's it . . ." She draws a finger across her throat. "I'll wash my hands of you and tell Mum and Dad how you're the reason I was expelled from school, you're the reason I lost my job and was dumped by my boyfriend, and now you're the reason I'm back home alone . . . Imagine if Oxford University found out about your lack of integrity. Do you think they might retract their offer?"

"You wouldn't . . ." I whine. She would. She could spin this situation any which way.

"Want to try me? I already left you in Australia, didn't I?"

"Oh, for God's sake, Tilly," I whimper.

She tuts. "Not like you to swear sis, but it's a promising start. It's about time you broadened your vocabulary. And about time we shook things up a little. Just remember, *the only way to achieve the impossible is to believe it is possible!*"

6

ALICE

The Impossible Things Game goes like this:

Tilly texts me my *Impossible Things* daily challenge. Ideally, I'm meant to achieve it before breakfast, but at the very least within twenty-four hours. It's like having a ticking time bomb hanging over your head. Of course, I could choose not to play along with her stupid game. I could choose to ignore her completely, but the consequences are too horrible to contemplate. And I have no money. And despite currently hating her guts, I also want my sister's forgiveness. It's true that I have wronged her. As much as I try to do the right thing, somehow life has a way of throwing things off track.

I'm woken by the sound of Tilly's first IT message at four in the morning and choke when I read:

Hitchhike to Queensland.

Chuffin' hell!
Hitchhiking is the one thing Tilly and I promised our parents we

would never do, even together. That's probably why she put it first on her list. She sends me directions to a place called Uncle Leo's Roadhouse and transfers just enough money for me to clear the rent and catch a train to Glenfield. After that I'm on my own.

I trudge three hot and dusty kilometers to the roadhouse.

Maybe she just wants to get me as far away from Guy and Sydney as possible. Or maybe she wants me to die a horrible terrifying death . . .

You know what any sane person says about hitchhiking?

Don't.

Not ever.

Especially not when you're a young female, lacking any sort of athletic prowess to enable you to run away or fight back, especially not when you're traveling alone . . . that is, unless you have a death wish and don't mind getting yourself chopped and barbecued along with some Aussie bush tucker.

It's the last thing I want, but like a zombie, I get up, write a thank you note to the landlady and leave it on the kitchen counter along with the keys. At least the apartment is immaculately clean. At least I'm already packed. At least I'm finally saying goodbye to Sydney and hitting the road.

I can do this.

One step at a time.

The only way to achieve the impossible is to believe it is possible, repeats in my head like a crappy mantra. If I could throw up words, those would be the ones.

Standing at the side of the ramp leading onto the Pacific Highway, I stand out like a misplaced letterbox. When the first truck approaches, rather than sticking out my thumb, I turn my back and pretend I'm busy rifling through my rucksack. My heart pounds as the truck thunders past, blowing hot air up my shirt and blasting its horn.

How in God's name am I going to do this? I'm already dizzy, half-fried by the Australian sun. Every breath I inhale sears my lungs and sweat sticks my clothes to my body. I gulp water from my bottle like I've sprung a leak.

Overhead, the sky is a perfect pristine blue.

A perfect pristine day.

A perfect pristine day to be murdered.

I only have to believe. I only have to believe. I only have to believe ...

Sweat trickles down the side of my face. Why am I so worried about being kidnapped by a psychopath when I'm more in danger of being baked alive by the sun? And hundreds of young people have hitchhiked before without mishap. So I should stop worrying. Easier said than done: Not worrying is not in my genetic make-up.

"This is hell," I mutter to a fly buzzing around my face. Flapping my hands and running in circles, ducking and diving to avoid it, makes me sweatier still.

A duck-egg blue VW van beetles along the ramp toward me, two surfboards strapped to its roof rack. My heart lifts. I stick out an arm and cock my thumb. Even as a fly settles on the bare flesh of my arm, I do not flinch—that's how determined I am to show my sister I can achieve the first Impossible. *Please God, don't let the next driver be an axe-wielding murderer. Or murderess.* Knowing what my sister is capable of, I'm equally wary of the female species right now.

But I'm doing this. Hitching a ride. Alone. In Australia. The land where men plunder, and I want to chunder.

There is a friendly honk as the van approaches. Psychotic murderers don't drive cute vans, do they? This is about as safe as hitchhiking is ever likely to get and it's now or never, so I plaster a huge smile on my face, heft my rucksack over one shoulder and stick out my thumb.

The van slows and the driver's face comes into focus behind the windscreen.

Oh no.

No, no, no.

The van pulls to a stop and the driver winds down the front passenger window. "You look like you're melting out there. Fancy a ride?"

A ride?

I am melting, but he's the last person on the planet I want to take a *ride* with.

"N-not with you, I don't!" Where the hell does Guy Balcombe get off driving a cute VW kombi van? That's just criminal. As if he needed any props to make him more alluring to the female species. But I'm not falling for it. There is no way on earth I'm getting in any vehicle with him, no matter how cute he may think he or his van is.

I spin on my heel as well as anyone can unbalanced by a backpack, and march along the hard shoulder. The van follows me at a slow crawl.

How is this possible? How is it conceivable? This cannot be simply a bizarre coincidence.

He pulls alongside me. "Can I give you a lift? You look hot!" shouts Guy merrily through the open window.

I stumble and take a couple of lurching steps forward before regaining my footing. He *must* have known I would be here. Was that phone he gave me bugged? I wouldn't put it past him. But I'd taken the phone out of its cellophane-wrapped box . . . so that seems unlikely. The obvious answer dawns on me. "Did Twister put you up to this?"

"Twister?"

"Tilly, my twisted twin sister!"

He laughs.

The van pulls up on the hard shoulder ahead of me and he jumps out, his hands raised as if in mock surrender. "She just wanted me to make sure you were still alive."

"What does it look like? I was doing fine until you appeared on the scene!" And why would Twister help me achieve an IT?

Of course, Guy doesn't give a damn about me. All he cares about is keeping Twister happy, but if this is her way of letting me off the hook, I don't want it. I especially don't want *his* help. Clearly, she thinks I'm incapable of doing something as simple as hitchhiking. Ha! I refuse to take the easy way out. I'll do this properly or die in the attempt. Best not dwell on that, but I don't want her sanctimonious ass telling me later I failed because I was picked up by her boyfriend.

I plant my hands on my hips. "Honestly, no offense, but I would rather get a lift with Ivan Milat." Yes, I've done my research on the Australian serial killer who murdered all those hitchhikers. "Or ride a camel all the way to Queensland. In fact, I would rather walk barefoot and bleeding, so no, no thank you. Whatever this is, I'm not interested!"

I happened to catch a glimpse over someone's shoulder on the train this morning. Guess who was plastered all over the gossip news? Guy Balcombe. I had no idea he was quite such a big deal on the Sydney social scene. For all *the wrong reasons*.

Sydney's *Sexiest Solo Singer* says, "So you'd rather catch a ride with a complete stranger and take your chances?"

I roll my eyes. "Duh. One hundred percent. Give me a psychotic murderer any day."

I already have my thumb out.

"Come on, Alice. You're not making this easy for me."

"Ha! Like I'm interested in making anything easier for you." I resist whirling around to look at him again because, you know, with that face, I might just forget how much I resent him. "Like I give two shits. So long. Farewell. Bugger off!" I stomp back in the direction of the roadhouse with my thumb out, silently cheering because (a) I have resisted the urge to grab the easy option and (b) I have put Guy and my sister back in their cozy little box and (c) he can't do a U-turn on the highway.

Back where I was five minutes previously, I stand like a muppet at the side of the ramp leading onto the Pacific Highway feeling proud. That is, until the cute little VW van starts reversing up the hard shoulder.

No. Way.

Through the heat haze to my right a white vehicle flurries. Frantically, I wave my arms and cock my thumb and step out onto the highway. The beaten-up jeep swerves but then, with a squeal of brakes, pulls up on the hard shoulder between me and van. I'm pretty sure—

at least 75 percent sure—I glimpsed a female driver. A friendly hand beckons me from the window, bangles jangling.

Picking up my backpack, I dash toward it.

The driver leans across and winds down the passenger-side window. "Where you headed, darl?"

I detect an American twang. "Anywhere!" I can't help checking the back seat—you know, in case there's a dead body stashed in there or something—but seeing no blood or body bags, I stuff my backpack in without even asking and hop in.

"Must be our lucky day," she drawls, smirking. "I'd invite you to get in, but seems like you already have." She has a shock of bleached-blonde hair, the cheeky smile of a modern-day pixie, several tattoos—a wave, a surfboard, and an octopus's tentacles wrapping around her neck, but a nice smile.

Guy beeps his horn and pulls up on the hard shoulder in front of us.

"You know that man?" she asks.

I shrug. "Unfortunately, yes."

"He bothering you?"

"Unfortunately, yes."

"Right then." Wheels spin as she floors the accelerator. Guy throws himself onto the bank as we hurtle past. For a moment we lock eyes, before he is lost in a cloud of dust and grit.

"I'm Lulu," says the woman.

"Alice," I say, turning to look out the back windscreen.

"Don't worry. We've lost him."

"Does this car go any faster?" I ask.

"Don't let appearances fool you. This here might look like a rust bucket, but this old jalopy hasn't let me down yet." She pats the driving wheel, eyes twinkling.

"Champion," I say, holding onto the sides of my seat and silently saying a few *Our Fathers*.

Lulu chuckles. "Well, Alice, I'm headed to Burleigh Point. It's a helluva drive and I'm glad of the company!"

"Me too. Ta." The twinge in my chest has nothing to do with

regret. My aching throat is probably dust and dehydration. But I would feel a whole lot more comfortable if Lulu put both hands on the steering wheel.

"Ta? Where are you from? You don't sound Aussie."

"I'm from Yorkshire. England."

"What's your story, Alice from England?"

I smile through gritted teeth, hoping my breakfast doesn't come up. There's no going back now.

"Spill the tea, girl," says Lulu, giving me a sideways glance. "I picked you up because I wanted company, not the silent treatment."

"Um. I'm just traveling around Australia, you know. Taking a gap year. No fixed plans." Not anymore. My plans have been well and truly sabotaged by Twister and her ridiculous ITs. I am now officially hitchhiking by the seat of my pants. The thought makes my heart flutter with a combination of pride and panic.

"That's cool. I can drop you off wherever you want. Where're you headed?"

"Erm . . . Other than to Queensland, I'm not really sure." I chew my lip. "I was meant to be traveling with my sister, but she's had to go back to the UK," I explain. "Family emergency."

"If it's a family emergency, why didn't you go too?"

Good point. "Uh . . . because . . . it was personal to her. A specific emergency. It's kind of private. Do you mind if we talk about something else? Do you surf?" I ask, trying to change the subject.

"However did you guess?" She laughs, showing me the wave tattoos rippling along her arm. "You?"

"Not really. I've tried it, but . . . it's not for me."

"You should try again. Don't be a quitter. Nothing like surfing. Such a ride. Life is one big wave, right?" Her laughter tinkles.

"Right," I say, although it seems to me that life is more like one big riptide.

While Lulu fills me in on all the reasons I should love surfing and love Queensland and love her friends, my mind wanders to Twister and Guy. What on earth was she playing at throwing Guy and me together again like that? What was she hoping to achieve? It was like she was deliberately trying to set temptation in my path. Hoping I'd fall. Honest to God, sometimes I do not understand my own twin.

"Don't you think, hon?" says Lulu.

"Sorry, what?"

"Gotta find your wave, right? You gotta be patient. Keep your senses alert. Often a wave is not so good as it looks. Sometimes it starts out sweet, but then it breaks early and you're in a mess of white foam."

"Yup," I say. That's me. White foam head.

"But sometimes, babe," continues Lulu, "the perfect wave comes along out of the blue. You never even see it coming, but when you catch that one, man, it lifts you off your feet. It feels like it's been made just for you. Gotta find your perfect wave, girl. Gotta find your perfect wave." She turns and smiles her impish grin at me. "Know what I'm saying?"

I have no idea. "I've got to find my perfect wave," I repeat. For some reason, Guy's face flashes through my head.

"You hitched a ride with me, honey, so technically speaking, you already caught it!"

I can't help smiling at her enthusiasm. She might not be my perfect wave, but ink and piercings notwithstanding, she seems pleasant and sane enough. And what's more, I am well on my way to achieving the first item on my IT list without any help or additional hindrance from Twister or Guy, thank you very much.

One down, only five ITs to go.

I've got this.

7

———

ALICE

It's late afternoon by the time Lulu pulls into the small coastal town of Burleigh Point. It's just over the border of New South Wales, but definitely in Queensland. I send Tilly the photo I took of Lulu and me with the road sign *Welcome to Queensland* in the background.

IT #1 accomplished!

Lulu's arranged to stop a couple of nights with friends before resuming her journey farther north. She tells me I'm welcome to crash with them. As I really don't fancy going anywhere in the dark, let alone taking my chances hitchhiking again, I take her up on the offer.

Her friend is a weathered surfer bloke with sharp blue eyes called Rider. He lives in a huge rambling house on a large plot of land adjacent to a campsite and right opposite the beach. He seems to hold open house to a whole pod of surfers. Their banter is like a different language, but I gather they're discussing surfing conditions. Not being a surfer, not inked and tanned and barefoot, I stick out like a sore thumb, despite them all being super welcoming and friendly.

I go so far as to remove my shoes.

"Woah, girl. Steady on!" teases Lulu, who seems to have got my measure pretty well already.

Half an hour later, when they're urging me into the water to go surfing with them, I'm tempted to put my shoes back on again so I can make a run for it. "Isn't it a bit late?" Isn't dusk shark feeding time?

"No way. Come on, girl. This is Australia!" says Lulu, as if it's a legal requirement to go surfing in a country famous for its shark attacks.

"I really don't have a clue how to surf," I say.

"No worries. We'll look after you," says Rider. For a moment, I'm too mesmerized by his pearly white teeth to respond. This is probably what it would feel like to come face to face with a great white shark.

"I ... I ... I'm reading this really awesome book."

"You can read it later," says Lulu.

At the back of my mind, I see Tilly rolling her eyes. *Stop being a wet drip.* Her words about living life to the full ring in my ears.

"Okay," I say.

The surfing fraternity jog toward the sea. I struggle to keep up, managing to look like a true tourist yelping because the sand is burning hot underfoot.

The others take flying leaps onto their boards before paddling toward the horizon.

I launch myself onto my board. Naturally, it flips, rolling me straight off the other side. I come up spluttering.

"You okay, Kook?" shouts Lulu.

"Never better! Catch you up in a sec!" I shout back, waving. "God, what the hell have I got myself into?" I mutter under my breath as I scramble onto the board again and paddle as fast as I can. Turns out, not fast enough. And I can no longer see the bottom, which, when the water is crystal clear, kind of freaks me out. I try to remember the one lesson I've had. *When you spot the right wave, paddle like crazy, go with the flow and when you feel the surge, try to pop to your feet. Easy as . .*

.

I spot my perfect wave. I paddle like a lunatic. I feel the surge of the wave lift the board.

Gritting my teeth, putting everything I have into it, I push down with my hands, up with my hips and heave my knees toward my chin. Incredibly, I make it to a kneeling position, enjoying the surge of the water beneath me . . . for at least a second.

Then my board jerks, pitching me into a washing machine. I am spun mercilessly; seawater shoots up my nose and I inhale a lungful of ocean. Then the battering ram takes over. My board slams into me from behind and I'm tipped head over heels, scraping along the sandy seabed. Panicking, I try to push off the seabed, but I'm pummeled from behind by what feels like a cricket bat. I scramble to get purchase with my feet, but my ankle attached to the board drags me backward—

Suddenly I'm yanked upward to the surface. Coughing and gasping for air, I clamp myself, octopus-style, around my savior.

"Man, you were axed."

Crap. I'd know that voice anywhere—Guy Balcombe—and right now my equivalent of dry land.

"Had me worried for a moment there," he says.

I can only cough and splutter. As I try to heave air into my lungs, I'm thankful to be attached to anything. Eyes closed, I rest my cheek against his solid shoulder. "Ta. I nearly drowned!" I whimper.

He cups the back of my head and leans back for a better look at me. "Nah, you're still breathing . . . thank God. But—"

I look up into his eyes and for a moment, I forget. Everything. I forget my sister. I forget myself. I forget I hate him. His body feels warm and reassuringly solid, his eyes hold bottomless mysteries and the droplets of water clinging to his ridiculously long lashes sparkle like diamonds in the sunlight. Fuck, I'm like a cat entranced by a sunbeam on the wall.

"No-one likes to be drilled by a wave."

His words snap me out of my trance.

"I never want to surf again. Ever," I say.

"I guess it's not for everyone." Guy gently but firmly unfastens my legs (which seem to have latched themselves of their own accord around his waist) and unpeels my fingers (which have speared themselves into his wet hair) from the back of his neck. For some reason, he no longer seems quite so enthusiastic about being attached to me.

Well, good. Good!

I let go, only to panic as I'm dunked back in the water. "Guy!" I flail.

Hands under my armpits, he hauls me to the surface again. "Alice, calm down. It's shallow. You can probably put your feet down. And if you're done splashing around, I'll go get your board."

He wades away from me and doesn't look back.

My head reels, my retinas blinded by the image of the sun kissing Guy's golden back, his muscles rippling and flexing like something poetic and . . . godlike.

Groaning, I drag myself out of the sea, shaking water from my ears like a dog. I sit for a while shivering on the beach rubbing my ankle where the leg strap has detached itself and left a welt.

Guy retrieves my board for me and looks like a Hemsworth younger sibling as he carries it back up the beach.

I croak a feeble, "Ta."

"You shouldn't surf alone," he says, looming over me.

"I wasn't!" I say. "What are you doing here? What part of, I do not want your help, do you not understand? Are you s-stalking me?" I struggle to spit the words out because my mouth is busy salivating at the sight of him in his board shorts. He's more ripped than I ever imagined . . . and those glistening muscles are doing something unfathomable to my insides.

Guy rubs the back of his neck. "Believe me when I say it's not out of choice. You can take it up with Tills. She wanted me to let you know I'm staying at the campsite next door . . . if you need anything."

"Oh, for crying out loud! Can you please inform your *girlfriend*, I'm perfectly fine? I'm having a whale of a time!"

His eyes roam over me, probably thinking *beached* whale.

He stares out to sea. "I think you'd best stick to the shallows, Kook, until you at least have a *basic* idea of what you're doing. I'd prefer not to have to rescue you again." Something makes his mouth tweak as he walks off, and my stomach does a deep dive of its own.

I watch him paddle out and then surf a wave. All the way in. He makes everything look so damn easy.

Every damn thing about him makes me feel difficult . . . and water-logged . . . and salty.

8

—————

ALICE

"Seriously?"

"Very seriously," says Tilly, giving me a smile that conveys all the warmth of a Chinese burn.

"But it's so stupid!" Not to mention time-wasting.

"Yes, but you have so much time to waste. And when do you *ever* do anything stupid? You spend your life with your nose in a book. You're so freaking sensible you might as well live your life in a straitjacket."

"That's not true. Yesterday, I went surfing."

"Oh, really." She laughs. "That's not what I heard. I heard you nearly drowned."

Great. Guy is obviously reporting back to her. Maybe she's just sent him along to spy on me. "And I suppose you think that's funny."

She cocks her head to one side. "Stop feeling sorry for yourself, Malice. It'll be extremely satisfying hearing about you doing something daft for a change. Try to enjoy life."

"And I suppose you'll have your spy Guy report back!" I snarl, but she has already dropped the call.

I *do* enjoy life. I just don't enjoy her version of what's supposedly enjoyable. *Bloody hell!* I should never have emailed her the photograph of the house and the beach, but I was kind of hoping Twister might see what she was missing and hop on the next plane back here.

Instead, IT #2 dropped into my inbox.

Alice, IT #2: Catch a brush turkey

Catch a brush turkey? How? It's like being slapped with a wet tea towel. I hadn't noticed the wild turkey in the background of my photographs, but Twister had.

The phone call with her is a reality check. It goes to show there's a fine line between me laying it on too thick in the hope she'll regret leaving and return, and me making it sound like I'm having a good time and thereby making her want to destroy me. Clearly, she wants to humiliate me to the max and have Guy witness it. Clearly, she still resents me serving up nut roast for Christmas dinner and not turkey. Clearly, I am meant to suffer.

"Bloody stupid!" I mutter, after she hangs up on me.

"What's up, babe?" asks Lulu, from across the yurt I'm sharing with her and her friends. If I thought Guy's lifestyle in Sydney was a bit Bohemian, this is next level. Don't get me wrong. I'm not complaining. I'm grateful.

Last night was even quite enjoyable . . . until I heard someone in the distance playing guitar. Goosebumps had instinctively informed me it was Guy. I wasn't about to invite him over because I wanted him gone. But unfortunately, Rider had other ideas.

"Hey. See if you can't track down whoever that dude is playing the guitar and invite him over," he'd said to Lulu.

Champion.

I thought she'd send him packing when she realized who it was, but ten minutes later she was back with Guy like they're best mates.

Bloody great.

Lulu seemed to have forgotten the dude was stalking me. I mean, I know she only got a distant glimpse, but now she's *really* into him. As is this whole surfing fraternity. Last night, I ground my teeth as they discussed music and bands, and I seemed to lose the ability to use my voice. I faded into the background rather than make a scene.

Guy fit straight in but also the man cannot help but stand out. He's in a league of his own, playing his guitar, singing in those deeply disturbing mellow tones of his that no matter how many times I tell myself are ordinary and average send shivers across my skin. Rider grilled him about RiffRaff and, looking almost apologetic, like it was no big deal, Guy reeled off all the music festivals and gigs they had lined up. When he mentioned they were minus a singer, his gaze raked over me, lingering and hot. I swear, if he'd mentioned I sang with RiffRaff at all, I was going to poke his eyes out with a kebab stick.

But he said nothing.

Didn't even acknowledge he knew me, which suited me fine. I made some lame excuse about being tired and went to bed early, but listening to him sing in the dark of the night, my whole body ached like I might be coming down with a virus. And I'm not feeling too hot this morning.

I groan.

"Hey, Kook," says Lulu. "You okay?"

It's only just getting light outside, but Lulu and the other women in the yurt are already in various stages of dress for what they call the 'dawn patrol' (and I called stark raving bonkers). As if surfing isn't dangerous enough when it's broad daylight.

"Fine. Sorry, just got a message from my sister. She's in a bit of a pickle," I say.

"Well, embrace the glorious Yorkshire pickles y'all are," says Lulu. "See ya later, Kook."

"Yeah," I say, "see ya."

I seem to have been stuck with the nickname Kook. At first I naively thought it meant I should make myself useful in the kitchen, but I was quickly enlightened by one of the guys that it means I can't surf for shit. A couple of them apparently witnessed me wipe out and

Guy coming to the rescue. Kook became the topic of much hilarity and entertainment last night, and I have a dirty suspicion it was him who gave me that term of endearment.

My priority now is to shower and find myself a job so I can get myself the hell out of here and shake off bloody Guy . . . that is, once I've accomplished Twister's stupid IT#2.

By the time I crawl out of my sack, the sun's throwing warm rays across the lawn and the air's already laden with humidity. Apart from the sound of cicadas and the crashing waves, the place is quiet. I stretch and inhale the serenity. The sky's a pale shade of lilac. I breathe it all in, reminding myself life is sweet and I have so much to be grateful for. Living is good. And if I believe, I can get done whatever needs to be done.

At that exact moment, out of the corner of my eye I spot movement.

Ey, up.

There's a trio of brush turkeys lurking not five yards away from our yurt, as if they've been placed there specifically for me. All I have to do is catch one, take a photo and then Bob's your uncle.

Maybe this won't prove impossible. I believe I can do this. Anyway, I'm willing to give it a crack while there's no-one else around.

I close in on my prey. The nearest turkey takes a couple of idle steps away. Somewhere in the distance, a dog barks.

Arms outstretched, I give chase.

It's a bloody fool's game, running around the back yard, leaping over bushes and tent ropes and surfing gear. As soon as I get within arm's reach of one turkey, it flaps its wings and flies up into the nearest tree.

"Hell!" Hands on my hips, panting heavily—I'm not exactly the fittest or fastest chick off the block—I look around. There's another one across the other side of the yard by the driveway and I'm not ready to call it a day just yet.

I amble across the grass toward it because I can almost hear Twister preaching in my ear like she does about men. *You scare them off by being too intense. It's not attractive. Gotta make them think you're dumb and not interested, right?* Yeah, right. What a joke. But for once I heed her advice and try to look as if this is part of my early morning wake-up routine. I stretch and yawn. The turkey scratches at the ground. *You gormless, pea-brained nitwit. You're so mine.*

When I'm within about three yards of striking distance, I switch into stealth mode: crouching, focused only on making the Impossible possible. *Oh yes.*

I spring out from behind a bush. The alarmed turkey breaks into a trot, wings flapping. I burst into a sprint just as a skateboarder goes flying past the gates. His eyes widen as the stupid bird flies straight into his path.

Oh shit a brick.

The skateboarder flips head over heels. There's a clatter of metal and a lot of squawking. Then, the bloody cheeky bird shakes its tail feathers and struts away. I swear those creatures are indestructible.

For a second, there's crickets and perhaps some distant flapping of wings, or that could be my erratic heartbeat because—*Oh fuck-a-doodle-doo!*—Guy is sprawled at my feet.

Unfortunately, he's still alive: I know this because he groans.

Eyes the color of thunderclouds snare me. My stomach plummets. Last night, he had a no-worries smile draped across his pretty face. This morning, it's definitely more of an ugly grimace.

9
____

GUY

"*Far out!*" Lying on my back, I gasp like a landed fish, trying to catch my breath. I see stars. I see double. I see Tilly. No, Alice. Fuck, of course, it's Alice. I wonder if maybe I have a concussion which would be a shame because I need all the brain cells I've got.

What just happened? One minute, I'm rolling toward the campsite on my skateboard and the next second a turkey flies at me out of nowhere. You'd think it had a death wish, only I think *it* may have done more damage to me than I did to it.

Alice stares down at me, her big brown eyes bigger than ever, horror written all over her rosy cheeks. She looks like she's been out jogging only she's dressed in . . . not a lot.

I roll onto one side as I try to get up. "Fuck! Far out!" That turkey may have cost me more than my pride. My hand looks . . . far from normal.

Nursing it against my chest, I flop onto my back again. This is a fucking disaster. As a favor, I picked up the van my brother, Ben, bought as a romantic wedding gift for Xanthe, his fiancé, and Muggins here was supposed to drive it straight home. I'm already in enough trouble for delaying (and I haven't even mentioned the detour to Queensland), so how am I supposed to explain this detour? The wedding flashes before my eyes—ruined. Not that I'd be too sore about that . . . But RiffRaff's summer tour—wiped out. My musical career—on the fucking line. My relationship with my brother— uglier than ever.

"What?" I growl.

"Nothing!" says Alice, looking alarmed. "I was just, um . . . coming to, um, help you." She leans a little closer, giving me a bird's-eye view of her ample cleavage. I shut my eyes and focus on the pain. It is everywhere. My head. My hand. My ribs. My knee. Maybe even my heart. Perhaps I'm having a seizure . . .

"Are you okay?" she whispers.

My eyes snap open. "Do I look okay?"

Her cheeks flame. "Sorry. No, um, you look pretty messed up, actually."

Yeah, like I hadn't realized. "I don't suppose you'd lower yourself to giving me a hand up?" I ask.

As I clamber up, I hold onto her for leverage.

I growl. Mainly because she is getting up my nose, and she smells . . . floral. Like spring. The image of her *springing* from behind a flowering bush, legs and arms flapping, pinwheels into my head. What the fuck was she doing? Yoga? Tai chi? Practicing her surf popping?

I make a mental inventory of my injuries. My head was already banging with a hangover, and I don't think I've done any more damage there, but I've barked my knee and blood trickles down my shin. Pain jabs me in the side when I inhale, so I may have done some damage to my ribs as well, but my hand is the worst. It is red and puffy. Fucking great. I try to conjure up a smile from somewhere as I touch it gingerly, but it's tender as hell and a wave of nausea hits me.

"I . . . um . . . Perhaps you should elevate that," says Alice.

"Thanks for the tip," I say.

She raises her eyebrows at me. "I think you should probably get it X-rayed."

"Fuck that. I've got to drive home today," I growl. "Man. That stupid bird flew out of nowhere!"

"Um . . . yeah . . . Th-that was . . . um . . . unlucky," she says, biting her lower lip.

I straighten up as best I can, but where the skateboard caught me, it feels like I've been stomped on by a bull. Alice makes a strange sound, a whimper, that doesn't help matters, though I do realize I'm still holding onto her. Perhaps a little too tightly.

I let go and hobble a couple of steps forward. My head spins. My bag of groceries is strewn across the drive, the baguette bent in half, the carton of milk spewing its guts into the flowerbed, my avocados probably ready-smashed and the box of eggs ready-scrambled. "Fuck!"

Alice hurries to gather them up. "Unfortunately, I think your groceries are—"

"Also fucked! So much for breakfast and a quick getaway. Toss them in the garbage, would you? Far fucking out!"

She flinches at all my swearing, but it's way too late to worry about offending her. My eyes could be deceiving me, but my hand appears to be swelling up. "God-fucking-dammit!" I've had enough wipe-outs in my time to know when something is broken.

"I'm so sorry," she whispers.

"What have you got to be sorry about? It's not like it's your fault!" I snap, unkindly, clamping my right hand on her shoulder again. She looks like she might buckle under my weight. Too bad.

"Would you please help me to the van?"

"Of course," she says, reluctantly putting an arm around me, "but I don't think you should drive anywhere."

I hobble a couple more steps, cursing. "I'll be fine. I don't have much choice. I need to get home to Victoria."

Her lower lip trembles as we hop a couple more steps together. I don't hold back on the grunting and swearing. "Jesus! Fuck! Bloody oath! This is the last thing I fucking need." I am royally screwed.

What am I going to tell the RiffRaff lads? They're depending on me. If my hand is broken, I'm going to have to put everything on hold. Quite possibly altogether. No, it can't be broken. I have to stay positive. I may just have to rest up for a couple of days . . . although I can't do that if I'm going to make the wedding on time. Damn!

By the time we make it to the van, I'm feeling well and truly mullered. I lean against it, panting.

"Who's Victoria?" asks Alice.

"What?"

"You said you had to get home to Victoria."

"The state. Not a person."

"Oh, right. Of course. That makes sense."

None of this makes sense, least of all why she is looking a bit tearful.

"Your hand looks . . . um . . . bad," Alice says. "I think it might be broken."

"Bull!" I snap. What's she got to cry about? I'm the one who's hurting and seeing her looking ridiculously upset over nothing makes me pissy as hell. "It'll be fine." I feel like a wolf caught in a trap who wants to take a bite out of her peachy ass, even though this is clearly not her doing and she is trying to be nice.

Our eyes lock.

She swallows. "I can drive you to hospital if you like."

"Did I say anything about hospital?"

"No, but I think you should get that x-rayed." She bites her lip. And gawps at my hand. Fuck, it has definitely swollen some more and might even be beginning to look a little purple.

"Why would you offer to drive me to hospital when you've made it perfectly clear you'd rather be anywhere else than within a hundred miles of me?"

She scuffs the ground. "You helped me out yesterday. And I honestly don't mind. I don't have any plans . . ." Her voice wobbles. "Though, I could call you an ambulance if you'd prefer."

"It doesn't merit calling an ambo, and even if it did, I haven't got cover. I can't afford it." If I can't play music, I can't afford shit anymore.

She can't hold my gaze. She wipes her hands on her skimpy pajama shorts. I tear my gaze from her skimpy vest top. God, I'm shameless. Even when in pain, I'm thinking about . . . an opportunity missed. Maybe it's her sleep-mussed hair. Maybe it's her nips pressed against her vest top. Maybe I have a concussion.

"If you don't get it checked, if it's broken and you don't get it fixed, it could cause even worse complications. Permanent nerve damage. Deformity. Osteomyelitis."

"Osteo-what?"

"Osteomyelitis."

"And you know this because . . . ?"

She shrugs. "I read about it."

I spot a brush turkey sitting on the branch of a nearby tree. I swear it's preening itself and giving me the evil eye, like it might be about to crow 'poetic justice' to the entire town. I think about being temporarily unable to play guitar, or permanently being impaired and feel myself break out into a hot sweat as another wave of nausea hits me.

"Do you even know how to drive? Are you old enough?"

"Yes! I'm nearly twenty!"

"Do you have a valid license?"

"Of course. I'm a very competent driver," she says.

"Gear stick?"

She frowns. "Yes." She fidgets like I'm asking her to jump in bed with me. "Look, if you don't want me to drive you to hospital is there s-someone else you can ask?"

I scratch my head with my left hand. "Do you see anyone? Far out!" I try to suck some air into my lungs and rein everything in like I do before a performance on stage, but my vision darkens, and I grab hold of the nearest thing to me.

10

ALICE

It's not every day a bloke swoons, but when Guy grabs hold of me, it at least seems to change his bolshy attitude.

"Okay. Let's go to hospital," he says, like it's the last thing in the world he wants to do, but he'll do it as a favor for me. Or maybe Twister.

"This would never have happened if you hadn't insisted on chasing me all the way up to Queensland," I mumble under my breath as I help Guy into the front passenger seat.

"Don't remind me," he grunts.

The outside of the van looks cute, but inside is predictably—having seen Guy's house in Sydney—a bit of a shambles. Guy clearly doesn't notice the stuff he discards without thought: chip packets, empty beer cans, probably women.

I take a deep breath, open the driver's door and jump in beside him. He looks very pale, a sheen of perspiration on his forehead. "I'll have you at hospital in a jiffy," I say, inspecting the seat to make absolutely sure I'm not going to sit on anything revolting. "You don't need to worry. I've never once had a prang. I'm a very careful driver, super responsible and this really shouldn't be a problem." My voice is a cheerful singsong despite the fact I'm trying not to panic because I've never driven anything this big before. I'm also ever so slightly concerned about Guy passing out on me before we get to hospital.

Guy tosses me the van keys. "Let's hope."

As soon as I put my hands on the steering wheel—which to give Guy some credit is neither tacky nor sticky nor grease-smeared—I fall deeply and irretrievably in love. With the van, obviously.

Call me callous. I do feel terrible about what's happened to Guy, what I inadvertently caused to happen, but it is also kind of his fault for being in the wrong place at the wrong time. Plus, this van is quite the distraction. In the right hands, treated with love and care . . . it could be *adorable*. There are some things in life that should be cherished. This is one of them.

Closing my eyes, I inhale the scent of leather and spice and the faint undertones of—I wrinkle my nose—Is that fish and chips? I wind down a window. Let me repeat that. I WIND DOWN the window. I know these vintage VW vans aren't exactly the most reliable, but there's something about them that is so damn cute. It's like stepping back into the seventies. A nostalgia trip. Call me old-fashioned, but I was totally born in the wrong era.

Guy grunts. "Any chance we could get going anytime today, Kook? I'm kind of on a tight schedule."

Oh yes, he needs to get to Victoria. I turn the key in the ignition and the engine burbles joyfully into life. *Mr. Blue Sky* starts playing in my head. As we pull out of the camp gates onto the main road, there's a full choir singing in my head. I even manage a smile. I may not be able to catch a brush turkey, but oh boy, can I drive an injured idiot to hospital in a dream vehicle. Not succeeding with my IT task today does not feel like abject failure. I will explain everything to Twister and plead. *Plead.* This is her boyfriend after all. She has to cut me some slack. Right now, I feel more like a heroine than one of life's tragics.

Guy gives me directions off his phone to the nearest hospital, and I drop him at Emergency then go and park up in the shade.

While he's inside, I can't resist having a nosy.

I love this van. I love the clean lines, the blue checkered curtains held in place with leather straps, the red leather upholstery, the dinky metal sink and gas stove by the door, the neat little footlocker with an icebox containing a bottle of water and beers. Beneath the main bench seat, a table is stowed, along with some bedding. I really shouldn't be doing this, but . . . I keeping poking around.

Beneath the discarded litter and clothes, the van is remarkably clean. But *how* can Guy live with this mess when it is such a small compact space? Why doesn't he tidy up as he goes? Without thinking, I find myself picking up his discarded clothes and sniffing. I check out the window. God forbid someone should catch me. Actually, despite being crumpled, they don't smell bad: they smell of detergent with a faint trace of sea and Guy. I inhale again. Not bad. I fold them into a neat pile.

How does he even stand up straight in here?

I spot the pop-up roof. Cautiously sitting down on the red leather bench, I find plenty more storage nooks and crannies. I guess the beds must all be folded away. It wouldn't take much to sort this place out and make it spick and span . . .

No! No, no, no. This van is not my concern. Not mine. I am not going to clean anything.

Although, I can't help but peep into a few drawers to see if there are any cleaning products.

I know I shouldn't, but I'm intrigued by how everything works. Imagine traveling around Australia in this. It'd be awesome. I'd have the van perfectly restored and meticulously maintained. Beneath the mounds of crap, I'm surprised to find it actually is in . . . great condition. So why doesn't he look after it better?

Opening the slatted windows, I let in some air. But it's just as hot and muggy outside. Sliding open a drawer, admiring the craftsmanship—the curved corners, the nifty retractable push-button handles—I discover the top one holds cutlery and kitchen utensils, the next an assortment of games—cards, Chess (which makes me think of Dad, the Grand Chess Master in our household), Scrabble and Backgammon—and the bottom drawer contains surf wax, guitar picks, and a curious black leather notebook. No, I must *not* pry.

I go for a walk around the nearby park. Lying down beneath a beautiful Jacaranda tree, I doze in the shade.

Back at the van, a couple of hours or so later, I'm ashamed to say my curiosity gets the better of me. I can't help myself. I spend the best part of an hour reading the lyrics Guy's written in his little black book. I'm amazed that someone who seems entirely detached from his emotions, morally adrift, can write words that are so profoundly moving. Maybe he didn't write these? Puzzled, I put the book back where I found it. In the drawer below I find a medical kit and . . . a large box of condoms. How much shagging can one man do?

Clearly, a lot.

I just can't help myself. Other than self-consciously scooting past the 'men's' section in a pharmacy, as tragic as it may sound, I've never actually studied a condom up close. My only sexual encounter was fumbled and in the dark and desperately disappointing. Overcome by curiosity, I pull a packet from the box for closer inspection. The wrapper is metallic blue—

My phone buzzes in my pocket and I drop the entire box. Condoms scatter like confetti, and I stare in panic at the name on my screen: GUY

"Hello?" I answer, heart pin-balling. What would be his reaction if he knew I was now on the floor retrieving his prophylactics?

"Are you okay? You kind of sound out of breath."

No kidding. I'm on my knees retrieving his condoms, panting like a dog on heat. "No, I'm champion. Absolutely fine. Just waiting on you. *Nowt* to report. Hunky dory here. Champion. Never better." Too many words are spewing from my mouth. "How're you?" I ask, finally recalling he might appreciate me showing a smidgen of concern.

"Bored," he says, sounding thoroughly dejected, "and you were right, my hand's broken."

I manage to drop my phone again. "Bloody Nora!" I scramble to pick it up. "I'm sorry to hear that."

What the hell is wrong with me? Even my palms are sweating. He's just a bloke. Admittedly one with a voice capable of disorienting me in a few syllables, but I should *not* be this nervous. "So what now?" I ask, as I attempt to brush sand off my phone without disconnecting the call and simultaneously—thank God!—spotting a couple more errant condom packets under the table.

"The good news is, they've agreed to squeeze me in last thing today. Apparently, I need a couple of screws."

"S-Screws? P-pardon?" I splutter, my brain misfiring as I stuff the last of his condoms back in the box.

"Screws, Alice, in my hand. They're going to try to fit me in straight away."

"Oh, screws in your hand. Fit you in. Ha, ha, ha!" Now I sound like a psycho. Holy shit, my brain is seriously malfunctioning. Must be the heat. And I need to get off the phone.

"Maybe you should go back to the camp rather than wait here. I've been told they can squeeze me in for surgery today, but I'm unlikely to be let out until tomorrow."

"Oh, what a shame." Hmmm. That didn't sound as sincere as it could've. "I'm happy to babysit your van for as long as you'd like."

"That would be helpful. Look, is there any chance you could pick me up in the morning?"

Damn. That soon? "Well, I . . ." I don't really want to be anywhere near him tomorrow. But this is kind of my fault. Okay, *totally* my fault.

"Please," he adds.

Ugh. Don't you hate it when people are polite? It makes it so much more difficult to say no when people ask nicely. Crap. And there is *the guilt* hanging over me like a sodding great thunder cloud. *Gah!* I can't exactly leave the bloke high and dry when I'm the cause of his broken hand, can I? Undecided, I do a good impression of a frog and croak, "Sure."

"Don't worry," he says. "Forget it. I'll get an Uber."

"No, I'll be there," I say. "Not a problem." Because I am a total beanbag.

"Great. Thanks. Hey, wish me luck. I hate hospitals." He sounds nervous, which seems so unlike him and as much as I hate to admit it, it's kind of endearing.

Not that I am endeared. I am pissed off with myself for buckling. Yes, I am a people pleaser. I need to add, *Stop being so pleasing* to my list of New Year's resolutions. "Good luck. You'll be right as rain," I say.

"Glad you think so. See you tomorrow then."

Champion. It'll be like driving myself to my own execution. More Guy time. More torture. More guilt and bloody suffering. "I've got to go. I've another call waiting," I lie. I am a bloody dithering muppet. When Twister finds out about this, she's going to disembowel me.

After Guy's call, I empty the condom box, shake out the sand that has somehow adhered itself to the inside and re-pack the condoms *extremely* neatly.

Then I drive back to Burleigh Point.

It feels like a lifetime since I chased those bloody turkeys, but when I get back to the campsite, they're still there, fossicking in the undergrowth, totally indestructible. Just looking at them makes me feel weary. Rather than return to Rider's house, I open up the back of the van and soak up the view of the ocean between the gum trees.

I think about writing in my journal, but there's a gentle breeze, the light is soft and dappled beneath the gum trees, and the gentle susurration of leaves and waves lull me.

Twister, clearly dressed as the Queen of Tarts, shouts, "You can only come to the Mad Hatter's tea party, if you catch me a turkey," from the end of a very, very, very long table which is covered with a red and white check tablecloth and piled high with plates of food.

Guy sits on my right side, his arm in a sling, his left hand inching up my thigh, with the white heat of a sparkler. I keep trying to push it away because Twister is bound to notice me giving off sparks and I'm worried I might set the tablecloth on fire. My parents and brother appear, distracting me, and the next thing I know, Guy has pulled me onto his lap and is kissing me in front of everyone. Everyone. And I absolutely know I shouldn't, it's excruciating, but I seem to be kissing him back even though out of the corner of my eye I can see Twister's head is doing 360-degree rotations and my parents are yelling at us to stop.

Guy appears oblivious. He lifts me onto the table and it's just the two of us making out among the wobbling jellies and piles of cupcakes and cucumber sandwiches and jam tarts and an enormous stuffed turkey that is very much alive, ogling us and clucking at me like it can talk. "Catch me if you can, you motherfucker!" the turkey gobbles.

I jolt awake, swiping lank locks of hair out of my face, my heart pounding in my chest like an alien. What the hell was that all about?

I hear a scratching sound. There is a goddamn turkey right beside the van, ferreting around in the undergrowth.

Like a light bulb switching on, all of a sudden, I have an idea. Perhaps there's a way to catch a brush turkey after all.

In the back of the van, I find the discarded broken baguette from this morning. Feeling a lot like the wicked witch in Hansel and Gretel, I leave a trail of crumbs starting not far from where the turkey is hanging out, leading right up to and into Guy's open van.

And then I sit behind a nearby bush and wait, camera on my phone at the ready like a private investigator.

Come on little birdies . . .

Not one, but two of the little peckers strut their way toward the open door of the van following my bread trail. First one, then another, hops right inside. While the dumb birds are busy stuffing their faces, I slide the door shut and fist pump. *Yay! How clever am I!*

Then I go around taking photos through the windows.

Unfortunately, the birds appear to be panicking, flapping their wings and generally having a frantic time. Feeling like the worst trophy hunter in existence, I snap a couple of very hurried very blurred photos and throw open the van door.

But the pea-brained creatures still can't manage to find the exit and OH. MY. GOD. They have their revenge. There is bird crap everywhere. There is a hellish amount of squawking while I shoo them from the front out the back of the van.

Panting, I collapse in a heap on the step. "Good God!"

I check out my photos. I am a terrible human being. The photo is a blur of wings, but I have my evidence. And there are no dead birds which is a serious bonus.

But there is a horrible stink emanating from the van.

Holy shit. Or rather unholy shit.

Although I text Twister to let her know IT #2 is done and send her the evidence, I've little to smile about:

1. I now have Guy's laundry to do. I hang out Guy's t-shirts, board shorts and 'smalls' to dry and decide I never want to be a housewife. This feels about as far from emancipated and independent as I can possibly imagine.

2. It takes me over an hour to clean up all the bird crap in the van, so I involuntarily give it a spring clean.

3. I waste the remnants of my tiny bottle of perfume in an attempt to fumigate the van.

4. I have to stand guard in case any of the damn turkeys think they might want some more of the action.

But, like the ray of sunshine that has probed its way through the clouds, I have accomplished my second Impossible Thing. That is better than nothing. That is something to be proud of. I log it in my journal along with IT #1, feeling more than a little smug.

Then, after locking up, I go in search of Lulu. I think I'd better spend the night in the yurt rather than risk inflicting any further damage on Guy's precious van.

11

———————

GUY

I get myself discharged as early as possible the next morning. Which, although I played the 'wedding card' and managed to jump the operations queue, is not nearly early enough for my liking. I am ready to strangle the sweetly smiling young female doctor when her rounds finally bring her to my bedside.

"You're all ready to be discharged," she says.

"Sweet," I reply, though I'm feeling decidedly sour by then. My hand is broken and my summer is screwed. Life is roses, without any blooms. The Havoc twins are the thorns of life.

On the plus side, my injuries are not as bad as I first imagined. Only my hand is broken and not my ribs, although I feel like I've taken a good kicking. I don't mention my possible concussion. The last thing I need is them keeping me in here for even more tests.

Alice, looking as angelic and composed as ever, is waiting for me outside with the van. I suppose I should be grateful for small mercies.

"Thanks for coming back," I say, climbing into the front passenger seat.

"No problem," she says, although it's fairly clear she's doing this under sufferance. So much for whatever spark we had going on New Year's Eve.

I sniff. It smells of perfume. And cleaning products. And every surface in the van is gleaming. Also, my clothes are folded on the bench seat. "Are those . . . ironed?"

"Um, I j-just had a little t-tidy-up," she stutters. "I had some t-time to spare and thought you might appreciate it what with your broken hand and all . . . What's the verdict with your injuries?" Blushing furiously, she starts the engine.

"A broken metacarpal. A couple of screws. Nothing major, but just enough to fuck up all the gigs we're meant to be playing this summer. I haven't had the heart to tell the lads yet."

"Oh, good." Her mouth twists. "I mean, I'm glad it wasn't worse. It could've been worse."

"You think?"

"Well, you could have broken your neck."

Is that the trace of a smile twitching at the corner of her mouth?

She clears her throat and focuses on the road ahead. Which is exactly what I should be doing, metaphorically and literally. But WTF? She did my laundry and cleaned the van? I wish she wouldn't be so damn nice. It makes what I'm about to do even harder.

While I've been in hospital, among other things, I've been mulling over how I'm going to get myself and this van home to the Mornington Peninsula. Honestly, going to my brother's wedding is about the bloody last thing I want to do, but family is family. I can't let him down. Even if I can't play guitar at the wedding, I can sing, and I still have to put in an appearance, more's the pity. I can't exactly not turn up at my own brother's wedding. Or fail to turn up without his precious wedding gift – the van. "So, Kook, I'm not sure how I'm going to drive this van home with my hand like this." I wave the blue cast on my left hand at her, hoping for some sympathy.

Her eyes stay fixed on the road. "I bet you're wishing you hadn't driven all this way north at my sister's behest. That'll teach you not to listen to her. Twister'll mess up all your best laid plans."

This much is true. Tilly Havoc is a key member of the band: the lads' attempts to harmonize sound like feral cats on heat. I am looking out for Alice because at the moment she is the only card I hold. She could yet prove useful. "Perhaps if you hadn't got it into your head to go hitchhiking, Tilly wouldn't have been worried about you and begged me to make sure you reached your destination safely."

"Oh, yeah. Like when has my sister ever begged anyone to do anything?"

"You'd be surprised," I say.

She pulls a face. "Ugh. Spare me the details."

Honestly, my friendship with Tilly is stretched to breaking point right now. When I called her in the hospital to give her a rundown of yesterday's events, she laughed. Considering how much wasted time and pain she's caused me, I was struggling to find my collision with a bird amusing. Tilly hadn't seemed surprised when I'd mentioned Alice had witnessed the whole incident and then driven me to hospital.

"That sounds just like Alice," she'd said. "Ever the Samaritan." Although, it kind of sounded like she'd called her Malice, not Alice. Maybe I misheard. Though maybe now I know Alice calls Tilly Twister, it kind of makes no sense . . . Alice is angelic.

"Hmmm . . . Maybe, Alice could be persuaded to drive you to Victoria for your brother's wedding?" Tilly had said.

"You think!" I toned down my enthusiasm in case she mistook it as me having the serious hots for her sister. "You think . . . I mean, that'd be awesome, but I don't think I'm exactly flavor of the month."

"Leave it with me. Besides, I owe you," said Tilly. She texted me at some point during the night to say, if I asked nicely, Alice might prove amenable.

But like I predicted, right now Alice is not looking too enthused at the prospect of spending even five more minutes with me, let alone agreeing to drive me home to Victoria. I grit my teeth thinking about all the brush turkeys I want to stone to death.

Perhaps I could ask Ben, my brother, to pay her, even though I fucking hate the thought of letting him know my finances are stretched right now. He'd jump on the family let's-get-Guy-back-to-work-on-the-vineyard bandwagon at the slightest whiff of weakness from me.

"So . . . um . . . Tilly mentioned you might be willing to drive me to Victoria," I venture.

"She what!" Alice fluffs the gear change—to which I say nothing —and tightens her grip on the steering wheel.

I press on. "I have to get to my brother's wedding. I'm already a couple of days behind schedule because of following you to Queensland—"

"Whose fault was that!"

"—and then this bloody daft turkey incident . . ."

She clams up again, biting her lower lip. She's not actually said *no*.

I take a deep breath. "If I drive with my hand broken and have any sort of accident, the insurance would be invalid. You told me yourself you've never had an accident and you're a very careful driver and super responsible. That's quite the resumé."

She shakes her head, a huff of exasperation escaping her pursed lips.

"It'd be good to know I'd be in safe hands," I add, trying to inject some sincerity into my voice.

Her elbows flap. "I'm meant to be here to travel and see Australia," she mutters, struggling now to put the van into fourth.

I put my good hand over hers and assist with the gear stick. She snatches her hand away and flushes bright scarlet.

"You *would be* traveling and seeing Australia. I understand you haven't been to Victoria yet. It's beautiful this time of year." I flash her my winning smile, but her eyes are glued to the road ahead. "I could pay you . . ." If I sell a kidney.

Still, she says nothing.

"If you're worried about me making a move on you, you needn't be," I say. "I promise I'll keep my hands to myself. Unless you're concerned, you won't be able to resist me."

"Ha! As if! Get over yourself! I've no interest in you whatsoever."

Ouch. That smarts. More than I thought it would. I guess she's still mad about me calling her Tilly.

"Look." I lower my voice. Nothing like having your back against the wall to make you discard any scruples. I need someone to drive this van and myself to Victoria, and Alice is the obvious solution. I'm running out of time. Tilly is clearly not going to be back by the weekend and has said Alice would help me. Time to apply the screws. "I wouldn't ask you if I wasn't desperate, but I am. I'm so sorry about what happened on New Year's, I know I fucked up and it won't happen again. This is my brother's wedding we're talking about. Imagine if it was Tilly's. I really can't miss it. Come on, Alice, please."

Her fingers strum on the steering wheel. "How much?"

"What?"

"How much would you be willing to pay me?"

It really depends on how much Ben, my brother, is willing to cough up. "Um, a hundred dollars a day?"

"A hundred dollars!" she yelps.

"Eyes on the road, please. Okay, two hundred dollars a day." Bloody oath, she drives a hard bargain—Ben had better be good for this because there's no way I can afford it.

Alice's cheeks are flaming again and she's doing a lot of blinking. Feeling hot under the collar myself, I wind down the window. Admittedly, this situation is far from ideal, but it's not like I have a lot of choice.

"Why couldn't I drive you to the nearest airport? I could van-sit for you until after the wedding," she says, a bright smile on her face.

"The van is a wedding gift from my brother to his bride. It also happens to be their going away vehicle," I say.

"Oh."

"Yes, oh."

We drive on in silence.

After five minutes, she pipes up again. "Just to be crystal clear . . . if I do agree to this little road-trip . . . You're willing to pay me two hundred dollars per day to drive you back home to Victoria and there would be *no strings attached*. Absolutely *zero* additional benefits."

I laugh. So that's the problem. She's terrified I'll jump her. "Alice, first of all, I hate strings unless we're talking about you know . . . erm . . ." I cough. Clearly, she does not know. Not that type of girl, I remind myself. "The offer is three hundred dollars a day just to drive me. I'm not looking for anything else . . . And if I was, I wouldn't be paying anyone. If you can get me and this van to the wedding on time and in one piece, I'll pay you an additional bonus of, let's say, five hundred dollars."

Alice moans like a cow in labor. "Would it be cash in hand?"

"Fine by me. Once the mission is completed." It's kind of beginning to feel like a mission. Mission Impossible.

She fails to look reassured. In fact, she looks dejected. "One proviso," she says.

"What?"

"You don't mention the money to Tilly. If I hear she's found out, I'll leave you in the middle of nowhere. I don't care if you miss the wedding. You'll have to walk to Victoria."

"No worries. Am I allowed to ask why?"

"Ask all you want. It doesn't mean I need to answer. Tilly needs her head examined. I don't understand what the hell she sees in . . . some people."

I sigh. Alice has me labeled as some sort of dirtbag and clearly hasn't talked to her own sister about our non-existent relationship, a twin she claims to be close to. If she wants to think the worst of me, it's unlikely anything I say will change her mind. Other than maybe a financial incentive. Her mouth does a strange little twerk side to side, and she glances in the rearview mirror. Her ramrod back sags a little. I fully expect her to give me a death stare and tell me to *be gone, Satan!*

She does give me a death stare, but instead of calling me Satan, she says breathily, "God help me. Then, okay, I suppose we have a deal."

Okay, so maybe, I imagined she said it *breathily*.

12

ALICE

I t's not like I have any choice in the matter. Twister sent me IT #3 before I picked Guy up from the hospital.

IT #3: Drive Guy home.

What happened to the ITs having to be achievable before breakfast?

Show me you're on the road and we can tick it off when you get there. You owe him!

None of this would've happened if you hadn't started the IT Games. Just remember - this is your can of worms.

Better the devil you know than the devil you don't, right? Okay, so I'm worried sick being stuck in the van with Guy, no matter how lovely that van is, may be the death of me, but I've no money to stay anywhere and if he's going to pay me . . . Money gives me options.

His roguish smile when I agree makes my stomach flutter with butterflies. No worries! Ha! No worries for him maybe, because I'm doing enough worrying for the both of us.

Life is full of crazy. Full of unexpected twists and turns. And a little too full of *Twister*. At this point, I'm not sure if my sister wants revenge on Guy or me, or both of us. But that does not make us partners in crime . . . Or partners in any sense of the word. I am his employee. *Yeeuurrk*. Sort of. I am an independent contractor . . . or whatever! I don't love this idea, but I haven't got any better ones.

"What's the plan?" I ask, cagily.

"We head to Sydney and stay at my place tonight. Drive on to Victoria first thing tomorrow morning."

"Oh no. No way. Thanks for the offer and all that, but I'm not staying at your place in Sydney. I'd rather sleep on the sidewalk." No sodding way am I staying in his house. I have flashbacks of the early hours of New Year's. Me on the kitchen sink draining board my emotional state little more than soap suds. Me in Guy's arms, melting. Me with my red dress and New Year's resolutions pooled around my ankles.

"It's not *my* place. I rent it with Brum, Fin and Scooter."

"Oh . . . But the traffic is terrible. All the drivers in Sydney are crazy, and although I'm competent, I haven't driven this van before and as it's a wedding present, I think it best if we avoid Sydney altogether, don't you?"

He gives me a look, forehead creasing. "Whatever. If you could put your foot on the gas, though? At this rate, I won't just be late, I'll miss the wedding altogether."

"When is it?"

"Saturday."

I shrug. "Plenty of time. No problemo. The hurrier you go, the behinder you get," I say, quoting *Alice in Wonderland*.

"What?" says Guy, looking bemused.

"This is as fast as the van goes," I say and focus on the endless tarmac and heat haze rising from the road ahead of me.

13

ALICE

·

I like to think, even though Twister believes I'm a deadbeat and incapable of living by the seat of my pants, this whole road-trip is proving her wrong. Admittedly, it's hard to relax; who could relax sitting next to old Tinderpants. The tension in the van feels like one strike and he might go *Kaboom*. Plus, I'm pretty sure that's the Tinder dating app he's scrolling through. Although, not being on any dating apps—not being on any apps in general—I wouldn't know for sure. Whatever it is, it's keeping him fully occupied.

Thankfully, the coastal highway looks fairly straight and easy driving. Not a brush turkey in sight.

"How's your hand?" I ask Guy, who, since I agreed to drive, seems to have lost all ability to make conversation.

"Still attached to my forearm," he mutters.

Point in case: Catatonic.

So maybe I'm not very good at the whole chitchat thing, but at least I'm making some effort. Admittedly, Guy has reason to be grumpy. He probably resents being stuck with me. I know Guy is perfectly capable of acting like Prince Charming when he wants something, but it's like the second he's got what he wants, he turns off that switch and goes into hibernation. He makes zero effort to disguise his yawns, which are now rolling out of him with the regularity of ocean waves.

I study him out of the corner of my eye, nursing his broken left hand.

While I battle with the gearstick and mutter under my breath, Guy grows increasingly catatonic.

"Do you mind if I put the radio on?" I ask after an hour of driving in silence.

"Sure," he says.

Wow. One word. I know I'm not the chatty type, but I may have met my match.

"Only two thousand miles to the Mornington Peninsula," I say with a tremor in my otherwise cheerful voice as I glance at the speedometer. I haven't been able to get the van above sixty kilometers an hour. "By my calculations, that's over twenty-four hours' hard driving, so you're getting your money's worth."

There's no response. He's fallen asleep.

There are probably a dozen girls, maybe more, who'd gladly run me over to be sitting in my position right now: next to the *wannabe* celebrity Guy Balcombe. But it's hard to warm to someone who has all the conversational talent of a Doberman.

Apart from the golden oldies on the radio, I drive on in silence for the next two hours.

TWO HOURS.

Finally, busting for a pee, I have to make a pit-stop.

I dare to look in Guy's direction again, but he's still out of it, his sun-bleached mop flopping over half of his face. It's an improvement. Relaxed, he looks like a different person. A softer, more vulnerable version. Of course, that's probably because his one brain cell is taking a rest. Once he's awake again, it'll be a whole different story.

A sign for a service station five kilometers ahead flashes by, and I pull off the dual carriageway. Unfortunately, when I pull up to the tjunction there's no indication of which way I need to turn. Seriously? I peer left and right. The car behind us beeps. There's a low red building to our right, so, feeling hopeful, I turn that way.

Unfortunately, the low red building turns out to be some sort of DIY gardening store. I drive on a bit further and spot a sign back to the Pacific Highway. I make the snap decision to swerve onto the ramp back onto the highway. I breathe more easily once we're back on the main road, but I still need to wee and pelvic clenching is only going to get me so far ... the pressure is becoming unbearable.

I notice the hoarding we're driving under indicates . . . we're headed back in the direction of Brisbane.

Shit! Shit! Shit! How did that happen?

Guy stirs and adjusts his position.

Somehow, I need to get off the damn motorway and turn this van around, but the kilometers flash by and none of the exits seem to offer a route that will allow me to get back onto the highway in the right direction. I can't risk waking him and letting him know I've added even more time to our journey. He already thinks I'm an idiot. I'm unwilling to risk getting off the motorway again, but we're heading back in the direction we came from. Eventually, when my bladder is close to exploding, I pull off onto a road that seems to lead into a rainforest and not a lot else.

I stop the van on the soft verge and make a dash for the bushes.

"Where are we?" asks Guy, waking up, as I clamber back into the driver's seat.

"Um. Not sure," I say, avoiding looking at him. "I think I just saw an emu. Had to stop to take a photo."

"Of course, you did. Think I'll do the same," he says, getting out. While he does his business, I open my phone and frantically try to find out where we are on the map. Our lack of progress makes me cringe, but at least I now have my bearings. Until I spot a message from Twister saying IT #4.

The van door opens again and I stuff my phone in the door pocket.

I do an excruciating *twelve-point* turn because, of course, there is no power steering, and I may be freaking out a little at the thought of my next Impossible Thing. Grateful no other vehicles are coming our way, I drive back *under* the motorway, breathing more easily when I see a sign directing us back onto the Pacific Highway and Sydney.

"Didn't we go past here already?" growls Guy.

"Of course, not." I register the familiar beat of Shania Twain's *That don't impress me much* and throw myself into singing along with gusto.

14

GUY

So this is a mistake. A disaster already. A terrible decision. Alice hates me. And at the moment, I don't exactly love her, or the knowledge she's only doing this for the money. I don't know why I'm so wound up about everything, but it feels like the girl I fell for in Sydney was a figment of my imagination. I mean, I knew she was faking being Tilly, but for a crazy moment there, I really thought I'd found someone special.

This Alice is so far from my type, it's not funny. She wanted to listen to opera on the radio for fuck's sake! For a while, we tussled over what music we listen to until I had to grab the steering wheel because we were in danger of ending up in a ditch. That shut her up. There's no fucking way I'm listening to opera for one second, let alone hours.

An old '60s track, *King of the Road*, fills the silence. I almost want to weep because it reminds me so much of my father. I'm reminded of family road-trips along the Great Ocean Road or up north to Queensland. Whenever Dad heard this, he'd turn it up full volume and the whole family would sing along.

I can't help but join in.

I don't know what surprises me more, the fact that Alice knows all the lyrics or that she's singing along with a cheesy grin on her face.

"Family favorite," she says, grinning sheepishly.

It makes my heart twang like a plucked guitar.

Besides, when she sings in harmony with me, it's like my head loses its bearings. I'm in love with her voice, that's all. She harmonizes so effortlessly and there is a tonal purity that transcends . . . description. It's like nothing I've ever experienced.

When the song ends, Alice smiles, but it doesn't quite reach her eyes. Which is unbearable and makes me feel grouchy as all hell.

"So where exactly is home?" she asks, attempting to make polite conversation again. I wish she wouldn't. I feel bad enough about chasing her halfway around the country already without her feeling she has to treat me like we're strangers.

"Balcombe Brothers' Estate Winery."

"A winery. Very fancy."

"Mmm." I look out the side window. "If you like wine. I prefer beer." I suppose we don't know that much about one another. Perhaps that's a good thing: the more Alice knows about me, probably the less she'd feel inclined to make polite conversation. I'm the black sheep of the family. I was always in trouble at school, messing about to disguise the fact I struggled to read because I'm dyslexic. I refused to do a trade because the only thing I was interested in was music. I went to Sydney to avoid the constant ear-bashing I was getting from members of my family. Unlike Alice here, who according to Tilly has always been a high-achiever, a scholarship student, with a place to study at Oxford University.

Bravo.

Give the girl a medal.

For all her smarts, when we finally make it back onto the Pacific Highway, I suspect I may need to stop taking painkillers and attempt to stay awake because we have undoubtedly been past this spot already. And she lied. Alice's driving might be acceptable, but her navigational skills and integrity are clearly questionable.

I flex my fingers, doing the exercises I've been instructed to do by the physio, and Alice gives me a wary look.

"I hope your hand's not causing you too much pain. I'm . . . I'm sorry about . . . everything," she says.

The last thing I want from her is pity. "You apologize way too much."

"I'm sorry!" she snaps.

I can't help laughing. She shoots me a freakin-hell look.

"Shit. I guess I do. National habit, I guess. Sorry. Bugger! Sorry, not sorry."

I chuckle. As much as I try to resist, I can't help but be amused by her. It's like she's from another planet and everything is new and fresh through her eyes. She's a bit of a dork—admittedly a very attractive dork—and light-years younger than me in terms of street smarts. How Tilly can be the complete opposite intrigues me. At least, that's the impression I get. I could be wrong. There's something confounding about the pair of them.

I hunt around for my meds.

"Have you seen my painkillers?" I mutter.

"You sure you're not sitting on them?"

"Right. Thanks so much for the helpful advice." I shake my head in frustration. My hand is throbbing like a bastard. We pull into a service station and, while I fumble to fill the tank one-handed, she goes in hunt of the toilets.

She's back in the van by the time I return from paying for the fuel and the strongest painkillers the service station sold.

"Look what I found under your seat," she says, holding out my meds.

Seriously? "Thanks," I mutter, snatching them from her hand. I'm too done-in to argue further, and despite the painkillers I've already scarfed, I take a couple of the prescribed meds as well.

Alice shoots me a reproving look.

You'd think she was a saint. But I know looks can be very deceptive. I keep thinking about that damn turkey and having flashbacks of her running around the garden, arms flapping as if she was trying to take off. A gruff laugh escapes me, and Alice glances my way.

"What?" she asks.

"Nothing." Or something . . . For a moment, I'd thought she was high as a kite on something one of the surfers had given her. Or perhaps dancing. But neither of those is her vibe. God knows what Alice's vibe is. She might look like Tilly and sound like Tilly (though her voice is even more bewitching), but it's like an alien has visited planet Earth and abducted Tilly from her own body. Alice is so unbearably strait-laced . . . it makes me want to snap a few laces.

I lose myself in that happy thought. Indulge in some lazy daydreams. The pain drifts away on a pleasant tide, my eyelids heavy again . . .

Muttering because I fucking fell asleep again, didn't I, and we should have got so much farther by now, I direct Alice along a dirt track to a secluded beach I know.

"Here? Aren't we like in the middle of nowhere?" she squawks.

Whose fault is that?

She looks around with dinner-plate eyes like I'm about to drag her off into the bushes, have my evil way with her and then dump her body. Tempting though that thought is, I contain myself.

"You've been driving eight hours straight," I say—How is it possible we have made so little headway?—"but we could keep going and stay at my place in Sydney tonight, if you'd prefer."

Her pretty mouth snaps closed like I knew it would. I'm not sure whether the panicked look in her eye is at the prospect of revisiting the past or staying out here in the wilderness with me.

We bump along the track and park up in a dirt carpark not far from the sea.

"I'm hot. I'm going to take a dunk. You coming?" I add as an afterthought. Ever the gentleman.

"No, thanks. Perhaps later."

"Suit yourself." Peeling myself off the hot upholstery, I get out of the van and stretch. Then I pop the roof and open the sliding side door.

I make hard work of stripping off my t-shirt because it's no easy matter with one hand. Alice takes a step toward me but backs off when I start swearing. I catch her checking out the bruising across my ribcage.

"Impressive, eh?" I can't help goading her.

Gratifyingly, she blushes scarlet and bites her lip. God, she's too easy to wind up. It's about the only pleasure I've got left to me.

"I was just . . . those bruises look painful," she says, now avoiding looking in my direction.

"I'll live." I toss my t-shirt in the van. The look she flashes me is one of absolute disdain. I have finally figured out something about Alice: she's a tidiness freak. Neat and tidy is her *vibe*.

Chuckling quietly, because I've found her Achilles heel, I tramp toward the beach and the setting sun.

Stomping across the sand, I feel only mildly ashamed by my lack of manners . . . but Alice hasn't been totally honest with me. She still hasn't mentioned her little detour. And I'm so thoroughly pissed off about my hand and this whole situation and all the gigs I'm not going to be able to play that Alice's welfare is the least of my worries. Surfing, sex and playing music are usually my sure-fire methods for releasing any pent-up emotions. At the moment, I can't do *any* of those things and that doesn't put me in the best of moods.

Added to that, the idea of my brother's wedding keeps popping into my mind . . . like getting in the water when someone has just spotted a shark. Not where you want to be. Plus I will have to look happy about it. There will be the usual interrogation about girlfriends, or lack thereof, by the family. There will be Xanthe reminding me of Tina and Tina, her mother, scrutinizing me like I'm a piece of meat on a platter ready to be served as part of the buffet. There will also be the best man, Marcus Sauvage, the celebrity chef everyone loves to hate. So, all in all, it's going to be such a happy reunion. Somehow, I just need to survive it and come out unscathed.

I plunge everything except my left hand beneath the water, wishing I could wash away the last few days and handle this whole situation like a top bloke instead of the prize wanker that I apparently am.

The water is a relief after the heat of the van, my head and Alice.

When I resurface, Alice appears from the tree line looking whiter than the sand itself, a hand held to her brow shielding her eyes from the sun. Or maybe me.

Pretending not to see her, I wade out even deeper, keen to keep some distance—and my sanity. Or what's left of it.

I sink beneath the surface again and try to chill. My head is a hot fucking mess.

That evening, after more effing and blinding, Alice nudges me aside and quietly takes over making supper. It's a simple spread of salad, cold meats, bread and cheese. She butters my bread and cuts slices of cheese for me, and I grunt thanks of sorts. I don't trust myself to speak more than a few words.

As if we've signed a temporary truce, we sit outside on a couple of deckchairs watching the sun go down like an old married couple. I try to tinker on my guitar, but it's too painful and I don't think I'm doing my hand any favors. Jotting down a couple of lyrics in my notebook, I hum a couple of bars.

All my dreams ripped away
Lost for words and broken
All my hopes stripped away
Promises left unspoken . . .

Alice asks to borrow my guitar.

"Help yourself," I say grudgingly.

She can't play for shit, but you can't fault her for effort. The way she bites her lower lip when she attempts to play a chord makes my hands twitch to help her out.

I grab myself a beer. Best to keep my hands occupied.

"Want one?"

"No thanks," she says. "One's enough for me."

Of course, it would be. Saint Alice. I Googled Saint Alice on my phone. Turns out, Saint Alice is the patron saint of the blind and paralyzed? How fucking apt.

I go back to writing my lyrics.

No virtue left to speak of
No desire to be a saint
I'd rather be consumed by fire
And damned for what I aint

I can't write for shit because listening to Alice mangle my guitar is beginning to do my head in.

"Know any actual tunes? Or even any chords?" I ask.

"Sorry. Not really. I wouldn't mind learning, though." A faint blush colors her cheeks as she focuses on plucking away at the strings, her pink tongue pressed to her top lip, flaring her pert nostrils in concentration. Enough to drive any man nuts.

Seriously, I cannot look at her.

And I cannot concentrate.

"Didn't Tilly tell me everyone in your family was musical?"

She looks up. "I am musical. I play piano, violin and the organ," she replies primly.

"And which organ would that be?" I say, being a prize dickhead.

She pulls a face. "The church organ! Does your mind always fall in the gutter?"

"No need to fall when it's already made a home there."

Putting down my empty beer can, with a sigh, I get up and lean over her. "May I? Show you some chords?"

"Oh. Yes, please."

I reposition her fingers with my right hand. "That's an A." I move them again, trying to ignore the bird's eye view of cleavage I'm getting. "And that's a D. There, now you've doubled your repertoire."

I hasten back to my chair, and she thrums the new chords . . . until my eardrums bleed. Even though I pretend it's got something to do with what I'm writing, I can't help groaning.

"If my playing is so horrible, how about you teach me something worthwhile?" she asks.

Oh, I'd like to teach her alright. I'd like to take her into the van and strum her until she screams my name—

Fuck. No.

Fuck. Get a grip.

I do not want that.

I give myself a shake and stand up. Anything has got to be better than listening to her current inept . . . *strumming*. But the only tune to come to mind is the bloody *King of the Road* tune we were belting out in the van earlier.

"You've already got the hang of the A and D chords, all you need is the D to play this." I position her fingers at E and start strumming the strings myself. "Sound familiar?" Crouching, I sing the lyrics and direct her through the chord shifts. Removing the guitar pick from her fingers, I take over the strumming, trying to be professional and not insanely hot and bothered by the satin smooth skin of her neck, and the floral scent in my nostrils and the swell of her breasts inches from my lips.

By the time she's mastered the Bb, Eb and F, which to give her due credit does not take long at all, she's looking at me with something close to forgiveness in her hazel eyes and I am in a world of trouble.

I get up and brush myself down. I might need another swim.

"Thank you. I really appreciate that. You have a . . . a gift," she says, hesitantly.

That could mean anything. I have a gift for picking the wrong sort of women. I have a gift for fucking up relationships. I have a gift for saying some stupid stuff. And hell, I have a gift for drinking beer like it could put out the fire under my skin.

From inside the van, I watch her head bend again over my guitar and listen to her try to repeat the performance on her own, and for some reason—maybe those ridiculous lyrics—I imagine her having her arms wrapped around me instead of around my guitar. How is it even possible to be jealous of my guitar? How is it possible to think such dumb-ass thoughts? One thing is undeniable. Her voice is incredible. Like a bell. The minute I hear her sing, the hairs on my arms stand on end and I get tingles down my spine as if I've been touched by an invisible hand. Even the insects seem to hush to listen to her.

Hot damn. This is not happening. We still have at least a thousand miles or so to go.

But maybe tomorrow I could teach her another tune without getting a hard on.

Maybe tomorrow she'll confess about her grand 'detour'.

And maybe we'll see some pigs fly.

15

ALICE

I'm surprised by how patient Guy is with me. I mean he's still cantankerous and moody, but it feels like some sort of peace accord has been struck between us. But I could be wrong.

After a couple of hours of playing his guitar, my fingertips are too sore to continue. I examine them, but it's too dark to see what sort of state they're in. Blowing on them to cool them down, when I look up I catch Guy staring.

I get to my feet. "Well, that's probably enough strumming for one day."

A smile flickers at the corner of his mouth.

"Thank you for teaching me those chords . . ." I can't hold his gaze. "I'm exhausted. I think I might . . . go for a walk."

"A walk? In the dark?"

"Why not? It's a beautiful night. I'm just going for a stroll along the beach."

"Do you want company?"

"No! Nope. No, thank you," I say. His eyebrows shoot up and his eyes narrow, so I guess no *peace accord* after all, but the last thing I want is him spotting me skinny-dipping.

When we stopped at a service station to fill up with fuel, I sent Twister the photo of me and the van on the road. I checked my phone when we got here and saw she'd sent me IT#4: Go skinny-dipping.

I swear she's deliberately making life as difficult as possible for me. She knows I'm with Guy. If I didn't know better, I'd think she was deliberately pushing me toward him. It makes no sense, but knowing her, this could be some sort of test. She's fiercely competitive. Probably dying for me to give up, but there's no way I'm quitting.

"Thanks, but I'm fine by myself and you look busy," I say to Guy. *Stay that way,* I pray.

"No problem. Enjoy," he says, like he's not interested in where I go or whether I get lost in the dark.

I trudge down to the beach, checking over my shoulder just to make sure he hasn't had the crazy idea of following me. But no chance. Who am I kidding? He barely notices me. He's in love with my sister. I'm just the driver.

I stand looking out at the ocean. *Beautiful* isn't a big enough word. It's magnificent. Awesome. Intimidating. I've never seen such a ceiling of stars. The sound of the waves thunders in my ears and I appear to have the whole beach to myself . . .

The quicker I get this whole shit-show over and done with, the better.

I stride down toward the water's edge before I can stop to think about what I'm doing and lose my nerve. The waves look even more powerful close up. Quickly, I pull my t-shirt over my head and shimmy out of my shorts and underwear. The wind licks around my bare ass. For a second, I hesitate. Am I really doing this? How deep do I have to go for this to be classed as skinny-dipping? One toe? Up to my knees? Twister will never let me get away with anything other than the 'Full Monty' and, of course, there needs to be evidence.

I take my first step. "Damn, that's cold!" I don't know what I was expecting . . . a warm bath? The water is *freezing*.

You can do this. You just have to believe. "I believe," I say firmly. I have to admit, as I stand with the waves lapping around my ankles, there is something thrilling about the air brushing over parts of my body that are usually well-covered. It could almost be . . . exhilarating. I almost want to yell out. *Mostly curses at my sister.* But God forbid if Guy should come running.

Turning on my phone camera's video function, I hold it up and start filming. "Twister, here I am, starkers." I wade deeper into the water, my legs fighting the surging waves. "The water isn't warm. Or pleasant. In fact, it is freezing and there's a bit of a current . . . If I get swept off my feet, you'll be to blame." I pause to give her the briefest flash of my nakedness and then lower myself under the water up to my neck. Holding my phone above the surging waves, I do a 360-degree turn to show her. I film the sea, the sky and the beach. All so huge. And empty.

Apart from a flip-flop floating in my direction.

No, no, no!

Panic-stricken, I turn off my phone and wade ashore. I find another flip-flop bobbing ten yards along the beach, but where the hell are all my clothes? They can't have just floated away . . . Can they?

The next ten minutes are a nightmare: Me rushing up and down the beach in the dark, hands groping blindly in the water and coming up with nothing but—*Ew!*—seaweed and more seaweed. My knickers, bra, t-shirt, shorts—all my sodding clothes—have been carried away on the crest of a wave.

Bloody hell. Seriously, bloody fucking hell!

What do I do?

What can I do except continue to scour the beach for the next half hour—in vain.

What if Guy starts worrying about me and comes looking? No, he won't. I'm pretty sure he won't. He doesn't care enough and I'm an adult—admittedly a cork-brained incompetent adult—and I made it clear I wanted to be alone. But what do I do? Jesus. I'm probably going to have to wait until Guy's definitely asleep before creeping back to camp.

Shit. This does not feel exhilarating in the slightest. My hair is dripping wet, I'm cold and miserable and, oh great, my skin is a carpet of goosebumps.

Who would've believed Australia could be this cold at this time of year? I am so pissed at Twister.

But I also need her advice. Angrily, I send her the video I took and a ranty voicemail explaining how IT #4 has gone to shit.

No problem, I'll send a Guy I know with a towel.

Don't you dare! He's asleep!

He's awake. We were just talking seconds ago.

Don't. Send. Guy! I'm fine. Tell him if he comes down here, I'm not going to drive him anywhere!

Twister

Twister!

In the distance somewhere, I think I hear a kookaburra. Or it could be someone, howling with laughter.

16

GUY

I can't help but crack up when Twister tells me about Alice's predicament.

"Poor fucking Alice!" I splutter through my tears of laughter.

"Poor Alice? You mean Malice. But, she'll probably die of hypothermia before she suffers the humiliation of you seeing her naked," says Tilly.

I get a flashback to our house and Alice in her underwear. The chance of actually seeing her without any clothes is disturbingly appealing. "Well, she's not going to die of hypothermia. It's a little breezy, but—" I crack up laughing again.

"Look, seriously, I feel kind of responsible. Do me a favor and take the poor lass some dry clothes and a towel."

"I'm not sure that's such a smart idea."

"You'd rather let her sit shivering on the beach until dawn?"

"No. I'm sure she'll come back . . . in her own sweet time."

"I know my sister. I'm telling you, she won't."

I sigh. These bloody Havoc women. "Honestly? Fine. I'll take her a towel."

"And some clothes."

"Yes, Ma'am."

"Thanks, Guy. I owe you big time."

"Don't worry, I'm logging it."

When I open Alice's backpack to grab her spare clothes, I can't help but notice she has a journal stuffed down the side. Her private journal. Only an asshole would read someone's private journal.

Only an asshole like me.

Just a quick peek . . . I can't seem to help myself. And it's not like Alice is going to brave coming back anytime soon, so I shall be undisturbed . . .

Feeling wicked, I open it up.

Holy shit!

1st January

I am Down Under in Hell. Seriously, Twister has left me in Sydney without any sort of explanation and I've just made a total tit of myself over a guy. It's the first day of the new year and instead of feeling excited and full of hope, I feel like total CRAP! I can't believe I fell for his utter bullshit. I can't even call Twister to talk about it because I haven't got a phone. And I can't help but worry I may have unknowingly screwed her over. Again. I'm not sure she's forgiven me for Colin yet, so God knows how she'll react when she finds out about me kissing Guy.

Who the fuck is Colin?

My new year's resolutions:

1. Do NOT even think about GB. He is not worth the time of day.

2. *Find out what's going on with Twister and do whatever it takes to fix this situation.*

3. *Do NOT look at another man while I am traveling . . . let alone men Twister has shown a passing interest in.*

4. *Stick to my resolutions for more than five minutes!*

There's not a whole lot written because she only started writing her journal on 1ˢᵗ January, but my eyes zip across the page. It's a fucking revelation, although I don't understand all of it. What are ITs? There's a hilarious account of her hitchhiking . . . and a not so hilarious account of her . . .

IT#2 Chasing a brush turkey.

I cannot believe what I'm reading. *She* fucking chased that turkey into my path? And admitted nothing? I'm tempted to let her spend the night on the beach. But an even stronger urge to have it out with her, to find out what the hell is going on, takes hold.

I stuff the journal back in her backpack.

Fuming, I stalk up the sandy path between the wind-tortured trees. I will make her pay for this: not only causing my injury, but never owning up to anything. How conniving and dishonest can someone be? My feet slow. If I want to have it out with her, I'll have to admit to reading her journal. Dick move. Then I'll look like the bad guy. Fuck. I suppose it could be to my advantage to hold my cards close to my chest for now. God, I'm torn. Fucking furious, but also—Damn—I can't help feeling a little sorry for her. She's not exactly had the best start to the year, and I'm not entirely blameless for this situation, and Tilly does appear to be pulling some strings behind the scenes, and Alice has agreed to drive me home . . . If I upset her now, she might refuse to take me any farther.

Wooden steps lead down to the cove and there on the shore is Alice, a small, hunched figure sitting on the beach.

I take a few deep breaths to calm myself down.

Okay, man, you can do this.

Tempted as I am to call her out, I bite my tongue. Plus, I don't want to startle her just yet. Not until I'm good and ready. Then I will blow her out of the water.

For now, I can't help staring, my mind and body in turmoil. How small and vulnerable she looks. I can't help but feel like a bit of a tool for thinking all I've been thinking.

Then she stands up and my brain empties.

Wow.

My mouth falls open. Ogling like this isn't a crime, is it? And it's not like she's not guilty of any wrong-doing. She's not as innocent as she makes out. But I know I should make her aware—

She turns slightly, caught in the moonlight, and I forget to breathe altogether.

The moon cuts a silvery path across the rolling waves in the bay and Alice's profile is cast in silver . . . I don't want any other fucker seeing her like this. This is for my eyes only. She's a work of art. Something to covet. Something to treasure. Someone.

And I think my brain melts because I groan aloud.

Alice whirls about, sees me and gasps. She tries to cover up her nakedness with her hands and does a deliciously bad job of it.

I stride the last few steps of the beach toward her, then toss her clothes in her direction.

"Are you out of your mind going swimming by yourself at this time of night?" My voice is a growl, every nerve in my body screaming. "What the hell were you thinking going in the water alone?"

She looks away. Turns her back on me, which is even worse. "I was, um, just skinny-dipping. What does it look like?"

Her skin glistens. She's haloed in silver by the moon.

It looks like fucking awesome.

And temptation.

And damnation.

Hot damn! I attempt to recalibrate my jumbled brain, but something has snapped. I'm seriously broken.

"It looks attention-seeking," I say, dry mouthed.

This is not the Alice I thought I knew.

Unless she's lost her mind.

Unless she's been putting on an act all along.

Unless she and her sister are playing me. Right now, I don't know what to think. I'm confused. Reeling drunk and stone-cold sober.

I shake my head and blink hard, but she's still there, showing me her perfect-pear bare ass. I think I might have died and gone to heaven. More likely I've died and gone to hell because I'm burning up.

Hot damnation.

"Well, you'd know all about that." She grabs her clothes and scuttles away from me faster than a crab on steroids.

I run a hand through my hair, my whole body trembling.

A safe distance away, Alice's legs scissor frantically as she wriggles into her underwear. Then with her back to me, she concertinas trying to fasten her bra.

Dear God.

I need to put some distance between us before I do or say something I'll regret. After her reaction to me so far on this road-trip, after what I've read in her journal, I suspect she might object. Vociferously.

Marching off along the beach, it's a moment before I realize I'm heading in the opposite direction to camp. I press the heel of my hands to my eye sockets. "Fucking hell! This is fucking hell!" I mutter, furiously.

In my head, the images of Alice, water-kissed and wet, are relentless . . . Drops of water shimmering on her bare shoulders. Sparkling on her eyelashes. I wanted to lick every damn drop off her.

And I appear to have unexpectedly developed a raging hard on. *I don't fucking think so.* My dick doesn't pay any attention. My brain is too busy imagining punishing her. Her naked body mashed up against mine. My hand on her hips. Our naked skin as slippery as fucking heaven. I ain't never making it through those pearly gates. Right now, I'm incapable of any sort of rational thought.

I try a different tack.

She's the reason my hand is broken. She's destroyed my summer and possibly my career . . ." I'm blistering with rage again, but my traitorous dick is still going, *Fuck, fuck, fuck, she would feel so good. It's a waste of time making out you're angry when you have wood and all you want to do is nail her!*

Fuck!

This is a disaster. My imagination has gone haywire, my body feels like liquid fire and I need to cool down. I don't think I've ever felt this out of control. Admittedly, I like Alice. Admittedly, I want her. But I also don't want to want her. How nuts is that? Perhaps, it 's the moon, but I'm tempted to howl. She's the last person I should want . . . but I can't remember ever feeling this worked up, about anyone.

Ever.

Alice is a siren and I'm as good as wrecked.

On the rocks.

Slain.

I groan. Fucking great. This can not be happening to me. I don't think I've ever wanted to bury myself in someone as badly as I want to bury myself in Alice right now.

I might as well be buried and lying in my own coffin, her hammering in the nails. I'm a goner. A lost cause.

Alice is better off without me. But I need her—or at least the band does. I hate this Catch 22 shit. I'm damned if she leaves and damned if she stays. I'm damned if I act on how I'm feeling, and damned if I don't. Do I just surrender to everything? Try to convince her after all this that I'm a good guy and I don't mind what she's done to me?

Fuck, yes.

Can I really justify making this potentially worse for Alice than it already is? Do I have sufficient reasons? Yes again, shouts the voice in my head even if that does make you a selfish prick.

I turn to face the sea, gasping for air and slam my fists against my thighs. "Fuck!" Fuck my broken hand, that hurts! It's not the only part of me that's broken.

I'm as empty and useless as a broken shell.

I glance back along the beach.

Alice has gone. The beach is quiet and serene.

Except for me and my ignorant dick, and the devil in my head who informs me I have to keep Alice tethered to my side at least until after the wedding.

17

ALICE

I wait for Guy to return, not quite sure what the sleeping arrangements are and, as embarrassed and humiliated as I undoubtedly am, I still need to know the sleeping arrangements.

Half an hour later, he finally stalks past me without saying anything.

Why's he so angry?

I wait outside the van while he fetches another beer from the fridge.

"Thank you. For my clothes," I mumble. "Sorry, you had to go out of your way."

"No worries," he says, opening the can. "Want one?"

"No thanks. I thought I might go to bed."

He takes several glugs of his beer, and I have to drag my eyes away from his throat.

"I was wondering what the sleeping arrangements are." He puts his can down by the fold-out chair he was sitting in when I left.

"Hold on, I'll sort the bed," he says. "It's rock and roll."

"Rock and roll?" I peer through the door as he lifts and pulls the bench seat out into a bed.

"Oh, that sort of rock and roll. Where's the other one?" I ask.

"The other what?"

"The other bed."

Silence.

"There *is* another bed?" I say.

He scratches the back of his neck.

"Um, no." He opens a couple of the panels on the pop-up so the netting lets through a slight breeze, and I get a flash of taut muscled midriff. "Some vans have an extra bed up top, but not this one. Perhaps I should've made that clear, but I thought you'd have noticed."

A snort escapes me. "I didn't. So where are you planning to sleep tonight?"

He looks at the bed. "In the bed. There's room for two. Of course, if *you'd* rather sleep outside."

"Outside! With all the insects and snakes and God knows what else? Are you kidding me?" I shriek.

He grunts. "Hey, I was told you were intrepid . . . but I guess not. I'm happy to share my bed with you, so long as you don't try anything on. After your escapade earlier . . ."

"That was not my fault!" I splutter. "Besides, it's what you might do that worries me. If all the stories I've heard are true . . ."

"What stories?" His brows draw together. "*Bedtime* stories?"

The way he's looking at me, my cheeks grow hotter and hotter.

"You shouldn't believe everything you read in the gossip magazines."

"For your information, I don't read gossip magazines. D-did you not think for one m-moment that this s-set-up might prove awkward? That you should've asked me?"

He shrugs. "For your information, nah. I guess it slipped my mind."

He's being a complete asshole again. "Why does this not surprise me? I mean, this is so . . . not on! We're practically strangers!"

"Well, I'm sure you'll know from all the stories you've heard that I've slept with plenty of strangers." Unfazed, he goes back outside, sits down and opens up his notebook.

I seriously detest him right now. "Guy, *you* might think this is a perfectly acceptable way to carry on, but I don't."

"That figures." He writes a few words, then crosses something out, while I clench and unclench and clench my fists. "I don't know why you're making such a fuss, darl. You're being paid for this trip and you were kind of at a loose end—"

"I was not at a loose end!" I snap.

He looks up. "Okay, let's say, you didn't seem to be headed in any particular direction." His attention returns to his notebook.

"Just because I don't have plans set in concrete, doesn't mean I'm lost or don't know where I'm going."

He doesn't miss a beat. "Oh yeah, that explains why you took such a scenic detour this arvo."

Crap. He realized and said nothing.

"The only direction I wish I was going in is the opposite one to you!" I slide the van door shut with as much force as I can muster. But it only slides slowly along its rails.

Grumbling, I get changed into my nightclothes and study the bed. How, in God's name, in practical terms, are we going to make this work? The only thing giving me any peace of mind is that Guy's made it abundantly clear he's not remotely interested in me. Even naked. But I need to make it equally clear I'm not interested in him either.

This is mutual disinterest.

I can't have him thinking I'm hankering after him.

There are three spare cushions, so I pile them down the center of the bed. It's not exactly the icy Wall of Westeros but even he can't fail to get the message loud and clear. But in case he doesn't, I pile on several layers of clothing.

I open the van door again.

"Do you sleep on the left or the right?" I demand.

He strokes his throat, focused on whatever it is he's doing. "Babe, I'm not fussed. I'm ambidextrous in that regard."

"That's not what that word even means. Ambidextrous means you can use your right hand as well as your left. It has nothing to do with which side of the bed you sleep on," I say haughtily.

"But I guess it does when you're using your hands . . . in bed." He smirks to himself. Smug bastard.

I hate him so much. So much it hurts. But someone has to be the grown-up here and clearly, it'll never be him.

"You can take the same side as when we're driving. So the passenger side. Just don't get confused in the dark," I mutter, trying to slam the door closed again.

"Goodnight, Kook," he calls.

"Don't call me Kook. I am not *your* anything. I'm a free agent. An independent woman!" I shout.

He chuckles.

"And I'm free to leave you in the middle of nowhere at any time," I add. "I can go where I want and do what I want. I refuse to be put in a box or tied down."

"How disappointing."

I smack my head on an overhead shelf. "Ow! Bastard!" I don't know what's got into him, but it's like ever since the skinny-dipping episode, he's kicked up a gear, winding me up something wicked.

I can't let it lie. I stick my head out the van door again.

He sighs and turns his head. "Yes?"

"If so much as your little finger strays to my side of the bed tonight, I'm not going to drive you to hospital to get it fixed after I break it. You might like to think on that," I snap.

He snorts. "I promise I shall waste no time thinking about you at all. You have my word."

"And which word would that be? Manipulative? Machiavellian? Silver-tongued?"

"Oh, Alice," he says, lancing me with his dark gaze. "Anyone would think we'd met in a previous life. I promise to keep my silver tongue to myself."

My stomach flips like a pancake. I shut the van door again. Clambering onto the bed and lying down, my nose presses up against the spare tyre. It smells of hot rubber. And it's hot as hell's armpit in here. I can barely breathe. I've no choice: I have to strip out of my jumper and tracksuit pants. I flop back down. Honest to God, it's like lying in a sweat box and the idea of Guy's body adding to the heat . . . and the memory of his fingers on those guitar strings . . . is making me steam. Lying there, panting because it's so hot, my mind strays to the vision of Guy stripping off his t-shirt earlier, exposing all that muscle and—

Stop!

And hard stomach muscles—

Stop! Stop!

And as for his silver tongue—

Stop! Stop! Stop!

I must stop thinking about him in that way. This is a short, uncomfortable interlude. A challenging adventure. As long as I can keep my mind off Guy, I'll be fine.

I try to count sheep, but the sound of scampering bush creatures and Guy's fingers tap, tap, tapping on his keyboard is keeping me awake. What is it he's doing so late? I thought Twister was bad with all the time she spent on social media. Maybe they're messaging one another. Having a laugh at my expense. Maybe I am paranoid and losing my mind . . .

I'm inexplicably homesick and still wide awake when the van door finally slides open again. The whole van shifts under his weight. Nerve endings on high alert, I roll onto my side with my back to him, listening as he goes about putting things away, brushing his teeth, gargling, going back out again, pissing on a bush, undressing . . .

The scent of him invades my space. Eucalypt and man and sea.

The additional heat from his body makes my spine tingle. I can feel his warm breath on my shoulder . . .

And seconds later he's snoring.

Champion. Bloody champion.

18

ALICE

I'm alone, dancing along the corridor at school, my footsteps slapping on the flagstones. I shout Twister's name and it echoes, but there's no answer. I don't want to be dancing alone. But I dance and twirl and call out her name . . . until I collide with someone.

Looking up, I see it's Colin. Ugh. Not someone I want to spend time with.

"Hey, are you alright, Tilly?"

"I'm not, Tilly, I'm—" But the words stick in my throat because Colin has morphed into Guy.

Laughing eyes snare mine. "Care to dance, Alice?"

"Yes!" I say, delighted, no thrilled, that he knows who I am.

"Do you want to know a secret place to hide?"

"Do I ever!"

Guy and I race along the streets of Sydney. Fireworks blaze overhead. Outside a terraced house, he stops, picks me up, and carries me over the threshold.

Raised voices disturb us. Tilly's voice. In a mad panic, I scramble out of *his arms and lunge through the closest open door. Tearing across the room, I hide behind the floor-to-ceiling curtains. Guy is there right behind me, panting in the darkness. He brushes my hair aside and plants a kiss on my shoulder. "Looks like you found it without me," he whispers.*

I catch his hand in mine. In the darkness, I gasp, dizzy with desire as I guide his hand downward over my breasts, my stomach, my hip and I want more.

"Oh, God, yes!" I moan, clasping his hand beneath mine, our fingers intertwined. "Oh, please!"

"Um, Alice . . . ?" a husky voice rasps in my ear.

I'm riding the crest of a wave, more turned on than I can ever remember, but something is resisting, pulling me to the surface.

"Alice, are you awake?"

Like being ducked beneath the water, I'm suddenly gasping for air. Something is very wrong. Blood thrums around my body drumming in my ears. "Colin?"

I am very much awake all of a sudden. Alert.

I open my eyes to stabbing shards of morning sunlight, instantly aware I'm in the van, only this isn't a nightmare about Colin, it's worse.

Understanding barrels over me like a crashing wave. I'm on Guy's side of the mattress, my hand over his, pressing it between my legs. For a second, I don't know what to do. It's like both of us are too petrified to move. Then, instinctively, we both move at once. He pulls his hand out from between my legs, and I flail, my elbow connecting with flesh and bone.

"Damn, Alice! My nose!"

Only seconds before I was moaning in the throes of ecstasy. What was I thinking? How could this possibly have happened?

"What the hell d'you think you're doing?" I yell, scrambling into the corner.

"Me?" Guy holds his nose. "It wasn't me who swapped sides of the bed and decided to snuggle up. It wasn't me who wrapped my hand around you. I was fast asleep, thank you very much. I didn't even feel—"

"You felt *everything*! You just had your hand on my . . . on my . . ." I cannot even say it. "Oh, my God, I think I'm going to throw up."

I put my head in my hands. This cannot be happening to me.

Oh. Dear. God.

How much of that was a dream and how much was real? Guy had his fingers literally on my . . . my *pulse*! And now I'm pulsating so hard, I don't know what to do with myself or where to look. I want to hide. I pull the sheet over my head. If I thought the skinny-dipping humiliation was bad enough last night, this is just . . . just . . . I want to gouge my own eyes out . . . except even then I'd still feel like *this*!

"If it's any consolation," says Guy, "I think you may have broken my nose. That's some right hook you're packing."

I speak from beneath the bedsheet. "It's not like you didn't deserve it!" *But did he? Or was this all me?* I can't help but notice what I'm wearing. Or the lack thereof. This is a bit like shutting the stable door once the horse has already bolted.

"I didn't do anything!" Guy protests.

Even if it was unwittingly, he *so* did. He *so* has. At some point during the night, I've shed most of my clothes—thankfully, not altogether: I'm still wearing my underwear. But still . . . it feels like, it seems like, he could have *plundered* me with his hands . . . but he didn't. And it was, *hand* singular, and even though it is undoubtedly a very competent hand—*Gaawwd!*—a hand *I* may have been steering . . . But still. *Shit! Shit, shit, and holy shit!* He reduced me into a writhing, slippery eel. I'm mortified and also still humming with all this useless . . . adrenaline. I'm not sure I can ever come out from under these covers again.

"I'm bleeding like a stuck pig," says Guy.

I emerge, glaring. "You are a pig!"

Even with a bloody nose, the bastard manages to look good.

I throw a pillow in his general direction. "Use that to mop it up!" Fat lot of good those did as a barrier.

"I'm sorry, Alice, but what were you thinking, rubbing yourself up against me when I was asleep, moaning in my ear?"

"I didn't *rub* myself up against you and I did *not* moan!" I yell, although if my dream was anything to go by, I'm pretty sure I did.

"Uh, yes you did. *Oh, God, yes! Oh, please!*" Guy mimics confirming my worst fears.

"Shut! Up! And. Get! Out!"

He opens the van door. "No need to make too big a deal of this. No harm done. I … uh … I always wake up with … uh … wood."

No harm done? Eyes shielded, I jab a finger at the van door and hope he gets the message. I feel scorched. Too hot with shame to speak. I press the back of my hands against my radiator cheeks.

Thank God, I didn't moan his name out loud. Or did I? Oh bloody hell! I should've known this was a terrible, no good, bloody awful idea. He'll never let me forget it. What have I done? What did he do? Kill me now! I'm dead.

Unfortunately, five minutes later, I'm still breathing, so I do what I always do: I unmake the bed and put all the bedding away, wishing I could unmake the whole incident. I roll the bed away so I don't have to look at it. I plump cushions and wipe down surfaces hoping to remove all traces.

My phone vibrates with a new message from Twister.

> Morning, Malice, How's it going? IT #5 Ask a
> stranger to dance.

"Alice?"

"What the hell now!" I snap. Can't Guy or my sister give me a moment's peace?

"It's pissing down out here," he says.

Oh. I hadn't even noticed it was raining, but at that moment thunder rumbles ominously overhead like a passing truck. This could only happen to me. I am cursed. God hates me.

The van door opens. "May I come in?" Water drips from his hair and clings to his eyelashes. His drenched t-shirt clings to his broad chest. It's not fair, even with blood smearing his upper lip and cheek, he still looks outrageously bloody divine.

"If you have to." God, he must think I'm such a heartless bitch. I sigh. "You'd better take a seat, so I can help clean you up."

Guy sits down, smiling ruefully. I get some kitchen roll.

"Head back," I order, "and pinch the bridge of your nose."

"Ow," he says, as I gently dab his face.

"Quit complaining. You're lucky it's not broken."

"What, like my hand?"

I pause. Does he know I'm to blame? Could Twister have told him about the turkey? Surely not.

His face is a mask. Inscrutable. "Out of interest, who's Colin?" he asks. "You mumbled his name in your sleep."

I take my time answering, "A piece of shit. A wazzock. A dick of the first order," I mutter.

"Right . . . I swear, I was asleep . . . until you called me Colin. Admittedly, *that* was a rude awakening."

Colin. I can't help the shudder that runs through me.

Outside it's bucketing down with rain. Literally coming down in sheets. I should've let Guy drown in it and yet here I am, standing hemmed between his legs, mopping up his blood. Hyper aware of his hands resting on his muscled thighs. His soft breath. His gaze averted to the ceiling looking anywhere but at me . . .

And yet, the intimacy of the situation almost undoes me.

This is an unmitigated disaster. I feel like an overwound coil. I've no idea if I pressed myself up against Guy this morning first or vice versa. I'd certainly been dreaming of sex, and admittedly I did somehow end up on his side of the bed, but *obviously* I had no idea what I was doing. He's the last man on the planet I'd have sex with, even if the buzz around my body right now is in hot denial.

Unlike me, Guy seems completely unfazed. He's probably so used to waking up with a different woman every day of the week, he thinks nothing of it. He just goes with the moment, grabbing every opportunity that rears its ugly head. Ugh. Me and my ugly head. And he's shameless. Perhaps he and Twister are well-suited.

I sigh again. This is too horrible for words. I'm not sure how I can survive the rest of this road-trip even if it is only one more day. With any luck we'll be at his place tonight and then we can go our separate ways.

I guess if I want to survive it, I just have to believe I can.

One. More. Day.

How hard can that be?

"Thank you," says Guy, looking at me now, his warm eyes . . . utterly crushing.

Dear God, help me.

This is why a crush is called a crush. Because of the pressure. How do I contain all the emotions trapped inside my body knowing they can never go anywhere? I have no idea how to behave normally anymore.

19

GUY

Back on the road, Alice is unusually quiet. She doesn't attempt to make polite small talk like yesterday, and I guess I should feel grateful. I have a lot of emotions swarming beneath my ribs: a hornet's nest Alice has stirred up in me. The memory of her tucked into my side, her hand guiding mine, her satin smooth skin beneath my fingertips, juxtaposed by her appalled reaction when she woke and went batshit crazy and gave me a bloody nose, have me stewing with concern. Was this morning somehow my fault? Did I do something I wasn't even aware of? God, I hope not. When I think about waking up with her pressed against me, my hand between her legs, it brings me out in a cold sweat. I suppose it could have been so much worse . . .

Worse, but also better.

I shift uncomfortably in my seat.

I'm slightly puzzled by how carefully she attended to my nose when she probably would have preferred to drive the van over me. I touch it gingerly.

Alice glances my way.

"Eyes on the road, Kook," I growl.

Mentally, I'm groaning. Somehow, even in my sleep, I've screwed up again. And I can't help liking her. Wanting more of her. All of her. But if I thought I'd messed up my chances by calling her Tilly, now I've truly screwed them. Even blind, she couldn't have missed my physical reaction to her this morning as it was there shouting 'Morning Glory and Hallelujah' in braille. Even if she were willing, which she is patently not, I cannot go there. I can't contemplate getting involved with Alice because, (a) Tilly would crucify me and I can't afford to jeopardize her return to the band and (b) Tilly has made it abundantly clear, Alice is not the sort to take sexual matters lightly, and as I am not the sort of man to take sexual matters seriously that's a bit of a brick wall, and (c) at the moment, I need Alice.

You need Alice, but you do not want a second bite at the cherry. Who are you kidding? says the voice in my head.

This is about the band, my brother and the wedding, I reason. Alice is here to get me from A to B. No diversions. No detours. No scenic routes.

Also pitiful given you're lying to yourself, says the irritating bastard messing with my head. *Besides,* the voice continues, *her feelings toward you lean more toward hate.*

This much is true. She detests me. Cannot stand me touching her. And seems to loathe the very sight of me.

So, we are exclusively in hate with one another.

Yeah, right. Stop deluding yourself.

I glance down at my twitching dick. Now might be a good time for it to realize it should go back to sleep. It would also be helpful if the ache in my balls subsided . . .

Time to remind myself Alice is only doing this for the money, and her sister. I am only doing this for my brother and RiffRaff and Tilly. Tilly, Twister, seems to be the common denominator. I can't help but wonder what hold Tilly has over Alice and why she seems to be more than a little compliant when that is clearly not in her true nature. Why would she agree to drive me to Victoria when obviously, she would rather be on the other side of the country? Is she that desperate for the money? What are these mysterious ITs mentioned in her journal?

And who the fuck is Colin?

Colin. What sort of dickhead name is that? Whoever he is, I want to meet Colin and pummel him into the ground. It's as if he's the one who just smacked me in the nose and now I'm bristling to fight a man I've never even met before. That's how messed up my head is right now.

It's probably best to keep my distance, keep focused on the road ahead, keep moving and doing what I do best: acting like nothing ever matters.

Just another lie you tell yourself.

"Shut the fuck up!" I mutter.

"Sorry?" says Alice. "I didn't even say anything!"

I clear my throat. Shit, I said that aloud? "Just talking to myself. My hand's a bit uncomfortable, that's all." But not half so uncomfortable as the thought of the wedding. I know I'm not going to escape without getting an ear bashing from just about everyone there. I'm going to have to suck it up, man up and accept the stick I always get from family and friends. It sucks big time.

I wouldn't mind so much if I knew someone else had my back. Someone like Alice.

20

ALICE

My dad, the good Christian vicar, would not approve, but I say a prayer to the god of transport, Hermes, and his winged sandals, as we approach the suburbs of Sydney. It is busy.

Guy makes a show of yawning and stretching but casually fires instructions at me as we drive through the city. Turn left. Take this slip road. Right here . . . I'm grateful he knows his way around, but the thought of being back in this city makes me jittery. It seems like weeks since we were singing on that yacht; me fizzing like a firework in Guy's hands . . . not just a few short days ago. The memories come back in a rush, making it difficult to think straight let alone drive.

And it starts to rain again, the clouds overhead dark and foreboding as if I'm racing toward another storm when I should be finding shelter.

Finally, out the other side, on route for Melbourne, I feel like I can breathe again. Guy leans against the passenger door window and closes his eyes. Okay for him. My stomach rumbles louder than the thunder overhead, but Guy is oblivious, gently snoring.

Great.

I focus on the road as best I can, but within seconds the rain starts to hammer us. Rivers run either side of the main road and the windscreen wipers almost buckle under the monsoon of water. How can Guy sleep through this? It's as if someone put a knife through an awning over our heads and slashed open the clouds. It's impossible to see the road signs, so I just keep going as best I can . . .

On a smaller road, I slow the van down to a crawl and put on some classical music. We're low on fuel; I'm just thinking if I don't get some fuel in my own tank soon, I might start gnawing the dashboard when the weirdest thing happens: I put my foot on the gas and the van doesn't respond. Or she does, but she's very slow about it. Sluggish. Reluctant. Running low on energy like me.

I rub the back of my neck. Maybe I was imagining it.

Guy is still sleeping like a baby. I'm loathe to wake him up over nothing.

But the van gives a hiccup which I'm pretty sure isn't normal.

I turn the volume of the radio down to listen, when there's a loud popping noise and the van jerks as if offended by her own emissions.

"Guy," I say.

He grunts.

I check the gas again. Okay, we have less than a quarter of a tank, but we're not completely out. I press my foot on the accelerator to test the situation, to ease us into more than walking pace, but it's like the vehicle is comatose.

Shit!

"Um, Guy!" I say, just as the van surges forward like I've woken her. "What the hell? Guy! I think you should wake up." I thump his arm.

He opens one eye. "What?"

Another *pop, pop, pop* has him sitting upright. "Did you just—?"

"No, I did not just *parp*. That had nothing to do with me. It's the van."

Guy frowns; the van judders.

"When did this start?" he asks.

"Just now," I say. "It was nothing to do with me! I didn't do anything!" Perhaps I protest a tad too vehemently because he throws me a dark look. "The van's not responding when I put my foot on the gas and she keeps making these horrible noises."

The van farts again, as if to confirm my prognosis.

"Oh fucking great," groans Guy.

"What is it?"

"Do I look like I'd know? I'm not a fucking mechanic." His eyes widen as we go past a road sign. "Why the hell are we heading for Shoalhead? Fuck Almighty, we're on the A1 Alice!"

"Um . . . are we?" I'm not sure of the significance of this other than Guy appears to be outraged. "What road should we be on?"

"The M31."

The van decides it'd be fun to start bunny hopping along the road. And surprisingly, Guy starts laughing.

I can't help smiling. Clearly, I have taken a very wrong turn somewhere, in fact, I can trace it back to New Year's Eve when I first kissed Guy . . .

"Pull over," he says, grinning from ear to ear. "You can't see shit anyway."

"I couldn't see the road signs very well because of all the rain and—"

The van gives one final splutter, all power fading. I manage to pull over into a parking lay-by. I would rather look at the water streaming past us into a gulley than at Guy's face.

Where the hell are we? We're surrounded by trees and bushland and more trees and mud. In the butt end of nowhere.

For a moment, we sit there.

"Welcome to Shit Creek," says Guy.

I can't help giggling.

"Could be worse. At least I have a phone signal," says Guy. "Fuck knows what I'm going to tell my brother if I don't get this van to the wedding on time though."

"What about you getting to the wedding on time?"

"I'm secondary, believe me. I'm just the delivery boy."

"What?"

"Delivering the van. It's Ben's wedding gift to Xanthe and their going away car."

A part of me swoons. How romantic! But also how sad I'll be to say goodbye to the van, despite her being so temperamental.

Guy calls roadside assistance. He sounds super polite, if bordering on desperate. Phone in hand, he steps out of the van into the pouring rain and goes round the back.

I feel like I should do something to help. At least take a commemorative photo of him trying his hardest. I also think this might make a good opportunity to send Twister a picture of him suffering, so she realizes it's not just me she's hurting.

The minute I step outside I regret my decision—it's like stepping into a car wash only without the car—but now I'm in it, I might as well continue. I dash to the rear of the van.

Guy has opened the tailgate bonnet. He's still speaking to the roadside assistance people, well, shouting, while leaning over the tailgate. He also looks . . . extremely hot for a very wet person. His t-shirt clings to his back, outlining his muscles. He stands up. Give the man a trident. He looks like a marooned Poseidon or Neptune.

I take a quick shot just as he looks over. Shaking his head, he looks at me as if I'm a fish-out-of-water, which I suppose, in effect, I am.

"WTF, Alice? There's no need for both of us to get wet. Get back in the van."

I don't need to be told twice.

Moments later Guy jumps in the van too, his phone wedged beneath his ear. "Right. Thanks." He's struggling to slam the door with his good hand, and I make the fatal error of leaning over to help him. I slip and sprawl across his lap. "Jesus!"

He looks down at me. It's a good job he can't see my face because now I'm seriously gaping like a guppy fish. I scramble to get back upright in my seat, and he tosses his phone on the dash.

Oh God, I am mortified. Again.

"We didn't both need to get soaked," he says quietly.

"I was trying to help. I was going to suggest maybe I call roadside assistance. They sometimes come quicker if they think you're female and alone . . ."

I trail off as I realize he is studying me a little too closely for comfort. My t-shirt is in the same state as his, sodden and semi-transparent, leaving little to the imagination. I try to unstick it from my torso while Guy looks in the opposite direction, out the side window.

"And now we're both soaked through," he says, his voice a rumble.

"It's not a big deal," I say, although I'm feeling like this is a HUGE deal. "I can just—"

We both stand up at the same time and there's a wet smack as our chests collide. My breath hitches. My boobs squish against his slab of muscle. I grab hold of his arms to steady myself, which seems to have the reverse effect.

As if zapped by lightning, I yank my hands away and plonk backward onto my seat again.

"I was . . . just g-going to change . . . into . . ."—Steam rises from my clothes, not to mention my radiator-hot cheeks—"something dry," I rasp. My throat is probably the driest thing in this entire van.

Guy sits down. "You first."

"You're wetter. You go first."

Our eyes lock. Unsaid words are loaded.

"I'd hate for you to catch cold," he says, his eyes flickering to the gooseflesh on my arms. Oh. Or maybe my nipples, which right now could hold up a circus tent. Unable to think of a single coherent sentence in response, I peel myself off the leather seat and wiggle my way past him, hyper-aware of my thigh sliding against wet Poseidon bicep. Hot adrenaline cruises around my body like a swarm of piranha. My mind implodes with images of Guy and me this morning. Wet and hot. Holy shit.

No. No. No. No. No. No.

Turning my back, I yank off my wet clothes and drop them in a pile on the floor, stomping them underfoot in my scramble to find something dry to wear. This cannot be happening. Not in a month of Sundays. Not in a Leap Year. Not ever EVER.

I yank any old item from my backpack and shove it over my head. Checking over my shoulder, I freeze. Still in his seat, Guy's peeled out of his wet t-shirt, his torso now naked. Acres of bronzed flesh. Holy Mother of all that's jacked, I'm in deep trouble. Deep water. Shark territory.

Guy stands up and turns around. Christ alive, his chest and abs have more definition than a corrugated roof. Why am I noticing this now when there isn't space to swing a cat and he's the coolest cat imaginable?

"Your turn," I squeak.

"You know you have your t-shirt on inside out and back to front," he informs me.

Of course I do, because I am a blithering idiot. "I like wearing it this way."

A wry smile tugs his lips. "Not like you to leave your clothes on the floor."

"I'll sort them after you've . . . you know . . . ." We execute an extreme heart-defying waltz in the middle of the van as we exchange places. I can't help imagining chasing the rivulets of water glistening along his ripped abdomen. With my tongue.

Dizzy, I slide back behind the steering and let my head fall back on the seat rest. Holy shit.

"I think this could be a long wait. Apparently, the roads are flooded," says Guy, nonplussed, and hopefully none the wiser about my total loss of sanity, from the back of the van.

"Oh, hell!" I say with a little more emphasis than necessary. In the driver's mirror I gawk at the sight of Guy stripping out of his shorts, the sight of his muscled buttocks enough to start a tsunami in my loins.

This is a dire emergency. I'm not sure I can withstand the assault much longer. I pull out my phone to text Twister.

"Fancy a brew while we wait this out?" asks Guy.

I give him a thumbs up without looking his way. There is only so much torture a girl can tolerate.

While he's tinkering around making a brew, I send her the photo of Guy at the back of the van, standing in what looks like a torrential monsoon.

> Mission Control, we have a problem.

Seconds later, I get a response.

> Phwoah! Guy makes a hot mechanic! You have several problems, Malice. Which one of your problems are we talking about today?

> Guy's as clueless as I am about this van, and now we're marooned when he's supposed to be home already. The wedding is tomorrow at 3pm. This van is supposed to be a wedding gift and it might prove challenging to find a stranger to dance with when we're stuck in the middle of nowhere. This sucks! Can you stop the clock for a while?

Her reply pops up a second later:

> Stop the clock? Are you out of your tiny mind? Rise to the challenge. Be audacious!

I get more scrolling dots and then nothing.
Typical Twister. Leaving me in the eye of the storm.

21

ALICE

"Want to play a game?" Guy suggests.

Is he kidding? After the IT Game, I never want to play another game in my life . . . But I suppose it does look like we're kind of stuck here for a while, and it would help to pass the time and distract me from both Guy and the stress of my next IT. Where am I supposed to find a complete stranger to dance with before breakfast tomorrow?

"Alice?"

"What sort of game?" I ask, absentmindedly.

He shrugs. "Maybe a board game or cards? I can't play guitar, so unless you've a better idea of how to pass the time . . ." A smile plays on his lips. "Or maybe not."

"No, we can play a board game." Anything to take my mind off how trapped I am here in the van, in danger of losing my mind.

As I maneuver my way to the back of the van again, parts of my body I didn't know even existed hum as if there's some sort of magnetic force field zapping around inside the van with us. With all the rain, I'd say we're in potential danger of being electrocuted.

Guy places two steaming mugs on the table. And I sit down to give us some more space.

"What games do you know?" he asks.

We ping pong a few suggestions.

"What about Scabby Queen? It's like Old Maid . . . One of the few games I happen to be good at."

His mouth twitches. "Scabby Queen sounds painful, and I think you've already inflicted enough pain on me to last a lifetime. How about chess, Kook?"

I sit up. "Sure. If you can refrain from calling me Kook." I'm not half bad at chess. I've wasted many a damp and dismal afternoon in Yorkshire playing the game. Dad is the reigning champion in our household, but then, as my family knows, he has the unfair advantage of having God on his side.

"Alright." Guy crouches to take his chess board out of the drawer, giving me another savory view. My mouth seems to be doing an abnormal amount of salivating. "I was actually going to suggest chess because I happen to enjoy it, but I can never find anyone else below the age of fifty who does." He grins cheekily as he slides the chess set onto the table.

"Maybe that explains why you need all those Nanna naps. You've got into bad habits mixing with the elderly." I sip my tea, and I swear his chuckle reverberates from his side of the table, across the floor of the van and up my legs.

"You do not want to know about my bad habits, Possum." He opens up the chessboard.

Possum? Again? "Do you know the *rules* of chess, *Wombat,* or is this here chess set just to impress the ladies with how esoterically gifted you are?"

He rubs his nose. "I know the rules well enough. Do you?"

"Some."

"I bet you're a stickler for rules," he murmurs, smiling to himself.

I roll my eyes. "I bet you *hate* any rules."

"Oh no, I like rules. After all, where'd the fun be in life if there were no rules to be broken?" He says it in such a way that has me squirming on my seat.

"Well, contrary to what you may think about me, I am *not* a stickler for rules." I check his face. "I'm *not!* You'd be surprised. I can . . . rise to the challenge. I've been told I can be quite . . . audacious."

Guy roars with laughter.

"What? You think I'm not audacious? What about my hitchhiking? What about this road-trip?" I'm heartily sick of being pegged as prim and proper, dull-as-ditchwater Alice, while Tilly is labeled as the 'fun one'.

"So Bodacious Alice—"

"I said audacious, not bodacious."

"Audacious bodacious, tomato, *tomahto*. You want to *bend* the rules a little here then?" Guy asks. "Up the stakes some?"

Dammit, I've walked right into that one.

He cocks an eyebrow at me, waiting. Boy, he is one savage piece of work. It's too tempting to teach him a lesson in humility.

"Sure. Why not? So long as it doesn't involve getting intimate."

He laughs again. "No reason to . . . but I like how you're thinking."

His gaze lingers, and I can feel myself blushing as I shuffle a couple of pawns behind my back.

I hold out my closed fists but pull them back again. "Before we get started. What sort of stakes are we talking about?"

His mouth purses. "Well, it should be something worthwhile for both of us."

"Such as?" I can feel heat creeping up my neck under his scrutiny.

"I was going to suggest whoever loses becomes the other person's slave for the day."

"Sorry," I say, high pitch laughing, "I thought you said *slave!*"

His mouth puckers. "A little too *extra* for you?"

A *little*? If he wins this, I am dead. But the way he is looking at me like there is no way on earth I'm going to agree to this is like a jab in the guts. I attempt to laugh it off. "Isn't that me, anyway? You know, designated driver, cook, cleaner . . . and I can't possibly imagine what you could possibly do for me, what with only one functional hand." The minute I say it, I want to die all over again. We both know exactly how effective his one hand can be.

"Harsh," he says.

"But also true." I swallow.

His devilish smile deepens and the gleam in his eye turns my insides to rainwater. "Come on now, I'm sure you can think of something."

Psychedelic visions of this morning flash before my eyes. My entire stomach sloshes. The van feels like Noah's ark. Awash. And despite all the liquefaction, I'm pretty sure my cheeks are on fire.

"Let's see now . . ." He rubs his jaw, grinning satanically. In a moment he will sprout horns. "I could be your errand boy, your whipping boy . . . or your personal tour guide. I am open to suggestions . . ."

I snort.

"Or are you actually worried you'll lose?"

"No!" I snap. I'm actually crapping myself. Another nervous laugh escapes me. I am audacious. Bodacious, to his salacious. There's no way out of this without looking prissy.

But I have no intention of losing. That is out of the question. I'm going to annihilate him.

"How about guitar lessons?" I suggest.

"It's a deal," he says, smiling like he's won already.

Okay, this has just got serious. *Ser-i-ous!* Me be *his* slave? Not on your Nellie. That could mean almost ANYTHING. My heart pinballs around my ribcage and I hold out my closed fists again.

Pick black. Pick black. Pick black.

He picks white and therefore has first move.

It'll be fine. I'm in my element. I face off his pawn with my own.

"So, Kook, what are your thoughts with regard to being thrashed?" he drawls in a way that makes my breath catch in my throat and my lower regions stir as he moves his knight to f3.

Ha! He can't throw me that easily. "N-not going to happen," I say.

I'm going to beat the hell out of him. Beat him so badly he'll be begging me for mercy. I am going to be BOSS in more ways than one. If I can just put a lid on the bubbles of nervous excitement in my chest. He'll regret this. He'll wish he were playing with anyone but me. My mind wanders, thinking of all the ways he could *play with me* . . . before I haul my mental ass back to the board.

Guy frowns—it's kind of cute that he's trying so hard—and bites his lower lip. A mental flash—his lip between my teeth—momentarily invades my thoughts, but I swiftly bat the image away. His face is a mask of concentration. He steeples his fingers—I have to admit, despite the cast, he has beautiful hands—and it's kind of attractive. Guy looking studious. Who'd have thunk it?

I can't help but giggle when he chews his knuckle.

He eyeballs me from across the table. For a moment, I'm totally disoriented by the flint in his eyes. It's like knocking back whisky. Every single nerve inside me feels instantly scorched. It's little wonder that Guy is such a hit with all the women. Waiting for him to move, my core muscles clench and unclench in anticipation.

"Who taught you to play?" he asks, waiting for me to make my next move. Perhaps hoping to distract me.

"My dad. You?"

"Same."

"I have to be honest, we play a fair bit at home. Perhaps I should've warned you. But as Dad, the vicar, would say: sometimes you win and sometimes you learn." My mouth twitches as I take another of his pawns.

"Yes, Yoda. You are so full of wisdom." He focuses on the game again.

I should be concentrating as well, thinking ahead, but instead I waste time surreptitiously studying him: Guy Balcombe could be exhibited in a gallery. Exhibit A: Portrait of a man concentrating. Put aside his musical talent, it's disarming and alarming how beautiful he is. Sculpted perfection. Marble. I'm sure that makes him doubly attractive to some women, I imagine. Not me, of course, I know beneath the surface lies an unscrupulous bastard. But I can't help musing: he must feel like his life has taken a surreal trajectory since being stuck in this van with me.

Our eyes meet again. Dove gray. He raises an eyebrow.

Oh. Has he moved already? Sometimes Guy has this way of looking at me that makes me feel like I'm in free-fall. Everything forgotten except trying to slow down and land on my feet.

I take a deep breath. He's being deliberately unnerving. It has nothing to do with sexual attraction whatsoever. Focus Alice.

I study the board.

What I fail to consider is the extent to which Guy is prepared to play dirty.

The moment his knees brush against mine under the table, in a dither, I touch the wrong piece.

"Oh shame . . . but also . . . Touch, move," he murmurs.

"Says the man who reckons he's not a stickler for rules!" I glare at him and pull my legs up to sit cross-legged.

"Go again. I won't hold you to that move."

"Oh, no. I don't want you accusing me of cheating. I have principles," I say, moving my knight to c6 like that was exactly the move I'd intended all along.

"Implying I don't?" He moves his bishop four squares.

"Oh, I'm sure even gutter boys have principles, the dirtier the better."

His chuckle is deep and throaty. "Audacious Alice, how do you keep your mind so pristine?"

Pristine? Hmmm. . .

Until he strips off his t-shirt.

Not fair.

Definitely far from pristine now.

Swallowing hard, I move up another pawn.

He moves another knight, which frees the board for me to move my bishop to e5.

Oh, yes! Bring it home, sister! I sit on my hands to contain my excitement, as he takes my pawn with his knight . . . but that's okay because now he's exposed his queen.

I sidle my bishop up next to her.

His mouth purses, then twists from side to side as he considers. Then—*then!*—the devious bastard only goes and moves his bishop to f7 taking my pawn and threatening my king.

When he touches my arm, I almost hit the ceiling.

"Woah! Just getting up for a glass of water. Would you like one?" he asks, smiling sweetly.

I will not feast my eyes on his gleaming torso. Nor his six-pack. Nor the V-pack . . .

"Do you mind not distracting me?" I snap, holding my head in my hands to make sure I'm looking at the board and only the board. This game is not panning out quite as I anticipated.

As he sits down again, I'm aware of his long, lean thighs in my peripheral vision. He puts his feet up on the bench next to me. I ignore them.

Blot him out.

Blot out the big feet and the big hands. Blot the big idiot out entirely.

Unfortunately, I'm no chess master because the longer I stare at the board, the more I realize I'm in a hopeless position, but I can't bring myself to surrender.

He leans forward, corded forearms resting on the table, long fingers twitching. The idea of them playing me this morning makes me see stars, and I blink rapidly. "I thought you were getting me some water," I hiss.

"What did your last slave die of?" he laughs.

I can't even spare the time for a quip in response. I'm desperately trying to figure a way out of this, but it's like I'm trapped mentally and physically. He's just too damn big for this van. And it's like he's flicked a switch in my brain that I can't turn off. He's too close for comfort. Too disturbing. Short-circuiting my brain.

"Oh, look at that. It's stopped raining," he says.

"Open the door. Please." I make the mistake of glancing up and immediately feel floored again by the view of taut thighs straining the canvas of his boardshorts as he slides open the van door.

I re-cross my legs as he unfastens the zips of the pop-up roof, my treacherous eyes deserting the chess board drawn to his . . . his . . . king . . . piece.

King piece? WTF?

I've touched my king. I blink and blink again. What am I even doing? Am I losing my mind? I glance up at him.

"I'm saying nothing!" Guy crosses his arms, grinning.

Smug bastard. Like I'm going to let him say he *let* me win, even if the king is the last piece I wanted to move. Damn.

"Could you just sit down? I can't concentrate with you moving around." Reluctantly, teeth grating, I slide my king forward a square.

"I'm sorry." Guy sits down once more. "I'd no idea I had such a dramatic impact on you . . ." If his hand wasn't broken, he'd probably be rubbing his palms together. He's looking very pleased with himself, pretending he's not sure what to do next. "Aha! Would you look at that?" He moves his knight once more and sits back.

It's altogether too hot and steamy in here.

I've maneuvered myself into a corner.

"Hmmm," says Guy, one beautiful finger tapping his chin.

"Shut. Up."

He smiles. "I believe that is—"

"No, it isn't!"

"—Check."

"Guy!" When I look at him, he's not smiling anymore, his eyes are searing.

For the longest time, there's silence. Just the sound of water dripping from leaves.

There must be a way out of this. There should be a way out of this. There has to be a way out of this.

He stretches both hands behind his head and leans back, chest expanding. "Honey, I hate to say it, but that's—"

"Then don't!"

"—Checkmate. I believe."

Good. God.

Damn.

I don't need to study the board. I know he's right.

But I sit there, unable to accept defeat.

Now, finally, Guy is still and silent. My whole world is awash, going down.

Glug.

Glug.

Glug.

Fifteen minutes later, I flip over my king. Closing my eyes, I sag against the back of the seat.

Fuck, fuckity, fuck!

I've miscalculated horribly. Underestimated him at my peril. So much for me being great at chess. So much for me out-smarting him. I am one dumb bloody chick.

"Sometimes you win and sometimes you learn," he says, quoting my words from before the game back at me. Bastard. "I think that officially makes you my slave for a day. But let's start tomorrow." Humming merrily, he picks up my mug.

"B-but t-tomorrow is your b-brother's wedding!"

"I know." His rueful smile doesn't make this any easier to accept.

"This was your plan all along . . . to make me your slave at your brother's wedding?" I break out in a cold sweat.

Has he suckered me into this? Is he like some grand chess master? I'm pretty sure he took advantage of my competitive nature. Could Twister have told him about that? OMG Twister! What will she say about this? This is my worst nightmare. We didn't even establish any ground rules.

"W-what are you going to m-make me do?" I stammer.

Anyone with half a brain would have asked that before we started playing. Before it was too damn late.

"I'm going to make you . . . have fun." His eyes twinkle. "Nothing too onerous, I swear. I was thinking you could sing with the band and be my plus one for the day."

I can just about deal with singing with the band again, but the second part of that sentence slays me. "You're p-plus one as in friend?

Or your plus one as in your f-f-f"—*Fucking hell!*—"f-fake g-girlfriend?"

"Girlfriend!" He looks delighted with the word. "Couldn't have put it better myself."

No, no, no! This only happens in books, not in real life. "No way, José!"

He crosses his arms, frowning. "Errr . . . Are you reneging? I didn't have you pegged as such a bad loser? I thought you had principles . . ."

Principles be damned. My mind is in a whirling vortex. How in hell do I wriggle out of this . . . this worm hole? "You assured me, this wouldn't involve anything intimate."

He scratches his stomach. "Did I? I don't recall." I actually don't recall either. I'm pretty sure I would have insisted if I'd even begun to suspect it might involve intimacy . . . if I'd had my head screwed on, if my day hadn't started out in such a head-detaching, out-of-body, mind-blowing experience. "I'd hazard a guess, your idea of intimate and mine are radically, um different, Kook," he drawls. "I don't expect you to have sex with me, if that's what's bothering you."

Nervous laughter nearly chokes me, and I slap my hand over my mouth. Sex?! "I'm not bothered by you," I scoff, "but I know someone who might be. What do you imagine Tilly will have to say when she finds out about this?"

He shrugs. "You're right, she won't be happy."

"Exactly!" I say smugly, dismissing the twinge of disappointment in my throat.

"I imagine, as it's you and she's more than a little protective where you're concerned, she may tell me to behave myself."

"Ha! Protective!" I cough. "You're right. I'm the *last* person she'd want you to have as your fake girlfriend!"

"Don't do yourself a disservice. You're really not that bad to look at and—"

I throw a chess piece at him, and he catches it . . . with his left hand.

"She's all for you stepping out of your comfort zone," he says.

"What?" What is this? What has she said to him about me? "I can't do this unless she agrees and I'm sure she won't." I cross my arms.

"Want to bet on it?" he asks, eyes laughing.

"Shall we ring her?" I say, trying to call his bluff.

He smiles. "Great idea."

I watch in amazement as he makes a phone call. For a while, I think he's acting.

"Tills! How's it going? Right. Right. Right. Sure."

There's no-one on the other end.

"I'm just here with her now. We've been playing chess . . . yeah. No, she lost . . ." He laughs. "Yeah, I think it was a bit of a surprise." He winks at me, and I literally twitch. Or something does.

"Look, Alice seems to be under the misapprehension that there is or was something sexual going on between you and me. I know, extremely ewww, right? But I'd like you to make it one hundred percent clear we are and never have been an item . . . Right now . . . Because she needs to know." He holds the phone out.

I snatch it from his hands. "Hello?"

"It's true." Twister's voice fills my ear and my heart sinks like a stone. "Nothing ever happened between me and Guy. We're just friends."

I look across the table at him. I feel like I'm under the microscope with Guy's eyes riveted to my face.

"Friends with benefits?" I hiss.

"Not even. We've an unspoken rule: there's no screwing between band members," says Twister. "Guy came up with that one himself. Said band mates were off limits in case it screwed with the vibe. Riff-Raff *always* comes first with him."

"But . . . you were so upset with me." I turn away with the phone. "You gave me the impression . . ." I slide out of my seat, going to the door so I can talk. "I thought I'd messed up so badly . . ." I step outside, my eyes tearing up. "What are you *punishing* me for, if not because of him?"

She sighs. "I'm not punishing you, Malice. I'm helping you."

I walk away from the van to make sure I'm well out of earshot. "*Helping* me? How do you call this helping me? Forcing me to drive him all this way. Do you have any idea of the awkward as *hell* situation you've put me in?" I snarl, checking over my shoulder to make sure Guy's not listening in. "Because of you, I now have to be his *slave* at his brother's wedding tomorrow."

She cracks up laughing. "Fantastic! That sounds like a lot of fun. Most of the women I know would give their right arm to be Guy Balcombe's sex slave for the day."

"Not his *sex* slave! His *slave* slave!" I pause to suck some oxygen into my lungs and pinch the bridge of my nose. "Twister, enough already. Are you going to tell me what's going on and why I'm doing this?"

"Not until you've completed your six ITs. Happy dancing, sis."

Welcome to Hell.

22

GUY

Winding Alice up is kind of irresistible but having overheard some of that telephone conversation between her and Tilly, I feel a little concerned I might be pushing her buttons too hard. She returned, looking visibly shaken and paler than her usual pearly white. Okay, it's true, I feel a *little* bad about making her my fake date as well as demanding she sings with RiffRaff at the wedding, but now I've said it, it's difficult to backpedal. Plus, to be honest, this new situation suits me perfectly. Her posing as my fake girlfriend will take the pressure off me in so many ways.

Mum, Ben and Electra will be delighted I've finally found myself a girlfriend. And perhaps it'll send a message loud and clear to Xanthe's mother who is a real dingo—the closest Australian equivalent to a cougar—that I am *not* and never will be interested in her. Plus, plus, I have a gut feeling the wedding will be a lot more fun with Alice by my side.

Fun without strings. Just how I like it.

Plus, plus, plus, I've yet to explain to the lads that it was not Tilly singing on New Year's Eve but her identical twin sister, Alice. With any luck, no-one will be any the wiser because I'm looking forward to singing with Alice again. Musically speaking, we are very well-attuned. There are too many sound reasons not to budge. Alice, however, appears not to agree.

"I want to play again," she says, looking determined as she sits down.

"No, you really don't," I say, depositing the last couple of chess pieces back into the box.

She grabs the chess board to prevent me from removing it from the table, her grip on it surprisingly strong. "Don't tell me what I do or do not want! If you win again, double the stakes, you can do what you want with me tomorrow."

I let go of the board. *Woah.* I don't know what to think. Audacious? Capricious? Certainly surprising. But I already have enough guilt on my shoulders and besides, Tilly really will murder me. I know better than to shit or shag on my own doorstep. "I have what I want already, thanks. I only need you for one day."

Her eyes blink owlishly. "You're not only a selfish git, you're mean with it."

I fight not to smile. "If you haven't figured that out yet, then more fool you." I'm beginning to think I don't understand either of these Havoc girls. Alice does a good impression of being smart and straight, but just when I think I have her pegged, she catches me off-guard doing stuff like hitchhiking and skinny-dipping and saying I can do whatever I want with her . . .

"Let it go," I say again, watching a ripple of emotions cross her face: hopeful to disappointed. She needs to watch out. She's becoming more intriguing by the minute. I'd say the odds are stacked in my favor. I've wasted a lot of hours playing chess, and although she's not a bad player, she walked into the Légal trap without even blinking. It was as easy as stealing cake from a toddler.

"Why should you be the only one setting the rules?" she demands.

I put my head in my hands and sigh. Temptation will be the death of me.

"Guy, please, let's go again," she pleads.

I look up. She doesn't break eye contact as she twists her hair in a great handful and clips it up behind her head.

"Best of three," she says, as if I've already agreed. Setting up the board, her mouth is fixed in a very determined line . . . a line I want to blur with mine. Loose tendrils of hair fall around her face and I want nothing more than to tease them around my fingers . . . and pull her across the table into my lap. She locks eyes with mine, as if we're in mortal combat. "Or are those stakes too *extra* for the likes of you?"

What can I say: I've always liked a challenge.

Will power? Zero.

Extra? About a million things I want to do to her right now.

I throw my hands up. "Okay, but don't say I didn't warn you against this." In all good conscience, I probably cannot collect on my winnings. Not like this. Even if I'd like a hell of a lot of *extra* from her, I don't want it under these conditions.

But it seems I cannot say no to Alice. "Fine. Let's play."

She smiles and that's the moment it dawns on me—I've already lost. I can't put my finger on it, but this girl . . . she's . . . audacious and bodacious and capricious and hot damn.

How is this even possible? I barely know her, and yet I have these unfathomable urges when I'm around her. Part of me wants to win to prove a point. Part of me wants to lose just to make her feel better.

If I thought I was dazzled, the situation gets more dizzying by the second.

Alice unbuttons her shirt. I do my damnedest not to look, but my peripheral vision is scorched. She peels it off one pale shoulders, then the other. She sets it on the bench beside her, as if this is the most normal thing in the world for her to do when we both know this is far from her brand of normal. But hell, you gotta admire her fighting spirit.

"It's hot in here," she says, like she needs to explain.

"Yup, it's baking." We are literally sitting in a steam bath.

And I suspect she's trying to play me at my own game.

I have to chuckle. But I'm also captivated by the mole in the dip between her clavicle and her alabaster neck that I want desperately to touch. With my mouth. And then let it explore the generous curve of her breasts that swell above her bra.

Oh man, somewhere along this road, I have screwed up big time and my brain is unhitched. I have Alice bad. I'm not sure of anything at this moment in time other than how much I want Alice Havoc and how I need to totally throw away the rule book to stand any chance of winning her over.

Meantime, while I'm trying not to gawk like a kid in a candy store and no doubt failing abysmally, she sets up the chess board. Fighting the urge to sweep everything off the table, lunge across and put her in her place—that place being straddled across my lap—I grip onto the seat. Swallowing down my baser instincts, I think about all sorts of mundane shit while shifting to rearrange the junk in my board shorts.

"What's wrong? Not so confident of your chances second time?" she purrs. So demure. So sure. But *is* she so pure? She could be talking about me and her. Do I have a second chance? If I thought there was any hope, I'd take it. But for once in my life, I'm unsure about how to proceed. Maybe because I care a little too much.

She is so contradictory. Hot and cold. Brave and beautiful. Clever and naive. One day, someone will take advantage of that naivety. Someone like me. I'd welcome the opportunity to wipe the smile off her lips and surprise her.

"Cat got your tongue?" she asks.

"I was just wondering . . . I know what I get out of this, but if you win, what do you get?"

She sucks her lower lip between her teeth. "I'd have thought that was obvious—my freedom. I don't intend to be any man's *slave*. Not now. Not ever."

"Good for you," I say, though, as we commence play again, I can't help thinking I wouldn't mind having Alice at my beck and call. I want to claim her mouth as mine. I want to hear her cry out my name when she comes. I want to teach Alice Havoc a lesson she won't forget in a hurry.

Do I go for it?–It's fucking tempting–or should I deliberately lose? I am undecided. And damn, I need a beer to quench the raging thirst I seem to have developed.

I offer her one and she accepts. It's a big mistake. On my part.

She slides her fingers around the neck of the bottle. Then her pink lips seal around the bottle head. *Okay, I am totally screwed.* If I didn't know better, I'd swear she was teasing me deliberately.

But Alice looks one hundred per cent innocent and focused on the game.

I'm just no longer entirely sure what *game* it is we're playing.

23

ALICE

In chess, a gambit is a strategic move in which a player deliberately sacrifices pieces in order to ultimately gain the upper hand. I realize now that's exactly how Guy's been playing. He lured me into his trap in the previous game by sacrificing his queen. I'm not going to be fooled agin. This time I will *not* lose.

I *cannot* lose. Even though there's part of me that wouldn't mind singing with RiffRaff again. It's a shame really. The wedding might even have been fun. But, hell no. I will not be any man's *slave*. Slave? Jesus! How medieval can you get? This man and his ego need to be brought down a peg or two.

The rain may have stopped, but we're in a fugue of steam in the van and the tension is salty to say the least.

I'm playing white this time. I start with Bird's opening, 1.f4. my brain already leaping ahead, deciding how I will counter his next move and second-guessing what that move may be . . . Putting my chess brain on ice, I run a hand through my hair and place my feet on the bench—between his knees.

His eyes flash to mine, all steel and lightning.

I expect him to go d.5 but he employs From's Gambit, sliding his pawn to e5.

Interesting.

Taking my time, biting my lip, I flip to King's Gambit moving my pawn to f4.

Elbows on the table either side of the board, a muscle pulses in his jaw.

"I think I'm developing a taste for beer," I say, rolling the beer bottle across my hot forehead.

Movement distracts me: a gargoyle face suddenly appears outside, pressed up against the window.

"Fuck me!" yells Guy, while I shriek and drop the bottle of beer. It crashes onto the table, chess board pieces scattering like skittles.

Knuckles hammer on the window.

Instinctively, I grab Guy, my closest and biggest weapon, putting him between me and the deadly assailant. This is not the appropriate moment to appreciate that Guy's body not only makes a sturdy shield wall, but he smells like petrichor and his skin is silky smooth, somehow both cool and hot at the same time—

"You guys need assistance or what?" shouts the gargoyle.

"Lovely as this tender moment is, Kook, I believe that may be roadside recovery services."

I push him out of the way so I can grab my shirt. The van looks like we've just had an orgy. While I'm struggling to shove my arms in my sleeves, Guy chuckles.

"What?"

"Your face . . . No hang ups, much?" He laughs harder.

"Hello?" calls the voice outside.

"Yes, we need help!" I shout, slapping Guy. Hard muscle and bare skin leave my palm tingling.

Guy's laughing so hard, he's collapsed back onto the bench.

"Guy, get up you idiot! Go and *talk* to the man!" I say, but in my hurry to do up the buttons on my shirt, I inadvertently step on a chess piece, yelp as my foot slips and face-plant . . .

Champion. My cheek is planted in Guy's crotch.

Holy Mother of . . . all kings.

Guy curls in a ball.

I scramble off him, back onto my feet, not sure if I've got my revenge and destroyed him permanently. "Guy? Are you okay?"

"I will be . . . I'm going . . . I just . . . I just . . ." Shit, is he contorted with pain?

"Is this a bad time?" shouts the man outside. "I could come back in say . . . in ten minutes."

Guy snorts explosively. Okay, the bastard isn't hurt at all, he's holding his stomach, tears of laughter rolling down his cheeks.

"No. Now's good! Now's great!" I shout, slapping Guy's thigh. Could this get any more humiliating? Could we look any more compromised? "Guy, get up. Get out there! I can't talk to him. Look at me!"

At which point, Guy's laughter fizzles. A weird idiot smile creases his face as he rolls to his feet and looks down at me.

"Guy! Move it!" I order in my best prefect voice.

He takes his time, glancing down at his thigh and the red mark my hand has left, his gaze raking slowly upward, his eyes scorching like the sun.

The echo of my palm slapping naked flesh—more than once— seems to fill the silent van. And the knowledge that I may have trespassed somewhat inelegantly upon something large and intimidating in his trunks probably means my face is visible from outer space right now. For a long drawn-out second, neither of us moves. A second in which I'm hyper-aware of every millimeter of his skin, every pore of his being, and every beat of my treacherous heart.

"Please go," I croak at the same time he declares, "I'm going." He pauses at the door, turning to look back at me. "But we're no way finished with this game . . ."

What game? The chess? The rolling about like sex-obsessed maniacs?

The crunch of Guy's feet walking around the van makes me inexplicably breathless. I stand there for a minute, pretending to be busy picking up chess pieces, drowning in my own boiling vat of unsatis-fied feelings.

I cannot, I will not develop feelings for Guy Balcombe. Even if there's nothing going on between him and Twister—which is like the biggest weight off my shoulders—he's still an alley cat. A panther on the prowl.

24

GUY

While the roadside assistance guy winches the van onto his truck, my skull and bones ache with the bruising images of Alice . . . playing chess across the table from me, her head bent, biting her lip in concentration; the expression when she realized she'd lost; the mayhem when the roadside assistance guy turned up; the shock when she found herself sprawled in my lap—*Holy shit!*

The memory makes me grin afresh.

I can't wipe the smile off my face. I feel lit up.

On the drive into town, Alice is silent, squashed between me and the door, staring out the window and everywhere except at me. Our arms and thighs are pressed hard against one another's. Two fish, very much alive, squished in a tin. Fuck my life. I would do anything to put my arm around her shoulders, but she'd probably gnaw my hand off. I should be worrying about getting to the wedding in time. I should be worrying about the van arriving undamaged. I should be worrying about anything else, but all I can think about is Alice and how I can make something good out of this crappy situation.

Slave for a day. What was I thinking? Maybe it's because Alice is such a domestic goddess in every sense of the phrase. She can't help tidying up behind me, but, like her name, she's also the cause of utter havoc. Pandemonium in my head . . . not to mention my shorts. Alice is forthright, but not forthcoming. She's about as forgiving as a brick through a window. She's both fierce and timid. A constant contradiction to my expectation. A riptide rupturing my peace of mind.

Ben calls as we pull into what looks more like a junkyard than a garage.

"What's up?" I ask.

"Where the fuck are you bro? You should've been home days ago. You swore you'd be back by now!" Ben sounds harassed before he's even made it to his wedding day. *Good luck with surviving marriage, bro.*

"Hold on." I put my hand over the phone and shout to the vehicle recovery guy. "I'll be with you in one minute. Sorry, this is urgent." Alice rolls her eyes. "Bit of engine trouble. Don't sweat. I'm working on it," I say.

"What? What fucking engine trouble? What's happened?"

I give him a heavily edited-for-his-own-mental-health run-down of events.

"What the fuck do you mean, *you're* working on it?"

"Okay, not me, a professional. Chill, bro. If you will insist on buying an old van—"

"It's Xanthe's dream. I don't want to disappoint her."

Of course, whatever Xanthe wants, Xanthe gets. The apple doesn't fall far from the tree. I nearly tell him she's not worth it, but I can't do it to him. Especially not this late in the day.

"And what about the band? If you and Tilly both fail to make it, the entertainment is going to be a total clusterfuck."

"Don't worry, dude! She's right here. We'll be there on time, I promise. You can trust me." Can he though? Is this me trying to make up for all the shit that has happened in the past? Him taking the brunt of family responsibilities? I can't help but worry his clusterfuck wedding assessment may come true in real life.

Once I've got rid of Ben, I hurry back into the garage. The road assistance guy recommended we didn't get towed back to the nearest big town because he knew a guy who's a VW expert not far south of where he picked us up. Against my better judgment, we've been towed to the small coastal town of Eden.

Alice follows me, blinking her owlish eyes. Knowing how much she hates grime and dirt, I'm amazed she's even stepped foot in this shed.

After a quick assessment, Eddy, the elderly mechanic, cheerfully informs us the van's only problem is most likely her distributor cap and rotor arm.

"Great! Do you have the parts?" I ask.

"I do."

"Awesome. How long will it take?"

He scratches his bald head. "I'm that darn busy . . ." So busy, I can't see him working on anything else. "Nah, I won't be able to get her fixed until morning."

I give him a long heartfelt spiel, worthy of an Oscar, about how important it is that we get the van fixed today because we're on our way to a wedding, but he's already made up his mind. "Sorry, son. No way can I get it done today."

"Did I mention the wedding was tomorrow?"

"You did."

"Right." *Fuck.* "And there's no way . . . ?" He shakes his head. Still no. "Right. Of course." I go outside to jab at my phone and update Ben.

He's not amused:

> What a shitshow! *What am I supposed to tell Xanthe?*

I don't *care* what he tells Xanthe. He can tell her the wedding is off for all I care. If I thought for a minute, the van's absence would put a stop to their marriage, I would gladly hunker down here for a week.

It's not the end of the world

I text, just as Alice comes bounding out of the garage. She's not really a bounder, so what's she looking so happy about?

Eddy follows her, a toothy grin on his whiskered face. "If you can pay cash and want to leave the van here overnight, I'll shuffle my schedule around and make sure it's sorted for early in the morning," he says.

"That's awesome!" I pump his hand. "Thank you. This will make my brother so damn happy. Thank you!"

"Mate, thank your girlfriend. She's very persuasive," says Eddy, winking at Alice, who immediately blushes. "You're one lucky bastard."

"I am!" Without thinking, I wrap an arm around Alice's shoulders, but the minute Eddy disappears back inside, she wriggles out of my grasp.

"How exactly did you persuade that old buzzard?" I ask, hoping the smart of her rejection doesn't show on my face.

"I noticed a picture of his family on his desk. Looked like he had a couple of sons and I hope you don't mind, but I asked how he'd feel if it was his son's wedding he was missing. He said he'd move heaven and earth, of course, and started telling me about his son's recent wedding . . . and then he groaned a bit and shook his head and sighed, and I explained you were my boyfriend and it was your brother's wedding and for some reason, he changed his mind."

"Alice Havoc, you are awesome and I could kiss you." She puts her hands up to fend me off; I guess my chances are less than awesome. "Metaphorically speaking," I add hastily.

Right. Of course, metaphorically speaking. Haven't been obsessed with the thought of kissing Alice at all lately.

"We can't stay the night in the van," says Alice, "but Eddy said there's a hotel in town. It's on the esplanade."

It's a bit of a trek, but Alice insists on carrying her backpack as we trudge along the road to the hotel. It's located on the cliffs with spectacular views of the bay below. I insist on paying for the hotel. "It's only fair as you're in my employ."

Alice mutters but doesn't object overly. That is, until the hotel receptionist informs us there's only one room left.

"Of course, there's only one room," she snaps, like this is my doing.

"Don't stress, princess. I'll take the couch," I say.

She rolls her eyes and stomps across the yard in the direction of our room; we have wonderful views, but no couch. There is, however, an uncomfortable-looking tubular armchair. We both stare at the child-sized 'double' bed for a while.

"Look, we've done this before—"

"And look how that worked out!" she snaps.

"I'll sleep on the floor," I offer magnanimously.

Alice mutters blue smoke.

I think I'd best make myself scarce. "You do . . . whatever . . . you gotta do. Take a shower or whatever." I will not think of Alice in the shower. "I need to, um, get to the bank before it closes."

Jesus! If looks could incinerate, I'd be ash by now. The mental image of Alice in the shower seems to trail after me as I jog back into town. Panting, I stop to ring Ben to let him know the good news about the van. Then I run my ass to the bank.

Alice and I are back at square one.

Me, persona non grata; Alice persona non starter.

I find the bank and withdraw the requisite cash. Strolling at a more leisurely pace back up the high street, I spot a dress in a shop window.

It would look awesome on Alice, and I know, having rifled through the contents of her backpack, that she hasn't got much in the way of wedding attire. The red dress she wore New Year's Eve is still held together with a safety pin and while that might be the rage for some designers, I'm not sure . . . The shop looks to be in the process of shutting up for the day. I stick my foot in the door as the shop attendant tries to close it. "I'm sorry. I wondered if you could help me. I've got a bit of a dress emergency."

25

ALICE

IT #5: Ask a stranger to dance . . . Don't
forget, I want evidence.

Champion. Just when I was looking forward to a quiet night in . . . but then I think about the Guy situation. The less time spent in this room with him, the better. Sighing, I fling my phone on the bed and check out the bathroom. Gingerly, I push the shower curtain aside. At least it's clean.

Before showering, I decide to give Twister a quick call to check in. I make the mistake of lying down. The bed is remarkably comfortable. My shoulders and neck ache from all the driving I've done and it's only once I relax that I realize how exhausted I am. I close my eyes as I wait for Twister to answer . . .

. . . a car horn blares and I wake up with a jolt, believing I'm still driving. My heart pounds. I can hear voices. Shit, where am I? Not driving, at least. It takes me a moment to recall I'm in the hotel room. I check my watch. Double shit. I've been asleep for over an hour. Where's Guy? Maybe he's been and gone. I look out the bedroom door. There's no sign of him outside. My stomach growls loud enough to be heard in the next room. I need a shower and to find something to eat.

Apart from the plastic shower curtain, which seems to want to wrap itself around my body, the shower is pretty good. I stand and let the warm water gush over me. Bliss. I'm halfway through washing my hair, working up a great lather of foam, only once thinking of Guy and his wet body and how I wouldn't complain about him wrapping himself around me, when I happen to glance up.

"Faaarrrrrkkkkk!" There's a spider the size of my fist, with legs as thick as my fingers, perched like a peeping Tom on top of the shower rail. I leap out of the shower so fast, I slip on the tiled floor and nearly do the splits. Yelping and sobbing because I smashed my kneecap on the wall and have shampoo in my eyes, I attempt to shuffle on hands and knees out of the bathroom at Olympic speed, but blinded by shampoo in my eyes, I win the gold for smacking my head on the door frame. "Owwww!" I howl, adjusting direction and crawling out the door, hopefully faster than the spider . . .

The door flies open rebounding off the wall with a thwack. "Alice? I . . . ah . . . fuck . . . sorry! But are you okay?"

AH FUCK!

I grope blindly and find the bedside table and . . . the hotel brochure. Great. I'm not sure it's big enough to swat a fly, let alone a spider.

Through my blur of tears, I curl in a ball and roll to one side of the bed. "Get out!"

"What the hell, Alice? You sure you're okay? Anything I can help with?"

The bastard is laughing.

I.

Am.

Not.

Okay.

I crouch in an awkward fetal position on the hotel carpet, trying to cover myself with the miniature brochure. Dragging the cover from the bed, I wave a hand in the direction of the bathroom. "Sp-sp-sp-"

"Spit it out?" Guy says, shielding his eyes—somewhat. "What's the fuss? I thought you were being murdered."

"There's a sp-spider in my shower!" I yell, half sobbing.

"Our shower," he says, his mouth sliding into an open grin. "Don't mind me." He squares his shoulders, strides across the room and peers into the bathroom. "You really don't like our Aussie wildlife, do you?"

"I wouldn't mind, but the bloody insects here seem to have been fed on steroids. That spider is hanging on to the curtain rail like a trapeze artist."

Chuckling, Guy steps into the bathroom and turns off the faucets. "It's only a huntsman."

"A huntsman who doesn't realize I'm not bloody Snow White!"

"Would you like me to deal with your circus friend?"

"Y-yes!" I whimper unashamedly. "Please. Pretty please!" I pray he's not going to ask me to make it worth his while, because right now I'd agree to anything. I freaking hate spiders. Loathe them. Abominations, every one of them. I mean, what sort of innocent critter needs eight eyes and eight legs if not to assassinate you? I admit, I'm a total coward about some things. Mainly creepy crawly ones. My heart is still going like the clappers.

Thankfully, Guy, my temporary hero, seems unfazed by the unexpected visitor. As I cower on top of the bed, Guy, chuckling, retrieves the hotel brochure from the floor and picks up a glass. He disappears back into the bathroom, where it sounds like there's a deadly scuffle.

Guy comes out victorious, the spider trapped beneath the glass and the brochure underneath. "Quite cute really."

"Cute? It's a monster!"

Guy, the spider whisperer, proceeds to talk soothing words to the disgusting critter while he walks it to the door.

I shudder. "Please take it as far away from here as possible. I don't want it coming back. Not ever. I read s-spiders have navigation beacons. Maybe you should—" I slap my hands together.

"Now who's sounding like the Wicked Stepmother? No need to kill anything. I'll give you some time to . . . um . . ." Laughing, Guy strolls out the door.

Shuffling to the window, I watch him walk the spider across the car park and out of the hotel gates, catching the eye of a couple of women passing by.

"Need some help, darl!" one calls.

Guy stops to chat. Honestly, he's incorrigible! As he flicks the spider into a gutter, I can't help shuddering. He can't resist, can he? The man is a sucker for flattery and female attention.

Shaking my head in disgust, I go back into the room and close the door. I check the bathroom for the rest of the spider's relatives, all probably now scheming their revenge, but thankfully there seem to be none lurking. Hurriedly, I finish my shower, and burning with embarrassment, get dressed.

Fifteen minutes later, there's a loud knock on the door.

"Are you decent yet, honey?" shouts Guy from outside.

Gawd. Why not broadcast it to the entire hotel?

I open the door. He's grinning like he just won a prize and looks so heart-stompingly handsome, and he *did* rescue me from that spider . . . Damn, I catch myself grinning back at him.

But that doesn't mean I'm about to roll out the red carpet and celebrate his spider-catching skills. The man already has a big enough ego. If I inflate it anymore, he'll probably take off like a hot-air balloon, and for once, I don't want him going anywhere . . . not without me.

26

ALICE

The hotel pub restaurant is bustling with people. I can't find the gumption to make conversation and Guy seems lost in his own thoughts, looking serious. All I can think about is what a fool I've made of myself—embarrassing flashes of me sprawled face down in his crotch or crawling naked across the hotel bedroom floor; and flashes of him, the hotel towel slung low around his hips and then toweling his hair dry wearing just his boxer briefs —keep my lips firmly sealed. He's probably wondering what the heck he's done to deserve being lumped with me.

The cheerful hubbub around us is a welcome distraction from my internal monologue. Fairy lights line the picket fence and sparkle in the trees. The main dining area of the pub is spacious, with a lot of bleached wood and seashells and waterscapes on the walls, but, large as it is, there doesn't appear to be a free table.

"Maybe we needed to book ahead," I say, following Guy as he weaves his way through to the back. The smell of food has my mouth watering and my stomach rumbling like an approaching juggernaut.

Sliding doors at the back of the pub are thrown wide, revealing a wooden deck with more tables, a terraced lawn below with even more tables and a band on a low stage just setting up.

"I can't believe I've never been here before. For an out of the way place, it seems busy as," says Guy, looking around.

"Super busy." And is it my imagination or are people staring at us?

"Why don't you try to hustle us a table, and I'll go and get us drinks," he says. "What would you like?"

"How about I get the drinks? I owe you. For the spider." I can feel myself blushing as my voice trails off. Plus, I'm not sure the few dollars in my pocket will even cover two drinks in this place.

"In which case, I get to choose." Guy's mouth curls into a warm smile. Perhaps he's also reliving my earlier humiliation. "Getting drinks is the easier option. Find us a table before I'm back and I'll buy dinner too. What're you having?" I face the sea and inhale, rather than look at him. "Water's fine for me."

"Alice." He raises his eyebrows.

I give him a resigned smile. "Okay, a cider, please."

Guy disappears into the crowd before I can ask him how he's going to carry two drinks with only one hand.

Down below, I spy a couple in the corner just getting up from their table on the grass terrace. I dash down the steps like the proverbial white rabbit and the woman hooking her handbag over her shoulder looks a little shocked at my sudden appearance at her side.

"Sorry. Are you leaving?" I ask, panting.

"Table's all yours. Hope you're not expecting a quiet evening, though." She raises an eyebrow and glances toward the table of outlandishly dressed women next to this one. A hen party. But I can't believe my luck. Wedged between the stage for the band and the hens, this is an ideal spot, overlooking the beach and sand dunes and ocean, the sun just sliding into the sea, throwing up its rose-gold rays and casting everything in a warm glow. It's perfect.

My phone buzzes, and I jump. "Where are you?" It's Guy.

"I got us a table downstairs on the lawn, next to the band. Do you need a hand . . . ?" I cringe. "Sorry, I mean help carrying the drinks."

"No, I've got it sorted. We need to get an order for food in quick because the kitchen is closing in five minutes," says Guy. "I just sent you a photo of the menu."

"I'll be fine. I'm not hungry," I say, although my stomach is rumbling loud enough to obscure the sound of the musicians warming up.

"You haven't eaten since breakfast. You need something." He's right, but unfortunately, I have next to no money. It was a stretch offering to pay for our drinks.

"Um . . . no, really, I'll be fine," I say.

"Of course, you'll be fine, but you'll also be hungry, and I don't want to be kept awake tonight by the sound of your stomach growling. What would you like to eat? Or would you like me to order for you."

"No." I'm certainly not one of those women who would let a man take over everything. Like I have half a brain. "Would you be able to deduct it from what you owe me for driving?"

There's a pause. "No worries."

I scan the menu. "Right, I'll have the Thai green chicken curry, please."

Moments later, Guy reappears with our drinks on a tray. I can't help but notice he's getting more than a few admiring looks from the hen party. Perhaps it's the biceps. It's impossible not to admire the arms on the man.

"I think you may have a few fans," I whisper, smirking.

Guy glances cursorily over my shoulder to the women. A smile warms his face. "Perhaps they've seen RiffRaff play somewhere."

Or perhaps he's genuinely unaware of how eye-catching he is. "This lot aren't half bad," he says, looking at the band which is playing a cover of the Proclaimers' *I'm Gonna Be*.

"Pretty fun," I say, my foot already tapping.

At the end of the song, I turn to Guy to find him staring at me with a curiously happy expression plastered across his face.

"What?"

For a moment, his gaze lingers, then he clears his throat. "So, I was thinking," he says. "I still haven't told the lads in the band that you're not Tilly. As this is just a temporary arrangement, we should stick with calling you Tilly."

I roll my eyes. "Are you still sure that's such a great idea?"

He nods. "Absolutely. One hundred percent." A smile plays at the corner of his lips. "But maybe we should get to know a bit more about one another. Don't worry, I don't need your life history, just enough to sound convincing, so I can pass as a doting boyfriend."

As I have no idea what one of those would sound or act like, I gulp my cider. "Not much to tell. You already know I have an identical twin, Tilly." Who I can't help but feel worried about. Call it my gut instinct, but something is out of whack there. I take a deep breath. Hell, this wedding. Another evening faking my sister. The very idea wears me out, and it never seems to end well.

"What about the rest of your family?" asks Guy.

Doesn't he already know this from Twister? "We've an older brother called Harry. He's at uni in Scotland. My father's a vicar of Little Pickering, the village where we live. He's a pillar of the community and all that."

"Which explains a lot," says Guy.

I frown. "Such as?"

"Nothing. Go on. Your mother?"

"Secretary at a local private school."

"And where is this Little Pickering?"

"North Yorkshire."

"Hmmm. What about previous boyfriends?" he asks.

Zero. "What about them?" I counter, not enjoying where this is going.

"Names. Hobbies. Reasons you split."

Of course, I think of Colin and the spanner I threw into Twister's relationship with him. I also think about what a loser I am going to sound like if I admit I've had zero boyfriends. Twister says I scare them away because I'm too academic, but I think that's her putting a positive spin on the situation. For some reason, all of this gets tangled in my head and Guy is still waiting for an answer and a name spills out before I can stop myself. "Colin. But I don't want to talk about him."

"It ended badly." Guy looks concerned.

"You could say that. What about you? Girlfriends?" I ask, desperate to change the subject.

"Nah, I don't really do relationships—"

"I find that hard to believe."

"Well, not in the conventional sense of the word."

I study his face. "What does that mean? You have unconventional relationships?"

He scratches his eyebrow. "I guess." He turns and looks back at the band.

"What, you're poly?" I wish I didn't sound so shocked.

"No. Like you so rightly said, I'm selfish." He smiles. "I prefer not to get attached to anyone."

I scoff, though this I can believe. "Because they slow you and your fast lifestyle down?"

He shrugs. "Call it self-preservation. Unfortunately, my family is a bit too interested in my love life and I'd rather things remained private."

"Oh." He's being very mysterious. "But you do have a love life."

He laughs. "Hmmm, I'm not sure love comes into it, but I have a sex life. Does that count?"

The mind boggles. Blood rushes to my head. The tips of my ears are probably scarlet. And I can *feel* his eyes on me. "Right . . . A proper rockstar lifestyle . . ." I grope for words like I'm still scrabbling to get away from that spider. "What, with all your groupies? Must be a real smorgasbord of women." Ouch, did I sound jealous? "Yeah, that must be really fulfilling. I bet they tell you how great you are all the time. Oh Guy! Yes, yes. Do it to me like that, Guy!"

Guy leans forward and traps my hand beneath his. "I'm pretty sure they sound a little more enthusiastic than that, Kook."

Heart pumping, I drag my hand out from beneath his. I don't

want to know more. "Why don't you tell me about your family?" I croak. "If you're expecting me to play the girlfriend, I'd better know what I'm dealing with."

He hesitates. "True." He shifts in his seat. "We've lived on the Mornington Peninsula ever since my dad and uncle set up the Balcombe Brothers' Estate Winery in the eighties, but then Dad . . . had a heart attack and passed away about three years ago."

"I'm sorry. I had no idea."

"Why would you?" He leans back in his seat and watches the dancers on the grass lawn.

"Were you close?" I ask.

"Yeah." He blinks a couple of times. "I miss him. Every damn day."

I take a large gulp of my drink, trying to ease the ache in my throat. It's the first time Guy's shown heart-felt emotion about anyone.

"Ben, my brother," he continues, "gave up his high-powered job in the city to take over at the vineyard when I . . . I refused." He rubs the edge of the table. "My little sister, Electra, is still at school, but she and Mum help out with the vineyard as well. Like I said, apart from me, it's a family affair."

Right then our food arrives, and my mouth and stomach start singing hallelujah in harmony.

"Not hungry much?" says Guy, back to his old self, smirking as I get stuck in.

I want to know more about him. I'm intrigued. There seem to be undercurrents of tension when he talks about his family, and I can't help wondering why.

"Tell me more. What about your brother's fiancée and her family?"

He takes his time. "Ben's marrying his childhood sweetheart, Xanthe O'Sullivan. The O'Sullivan family and ours have been close since before I was born. Xanthe's father and my dad went to school together in Melbourne. And Xanthe's mother, Tina, is Mum's *dear* friend and therefore feels she has the right to speak her mind about *everything*."

It sounds rehearsed, but it's like he's chewing on gristle. His face is deadpan, but it's as if family and friends are something to be endured rather than enjoyed. A lump you'd rather spit out than swallow.

"Do you not like the O'Sullivans?"

Guy stops chewing. For a split second, there's naked pain in his eyes, but in a blink it's gone again. "They're fine."

I can't help wondering what's going on inside that head of his. Why is he not more excited about his own brother's wedding?

"What do you think we should tell them about how we met?" he asks.

He's deferring to me? "Errrm. We should probably stick to the truth as much as possible. Less chance of us contradicting one another. How did you meet Tilly?"

"At The Axel." That's the nightclub Tilly was working at and where she hooked up with the owner—Axel. Temporarily, thank God. I met him once. He was a creep in leathers. Tattoos up to his ears. I prefer not to know the ick details of her love life, but I wish I'd asked her more about Guy. Not that there was a love life there, I remind myself.

"Tilly was always great with the customers in the Axel. Big smile. Awesome dancer. We got talking one time after we were doing a gig and she asked if she could do a song with us. Normally, I'd have said no, but as she was with Axel . . ."

"You felt obliged?"

He shrugs. "Singing at the club was a big deal for the band. And to be honest, the audience loved her. We had a great vibe between us on stage."

"And the rest, as they say, is history."

"Yeah, but not the history you fabricated in your head. That was pure fiction. I hope you believe me now."

I stir the rice around my plate. "I do."

"Good."

I can't hold his warm gaze. It feels loaded. And it's impossible, totally impossible. Not after our false start and all the stuff I said to him. Plus he's in this cool band and on the road. Plus plus I'm only in Australia temporarily. Besides, he's only interested in one thing . . . *sex*. That's not on my mind at all. Much.

I proceed to stuff my face, chewing fiercely, struggling to swallow.

This is crippling me. Being stuck with Guy is . . . panic-inducing and frustrating. He's gotten under my skin and although he acts genuinely interested in me, but he could also be toying. Like big cats do. I need to protect myself. I do not need this complication. This hump in the road. *Gah!—Hump!*—even my brain seems to be trying to trip me up.

"So, I know you enjoy chess—"

"Only sometimes," I mutter.

"—and hate spiders—"

"Not exclusively."

"—but what else should I know about you?" he asks. He should know that right now, I'm about to implode. He should know, I'm not in control of the way my body responds to him no matter how many times my brain tells me it is a terrible idea.

"Nothing to tell!" I say.

He puts his hand on mine and I snatch it away.

"Tilly mentioned you'd been offered a place at Oxford. What are you going to study?"

What else has she told him? "Law."

His mouth twitches.

I take a slug of my drink and close my eyes.

"I'll go and get us some refills," he says, wandering off with our glasses before I can protest.

If there really is nothing going on between him and Twister, it changes everything. And nothing. He is not boyfriend material. Not that I'm looking for a boyfriend. I am passing through. And God Almighty, it's not like he's seriously interested in me! This wedding plus one thing is another gig for him. All show.

But I can't help but wonder what sex with him would be like. The fumbled efforts with boys to date have been . . . uncomfortable, and that's putting it mildly.

I watch him muscle his way through the throng, back in my direction. Several women watch him as he passes, their gazes lingering. He's undoubtedly what Mum would call 'a strapping lad' and the face on him could belong on a Calvin Klein billboard, but . . .

Eyes on the road, Alice. He would melt you like tarmac under the Australian sun.

He puts our drinks down, his forehead creased with concern. "What's up?"

"Nothing."

"You look stressed."

"No, I'm just enjoying the view. The music. The general ambience."

His mouth twitches. "Yeah, it's extra. Hope you don't mind me saying, I don't know what's going on with your sister, but I'm bloody glad you're here . . . to step in and save the day."

"Is that what I'm doing? There was I thinking I was here to create havoc."

A smile creeps onto his lips. Lips I am now fixated with. How could lips be so, so . . . his lips are perfect. Not too full. Not too thin. Quick to smile. Full of mischief—

"Havoc by name, Havoc by nature, hey?" he says, smiling. "I'm willing to take the risk. So, you and Tilly. Tell me more. What do you think is going on?"

I tear my gaze away from his lips and shrug. "We had plans," I take a thirsty slurp of my drink, "before we came to Australia. We'd barely left the UK before. Like ever. My parents are real home bodies. And there wasn't a lot of money to go around being vicar's kids, so it took a while to save up." I frown. "This was meant to be our grand adventure, seeing the world together, finding ourselves . . ."

"Although Tilly seemed pretty set on staying with the band."

"She wasn't."

He gives me a look. "If you say so."

"Ugh. You think you know her so well."

"And perhaps you don't know her as well as you think."

"And undoubtedly you have an answer for everything. You are quite possibly, no, probably, hmmm, actually, *definitely* the most infuriating man I have ever met."

He smiles. Warm eyes. Dimples. Sweet perfection.

I want to hate him, but he makes it so difficult. I try not to let his face derail my whole evening.

I'm startled when his finger lifts my chin. "Alice, if it's any consolation, I'm genuinely sorry I called you Tilly at New Year's. I can't ever undo that, and I know it was about the worst timing ever. I've been kicking myself ever since for making such a stupid blunder."

Oh no. He can't do this now. Be nice.

I struggle to swallow my mouthful.

I want to believe he's being genuine. I want to trust him, but my confidence is shaky to say the least, and I don't trust that I won't make a fool of myself. What's more, I have the very strong notion that I'd get burned. I'd be too involved, too fast, too much for him, and next week he'd be like, do I even know you? So, is it really worth putting myself through the wringer?

Yes, whispers my traitorous brain.

"Alice, we both know *us* at the wedding is just for show, in front of my family and the wedding guests, but maybe we should discuss what that's going to look like for real. We *are* going to have to dance."

I stuff another forkful of green curry into my mouth to stop myself from saying anything untoward.

"If you don't dance with me, no-one's going to be convinced we're together, and there's no point doing this thing half-assed. We need to look convincing, don't you think?"

I shrug my shoulders.

"I don't want you freaking out on me like I'm another spider if I kiss you—"

I inhale a grain of rice.

My brain is torn between working out how to dislodge the food in my esophagus and how to dislodge the image of Guy kissing me . . .

and realizing, as Guy starts thumping my back, that I am way out of my depth.

"Stop!" I wheeze, gulping my drink and spluttering it everywhere.

I'm too appalled to look at him. The epitome of uncool, I get to my feet and rush to the Ladies.

Shit. A. Brick. House.

I blow my nose and stare at my glassy-eyed reflection in the mirror. *What are you even thinking, you idiot? You should know better. You and Guy? Not ever going to happen, so pull yourself together!*

When I get back, Guy's watching the band and the clutch of drunken hens whooping it up on the lawn, grinning at their antics.

"Sorry about that. Um, so, I was thinking, won't your family wonder why you never mentioned a girlfriend when you were home at Christmas?"

"I didn't go home. I was too busy." Is he serious? "Maybe we should say we spent Christmas together?"

"Oh." Why didn't he go home for Christmas? "Right, so what did we do on our fictitious Christmas Day together then?" I don't know what it is about the way he's staring at me, but it's increasingly difficult to remain cool under the assault of his hot gaze.

"I imagine we lazed in bed. Took our time . . ." His smile gives me goosebumps.

"I imagine we opened our presents, I cooked breakfast and then we went for a walk on the beach," I say, brusque as I can.

"I gave you a surf lesson." His dimples reappear.

"We took a picnic with us."

"And then we were so exhausted we went back to mine again. It was hot as . . . because I barbecued. Obviously." His eyes glint mischievously.

"And then we watched a Christmas movie together. *Love Actually.*"

"Huh? No *actually, Die Hard.*"

"*Die Hard!* That's not a Christmas movie."

He looks surprised. "It is in my family."

"Not in mine."

"Well, maybe we were too obsessed with one another to watch anything at all . . ."

"Ha!" That shuts me up. For a second or two. "You wouldn't say that though, would you?"

He grins, mischievously.

"I called my family because I was missing them so much," I say. "Did you call yours?" I add as an afterthought.

"I made a short phone call. But I was far too busy comforting you because you were homesick."

I can't help giggling. I wish I had spent Christmas with him for real. It would've been much more fun than the row I had with Twister. "I was. It was *not* a Christmas I want to repeat . . ."

"Oh really? I'm pretty damn sure I had the best time with you! I may have even won at chess." He cocks an eyebrow and grins wickedly. "What did you really do Christmas day, Alice?"

"Tilly and I had a stupid row. I read a book."

"Sounds desperate." He's studying me with a horrible, sympathetic lopsided smile on his otherwise perfect face.

"W-why wouldn't you w-want to spend Christmas with your family? I don't get it," I say.

Guys leans back and runs a hand through his hair, and my traitorous eyes stray to the impressive curve of his bicep. "I . . . it's . . . complicated. RiffRaff had a lot of gigs scheduled and I also told Mum I was seeing someone." His mouth twitches.

"Seriously?"

"Seriously. I'm very serious about you." He stares at me across the rim of his glass as he takes a glug of his beer. "To be honest, my family wants nothing more than for me to settle down . . . and then join the family business. It's kind of wearing just speaking to them on the phone, let alone visiting. Having a girlfriend who's also part of the band makes perfect sense."

"So, I am your perfect excuse."

"Exactly, Alice. You are my perfect excuse." Again the look that triggers something in my chest. Again warmth pooling and spreading inside me. I clear my throat. "Even though RiffRaff have a no sex between band members policy?"

He laughs. "Well, my family doesn't need to know that. I haven't been home in over a year because it causes . . . arguments. I don't love conflict." He drinks again.

"Good to know."

He scratches the scruff of his jaw. "Of course, I feel bad about not going home for Christmas, but as I was obliged to go home for the wedding anyhow, I didn't want to make my visit any more protracted than it needed to be . . ."

"Oh." I'm still mystified.

"Look, if I want a career in music, if I want RiffRaff to succeed, I have to make sacrifices."

It kind of makes me feel guilty that I'm not more committed to, well, anything. It also makes my stomach sink knowing I'm a minor interlude, a small note in his musical world. A quaver. If that. "Well, I guess our Christmases would have sucked had we not had each other." I stop.

"Yeah. I was your consolation prize."

I snort. "Of course, you were." I wish he wouldn't play with me like this. His faux flirtation is making me hot and flustered. A perfect excuse and a consolation prize. I'm not sure which is worse. "Does the band spend a lot of time on the road?" I ask, desperately deflecting.

He shrugs. "Yeah, a fair bit. Mostly music festivals and smaller gigs, but I think we're slowly gaining traction. Finding a few fans."

Plenty of female ones I imagine. "Does it ever get lonely? I mean . . ."

Our eyes meet.

There is raucous laughter among the hen party, and his gaze slides toward them.

"Nope. No time to think about lonely. I can't afford to get distracted by anyone or any place. That's why you really *are* my perfect excuse, Kook." He looks back at me and smiles.

Wow. I think I might be a little bit heartbroken by my fake

boyfriend. He really is only serious about his music. Only committed to the band. And more than a little cut-throat about it.

I can't shift the goosebumps on my arms. I pick up my drink, but can feel his eyes on me still. I must not fall for this man. I must not want him. I must tamp down all the emotions which seem to be prickling beneath my skin and threatening to erupt.

Like Twister said, I have to get on with my own adventure. By myself.

As soon as this road-trip and wedding are done. Ugh.

"You disapprove," he says.

I shrug. "I don't really understand why you'd lie to your family."

"It's a white lie."

"Call it whatever color you want."

"And you've never lied about anything, I suppose . . ."

I can't hold his stare. Shit. Of course, I've lied. Maybe now is the time to come clean about the whole brush turkey incident. "Actually, Guy—"

"I knew it," says a voice behind me. A woman leans a hand on my shoulder. "You're Guy Balcombe. The singer." She checks me out. "You were both in the news recently. You're from that band." It's one of the drunken hens.

"RiffRaff." He smiles at the person behind me. "Color me guilty." His eyes flash to mine.

"Oh. My. God. I can't believe this. Are you performing tonight?" asks the woman.

"No, I'm having a quiet evening out . . . with my girlfriend." Again, his eyes rest on mine.

"Oh, come on, Guy. You wouldn't want to miss any opportunity to perform," I say.

She looks down at us. "Exactly! It's my brothers' band. You wouldn't mind if we stole Guy away from you, would you?"

I look at Guy. My mischievous side gets the better of me. "Of course, not. I know for a fact there's nothing Guy likes better than singing, so be my guest. Please!"

"Girls!" shouts the woman. "You'll never believe who this is. It's only Guy Balcombe from RiffRaff. You know, that fella I was telling you all about."

In a flash, we're surrounded, and Guy is practically beating them off. He looks to me for help, but I just laugh and shrug.

"I'm going to have a word with my brother," says the woman who interrupted us marching off toward the stage.

"Excuse me, ladies. The only thing I want to do right now is dance with my girlfriend," says Guy, getting to his feet, shedding women. He holds out his hand to me. "Come on, we need to do this."

27

———————

ALICE

"**I** didn't realize you were such a hit. Those women were gunning for you," I say, once we've found some space on the lawn to dance.

He reels me into his arms.

"I didn't realize my girlfriend has the face of an angel and the mastermind of an evil genius," he growls in my ear.

Oh God, save me. When Guy thumped me on the back a few times to stop me from choking to death on a grain of rice, I think he may have dislodged a few brain cells. It's like I now want to drape myself all over him. I laugh nervously, achingly aware of our pelvises mashed together, my hands around his neck, his on my hips.

"And the point of this dance is to humiliate me, is it?" I say.

"The real point is if we practice dancing here, it shouldn't feel so damn awkward at the wedding."

"I suppose. I, uh, for the wedding's sake . . . But I, uh, also think we should establish some ground rules."

"Agreed. But first, we need to loosen you up a little."

I'm dancing like a mannequin. Stiff as anything. Only he smells so deliciously shower-fresh and at the same time masculine, like a human-hot-engine, that my body is humming in response. I'm terrified I'm going to give myself away.

He hooks my chin up, so I'm staring into the vault of his dark slate eyes. There is absolutely no need to loosen me up. I'm unravelling like thread, unspooling like I've been hypnotized. It's like staring into the night sky and wondering what galaxy I'm on.

"I'm loose," I croak, "in the dancing sense of the word."

"So why do you look like you're about to have several teeth removed? Am I so hideous that you can't look at me . . . occasionally." Shit. He knows he's not hideous. The man is outrageously handsome. And I am like something untethered floating off into outer space.

"Kook, lose the frown," he says.

"I'm concentrating on not treading on your feet."

"I don't mind you stepping on me. I expect a little collateral damage where you're concerned." *What does that even mean?* "Stop squinting, try smiling. Pretend like you're having fun."

"Any more instructions you want to dish out, Mr. Ballroom Dancer?"

His lip lifts into a crooked smile and my stomach swoops again. His hand on my lower back presses me close. "Oh, I can think of plenty. I'm saving them for later." His hips are hard against mine. I can *feel* him, and while I have few comparisons to make, I do not get the impression that God has been ungenerous.

Hot damn.

My entire body simmers.

"Damn, Alice, how am I supposed to think about rules when you smell good enough to eat?"

I do? Or is he playing with me again? "Cake or steak?" I ask, trying to laugh it off.

He leans up close to my ear again. "Ice cream."

Holy mother of God. Lick me now. "You're ridiculous," I say, unable to stop myself from smiling. Just a bit. Inside I'm grinning from ear to ear. Inside I'm disco dancing. Inside I'm already imagining his silver tongue devouring me.

"What are you so worried about? I'm not going to bite you." He leans closer, "Unless you want me to. Should that be in our rule book? No licking or biting in public?"

Heat flashes from my ear through my core to my navel. I slap his chest, pushing him away before I combust completely.

"You're such a douche," I laugh. No, *I* am such a douche, totally turned on by his innuendo. I'm worried I might zip off into the stratosphere at any second. "Why would I ever date a guy like you? Tell me that?"

He swings me around and I stumble against his chest, off balance. "Maybe it's our sexual chemistry on stage that spilled over into something more."

Oh God. He has no idea. "I don't think anyone would ever believe it," I say, feebly.

Guy runs his fingertips down my arms and I feel it everywhere.

EVERY.

WHERE.

"If you pretend it's just the two of us," he murmurs, spinning me so my back is now pressed against his chest and his arms are wrapped around me, "perhaps you'd find this easier."

Easier? I'm so easy right at this moment I might as well give the man a trophy. Goosebumps have spread like wildfire along my bare arms, my knees feel so flimsy they might give way and I'm swilling in a hot sauna of lust. At this rate, he'll have to pick me up and flipping carry me off the dance floor. God help me. It takes every ounce of my remaining willpower not to collapse.

"This is not making anything easier," I somehow rasp. "It makes it harder." I cannot think of *hard* where Guy is concerned. "Guy! I can't dance like this!" I wriggle out of his grasp and put some much-needed distance between us, gasping for air. I cannot let *that* happen again.

"Just because I'm your fake girlfriend, that doesn't mean we have to be super clingy with each other." I know I'm no expert when it comes to sexual relations, but the effect he has on me is bewildering. Shocking. Seemingly with no effort at all. If he does this to me at the wedding, I am likely to, at the very least, climb him like Hadrian's Wall.

"Rule number one," I say, "no slow dancing!" Closing my eyes, for a moment I let myself feel the beat of the music and the cool sea breeze tousling my hair. I will the rave of hormones rampaging around me to subside. It would be so much easier to dance if I didn't have to think about Guy at all.

I focus desperately on the music and rhythm, dancing on the spot with my eyes closed. Anything rather than actually look at Guy. At the end of the song, I hear a low chuckle, open my eyes and Guy is right there, looking down at me.

Dancing with a complete stranger seems like a much safer option right now than dancing with Guy. And I still need to complete IT #5.

"Well, thank the Lord that's over," I say, brushing myself off like I've survived the Hunger Games, but he's not having any of it.

"Kook." There's a strange gleam in his eyes as he brushes my hair from my face. I guess dancing by myself with my eyes closed must have looked pretty kooky. "That wasn't even a full dance. Clearly, we need more practice." There's a steely glint in his eyes, and I feel like a rabbit on tarmac, headlights blinding me.

"I really don't think that's necessary. I'm fine."

But then the band strikes up with *King of the Road* of all songs.

We grin at one another. This bloody stupid song might just become our anthem.

The hens and bucks start doing some sort of crazy line dance and Guy joins in. Blundering about like he hasn't a care in the world. Like he does this *all* the time. "Come on Kook, you can't complain about this. Look, no hands," he says waving at me. Idiot.

I bumble along in his wake, unable to stop laughing whenever I get it wrong (frequently) and crash into his shoulder (often). At the end of the dance, I'm breathless, but I have to admit, it was fun. I can't remember when I last had so much fun. He throws an arm around my shoulder and murmurs in my ear. "I'd almost given up hope that you knew how to enjoy yourself. It's good to see I was mistaken."

I open my mouth to reply, but we're caught up in a sudden surge toward the stage. Guy is swarmed by a chorus of drunk women in tiaras and veils shouting, "It's his turn now! It's your turn! Let him sing!"

Beckoned by the lead singer, Guy reluctantly mounts the steps onto the stage and I manage to slip his grasp. He's ushered toward the microphone.

"Okay. Evening folks. I'm Guy Balcombe," I hear him say moments later. There are cheers. "Thank you for inviting me to sing. My brother's getting married tomorrow. Maybe it's not an entirely dumb thing to do. This one's dedicated to everyone in love." That voice. He creates a frisson of excitement and he's not even started singing yet.

The band starts the very recognizable tune of Bruno Mars' *Marry You,* and the hen and buck party goes nuts. Back at our table, I'm hoping I'll go unnoticed, but Guy stares right at me as he sings. My stupid stupid heart flutters like a butterfly trapped beneath my ribcage. I'm feeling so many things. Like this could be real. Like he's maybe the most gorgeous man I've ever laid my eyes on. Like my body is alive and also on high alert while my head is arguing that this is mad and bad and oh, let's not forget, totally FAKE.

Fake. Fake. Fake. Fake. Fake.

"Who cares baby?" croons Guy.

I care. It would be all too easy to believe, to get carried away with his molten stare beneath the velvet sky stage lit by a canopy of stars. I take a photo of him because this feels like a 'moment'. A moment to remember. A stepping-stone. There is no way Guy Balcombe is not set on a path to greatness. I check out the photo of him and I'm about to send it to Twister when I'm reminded I still haven't done IT #5.

Bugger.

I look around for someone I can ask to dance. There don't appear to be too many single blokes in the pub other than a group of tradesmen wearing fluorescent vests, shorts and boots in the far corner. One of them will have to do. It's now or never.

Draining the rest of my drink, I skirt around the lawn that is now bristling with dancers, to the huddle of tradesmen. The man talking stops mid-sentence. Looks at me.

"Sorry." I wipe my sweaty hands on my jeans. "Excuse me. I wondered if one of you gents would be kind enough to dance with me?"

There are snorts of laughter and some elbow shoving. Technically, my brain tells me, I have completed my Impossible Task. It only said to *ask* a stranger to dance, not that I had to *actually* dance with them, although, I remind myself, I don't have evidence yet. While they're pushing and shoving one another forward and having a gas about who should dance, I take out my phone. "Sorry, I'm just going to repeat that." I switch on the video camera and they look at me like I have two heads. "I'm not asking you to marry me, but would one of you gentlemen please dance with me? Just one dance?"

The middle-aged man in front, who has tattoos right up to his cleft chin, raises it defiantly. "It'd be my pleasure," he says, rubbing his hands together and grinning shamelessly over his shoulder at his mates. "I'm Big Dick," he says.

Of course, he is. This could only happen to me. "I'm Alice."

The band starts singing *Islands in the Stream* and I realize Guy is still singing, but also watching me with a dark expression on his face.

Big Dick holds out his calloused hands like he expects me to step into them and waltz.

Dear God.

I can survive one dance.

I'm not so sure he will though.

"Good job you're not wearing boots like me," he says, cheerfully, halfway through the song, as I step on his foot for the fifth time.

"Sorry. Dancing isn't really my thing," I say.

"So why d'you ask then?"

I shrug. "Long story."

"We've all night."

Mother Earth, please swallow me up already. "Actually, I have to leave after this dance," I say.

"Oh." Surprisingly, he looks disappointed. "Just when I was starting to have fun."

"Sorry. Early start in the morning . . ."

"Oh, come on love, I bet mine's earlier." The song has come to an end, but he won't let go of my hands.

"Alright. This next one is a special song for my girlfriend," announces Guy's voice loud and clear over the speaker system.

"That's me," I say to Big Dick.

"Yeah, right," he scoffs.

"No, really it is," I say.

"Ah, there she is," says Guy, pointing right at me. Heads swivel in our direction. "Sorry mate, that one's taken. You're going to have to give her up because she's needed on stage. Won't you come up and join me . . . Tilly."

The man steps away like I've electrocuted him.

There's some whooping and hollering and clapping, but I'm guessing probably a few death stares as well. I'd quite like a tsunami to roar in right now and carry me away. Talk about being stuck between a rock and a hard place. I'm not sure whether to be grateful for being rescued or terrified he expects me to step on stage.

The band starts playing *Crazy Love* by Van Morrison, and Guy's eyes never leave my face. Thankfully, Big Dick doesn't like being center of attention any more than I do. He shuffles off, receiving a good ribbing from his mates.

As he starts singing, Guy steps down from the stage with the microphone in his hand. I know I've been the subject of his attention before, but this feels different. This feels as if a laser-guided beam is powering straight through my dress and my skin and my muscles and ribs and slicing into my core.

I'm not sure at what point I go from being terrified to mesmerized, but Guy has that effect on me. Our hands connect. Mine cup his around his microphone. Our eyes lock. And I start singing.

Our voices weave around one another. And it's like coming home.

It's like we're made for each other and the only two people left in the world. It's like I lose touch with reality and can believe I'm in love and it's crazy in every sense of the word.

A few minutes later and it's over. I struggle to break his gaze. But I can hear the applause and his mouth tugs into a smile. Then he kisses me.

Damn.

In front of everyone.

I'm not sure if it was the moment his lips touched mine or the moment they separated from mine, but I know I'm lost and this is no game. Not for me.

Much, I imagine, like a heart surgeon might pack away their tools and ready themselves for the next patient, Guy ambles back toward the stage, accepting congratulations and adulation along the way. He chats to the band. He never once looks my way.

And I am ... broken.

What just happened? I have *crazy* radiating out of me and feelings that should be declared illegal. I want to march up the steps and onto that stage and tell the world, that, fuck it, I have not only fallen hard for Guy Balcombe, I am mad for him.

It's so ridiculous a snort of laughter mixed with a strangled sob escapes me. I turn away, desperate to hide what I'm feeling from everyone.

For a moment, I am too shellshocked to know what to do with myself.

It was all part of the act. His act. His *practice* run, I tell myself.

Oh God.

I come back down to Earth with a crash.

Guy is getting swarmed. He's forgotten I'm even here.

My head reels with alcohol and my gut roils with the knowledge that Guy Balcombe is undoubtedly on the cusp of a new remarkable career. He is going to be huge. He is going to be stellar. I just know it. Just as I know, I have fallen stupidly in love. I am happy for him. But I'm also devastated because there is no place for me in his world. I am passing through. A falling star.

I slip away.

Back in our room, I send Guy a quick text.

> Thanks for supper. Looks like you've made plenty of new fans. I'm cream-crackered and off to bed. Don't wake me up. C U tomorrow.

Checking my reflection in the bathroom mirror, I look like I've survived a tornado. Or open-heart surgery without anesthetic. If this is love, it sucks. I've never felt so . . . shit. I don't want this. I never wanted this. And I don't want anyone witnessing me falling apart. Least of all Guy. *This is not love*, I tell myself. *This is lust. Plain and simple. Unrequited lust. And I am the Queen of Fools.*

My phone pings and I pounce on it. "Oh, for God's sake," I half sob when I see it's only Twister:

> Asked anyone to dance yet?

I send Tilly the requisite video and throw myself onto the bed.

How in God's name am I going to survive another twenty-four hours of this? Worse, I'll be at Guy's beck and call tomorrow.

And we still haven't established any rules.

I like rules. I like to know what to expect. I expect tomorrow I may fall apart entirely.

Just kill me now and put the crazy lady out of her misery already.

And what happens when Guy comes back to the bedroom tonight?

28

ALICE

Someone hammers on the door at an ungodly hour. Crap. I'm alive and it's tomorrow already. I groan, "Go away!" And stuff the pillow over my head.

"Alice, are you up yet? We need to get going."

Ugh. Leave me alone. Did Guy even come back to the room last night? I check out the bed. Sniff the pillow. It smells sterile. No delicious Guy scent.

"Alice, wake up!"

"Hold on!" I shout, throwing the pillow aside, crawling out of bed and staggering to the door.

Judging from Guy's startled expression, I'm not looking my best. He looks somewhat disheveled himself, his hair sticking up at all angles. "I need a shower," he says, as if reading my mind.

Where the hell did he spend last night? Anywhere, but with me, I guess. I also guess he had plenty of better offers.

As he hands me a coffee, I want to disappear into one of the cracks in the floorboards. I feel about as attractive as a cockroach. No doubt he spent his night wallowing in adulation, having his ego fluffed while pissing it up with multiple women. From his perspective, the ultimate night out. Thank God, they took the hen party elsewhere.

"Ready to rock 'n' roll?" he says reemerging from the bathroom all sparkly and shiny clean.

'No." I'm not ready, because my body is still rock 'n' rolling from last night and not in a good way. "I need a shower too," I mumble. God, I hate this.

"Are you alright? You look . . . peaky," says Guy.

I have peaked. I'm on the downward slide. "I'm perky," I say, unconvincingly, shutting the bathroom door behind me, checking for unwanted eight-legged friends.

"Good, because I need you hale and hearty!" Guy shouts through the door.

"What for?"

"What do you mean, what for?!"

It dawns on me . . . Crap a doodle doo! Today, after driving God knows how many hours, I'm meant to perform like a circus pet. I take my time in the shower hoping to wash the residue of disappointment down the drain.

"Can we get going, Kook? We're running late already, and if we're to stand any chance of getting to the wedding on time, we needed to leave yesterday!" Guy shouts again.

"Keep your hair on. Give me two minutes."

I take a moment to drag some air into my lungs and blink back the tears. I check my phone. Faaarrrkkk!

> Morning Malice! Final IT: Perform your best rendition à cappella of Carmen's L'Amour est un oiseau rebelle on stage at Guy's brother's wedding.

> Because that'll go down as well as a pint of puke.

> It's one song. No-one's going to kick your ass off stage.

> No-one is going to want me to sing opera either.

> Twister.

> Tilly!

As usual, she gives me the silent treatment when I want to speak to her most.

Guy hammers on the bathroom door. "What are you *doing* in there?"

I've had about all I can take of Guy and my sister. I wrench open the door and barge past him. "I'm done." I stalk across the room.

"Woah! Where do you think you're going?" he demands, stepping back.

"To the garage. Where does it look like I'm going?"

"Aren't you forgetting something?"

I stop and turn around. His eyes flick down to his bag.

Is he serious?

Okay, the dipshit is serious. I am his slave, and he is definitely going to make the most of it. Bastard. Asshole. Wanker.

Muttering names under my breath, I pick up his bag. Thankfully, there's bugger all in it.

Guy strolls at my side as I march toward the garage. "Why did you leave all of a sudden last night?" he asks. Like he doesn't know.

Flashes of Guy's brilliance come back to me like a migraine. "Like I texted you: I was tired."

"Really? Who was that man you were dancing with?"

"What's it to you? A stranger. You seem to have no problem ingratiating yourself with strangers."

"Ingratiating? Interesting choice of word . . . Are you mad at me, Alice?"

No, though I've pretty much established I'm mad for him. I scoff. "Nope."

"Why?"

I stop and glare. "I am carrying your bag. Do you need another reason? Would you like me to walk behind you so I can kiss your ass while I'm at it?"

For a moment I glare and he has the audacity to look bewildered.

"Okay, today is going to be heaps of fun," says Guy.

"Such fun," I say, without an iota of enthusiasm.

"You are without doubt the most confounding woman I've ever met, perhaps after your sister."

"Why thank you," I say. "I've always enjoyed being second best."

"Oh, for God's sake. Give me something, Alice, other than a screaming headache."

I stop, rifle through my bag and shove a packet of Tylenol in his hand. "Take a pill. Take the whole damn packet."

"Seriously? As my slave, I demand to know what's going on."

I glare at him. "Nice try, asshole. I may be your slave for the day, but you don't own my mind." I cannot believe quite how malicious I'm sounding. Perhaps today I deserve my Alice McMalice name.

Little does he know he already occupies a vast amount of real estate in my brain. I am spending far too long thinking about Guy and his hands and everything I want to do to him and everything we are not allowed to do to one another and everything he has probably been doing to some other woman . . . *Bitch! Bastard!* I want to burn the whole place down. Not that I'm psycho much. And if I am, what of it? You can blame that on Guy and Twister and her sodding IT GAME!

His expression sets like concrete. I shouldn't have called him asshole, but then again, I shouldn't have fallen for an asshole.

Too late.

Besides who cares?

Today, I hate myself more than anyone.

"Didn't you want to get a move on?" I snap, marching around him and up the street.

"Is this because I didn't come back last night?" he asks behind me.

Ugh. I grit my teeth and keep stomping, one foot in front of another.

"Are you going to give me the silent treatment all day?" he asks. "That's not going to look like we're girlfriend and boyfriend."

"Maybe our relationship is going through a rough patch," I say.

Little does Guy know that his 'girlfriend' is planning to hijack the wedding entertainment. I wonder how well that will go down with his precious brother. And I can't tell him how I really feel because it is already too uncomfortable and awkward. One-sided. A waste of time and energy. A one-way street to heartbreak.

I can't tell him anything about the IT Games because it's against the IT rules.

And I'm so close to achieving them.

This close.

Only one to go.

That's today's focus. I need to be more single-minded. Like Guy.

As I stomp along the sidewalk, my brain works overtime trying to figure out a way I can achieve my IT #6 without drawing attention to myself and spend a day at a wedding as Guy's *slave* without betraying myself to him. Like that's remotely plausible.

A rough translation of the opera lyrics run through my head. *Love is a rebellious bird that no-one can tame. And if you call for it, it'll be in vain. Nothing helps, not threats nor pleas . . . Love is a gypsy child who never plays by the rules . . .*

It's a little too close to the bone right now, and I can't help wondering if this performance is for my benefit or Twister's. All I know is I'm going to need to drink excessive amounts of alcohol to get me up on to that stage with him again, let alone sing a solo opera song about unrequited love. The very idea just makes me want to sob.

At the garage, I watch as Guy switches seamlessly from peeved to matey in the blink of an eye. He's appears chatty even though he's in such a tearing hurry. He sings my praises even though I know he's super pissed off with me. Love isn't a rebellious bird, I think. Well it might be, as far as my sister is concerned, but as far as my life goes, it's a bird trapped in a cage desperate for someone to open the door and let me fly.

Ugh. I'm not liking where my head is taking me.

How would I explain the IT Game to Guy anyhow? It's ridiculous. It's not something I'm proud of. It's hardly going to raise Guy's opinion of me or Twister or make this situation any less impossible.

If I say anything, I lose. If I say nothing, I lose.

Somehow, somewhere along the road, Guy has inked himself under my skin. Like a tattoo. I'm desperate not to care, but I do. I don't want him to think I'm an awful human being. But I suspect I am. God, this whole situation is so hopeless. Just driving another six hours with Guy is going to be challenge enough. I don't even want to imagine how pretending to be his girlfriend at the wedding will turn out.

Not good. I can feel that much in my bones.

Today life feels like one Impossible Mess.

29

GUY

"Just in case you were worried about my whereabouts last night, I slept on the beach," I say, once we're on the road again. I don't know why I feel the need to tell her, but I do.

"Oh." She doesn't look at me. Okay, she probably wasn't wondering. I spent the whole night worrying and stewing over why Alice had left and feeling upset because I liked her way more than I wanted to admit and last night I'd almost decked a complete stranger just because she was dancing with him and feeling as uncomfortable as fuck sleeping on the sand and she probably didn't even notice I was missing from the bed until this morning.

Fuck.

I don't know why I feel the need to explain further, but again, I do. "I didn't want to make the same mistake as yesterday in the van, you know when we woke up and we were—"

"Rules!" says Alice. "We still haven't established the ground rules for today."

"So even though you're my slave, I don't have carte blanche?" I tease.

Her cheeks immediately blush fuchsia pink. "No, seriously, Guy. I think we need to set some clear, you know, boundaries." Her elbows flap and her hands squirm on the steering wheel, clearly uncomfortable having to broach the subject.

"Play it cool?"

"Exactly."

A scoff escapes me. There is nothing whatsoever cool about the way I feel about Alice. Boiling, yes. Baking, yes. Blistering, yes. Combusting, yes. Explosive, yes.

"The reason I'm worried is not because of you, *per se*," she says, worryingly. "I'm just not very experienced in the girlfriend department. I mean *being* a girlfriend. I might let you down." Her voice gets quieter and quieter.

I laugh. "Come again? I'm not sure I heard you right." She let me down last night when she disappeared without a word. Her text couldn't have made it clearer how uninterested she is in me.

"What I mean is, to be honest, I've *never* had a boyfriend as such." She gives me this nervous glance, as if she's expecting me to laugh at her.

"Okay but you must've had relationships."

"Um . . . Well, sort of, but, um . . . Nothing long term as such . . ." She studies the road ahead, gnawing her lip.

"What about Colin?" I ask, feeling a twinge of jealousy.

"Colin? He doesn't count." Colin and I may have more in common than I thought. "I just thought I should explain," she says. "You know, I'm probably not ideal girlfriend material."

A harsh bark of laughter escapes me. "Well, me neither. I'm light-years away from being ideal, so that should make us the perfect match. On paper at least."

She opens her mouth as if she's about to disagree, but then closes it again. She licks her lips. Those lips. They're enough to distract me from all my other worries.

With a sigh, I drag my sorry ass to the subject in hand. "Okay, you want rules for today. I'm presuming you're going to be okay if I touch you in public?"

She hesitates. "Where?"

"As in location or body parts?" I ask.

She glances at me. The color in her cheeks spreads to her neck. Sun lances through the clouds and Alice pulls down the sun visor. Honestly, I feel bad because she looks scared.

"Perhaps it would be quicker if—"

"Fuck!" she yells. I'm thrown sideways as Alice swerves the van onto the verge, brakes, opens the driver's door and leaps out.

What the hell? WTAF?

For a moment, I presume I've said something to upset her, again, but then I spot a small insect on the windscreen. A spider. It's incy-wincey—about the size of my pinky fingernail—and must've been hidden behind the visor this whole time.

I can't help laughing—mostly with relief. Thank fuck it wasn't just her reaction to me. I lean forward to grab the spider but it scurries across the windscreen to the far corner; outside Alice shrieks, like it's somehow going to leap out and attack her. She backs even farther away putting distance between herself and the van.

"I can't understand why you'd choose to travel around a country like this when you are terrified of pretty much everything that moves here, me included," I mutter under my breath.

The spider backs itself into a corner, trying to make itself invisible.

Alice is watching me and my arachnid friend's every move. I can't bring myself to squish the poor bugger. That would be bad karma. If I harm it, bad luck will probably return to me tenfold. And I guess from her reaction we're not going anywhere until I catch the spider, wedding be damned.

It takes me fifteen minutes with a piece of paper torn from my song-writing notebook to entice the critter out of its crevice. With the spider perched on the paper, hoping it doesn't make a mad dash up my arm—because let's face it, I'm no hero and if I shriek like a baby any chance I have with Alice would most likely be compromised. Not that I have a hope in hell—I march it a safe distance away from the van.

"Done," I say, smirking at Alice and feeling more than a little gallant. "Can we go now?"

She returns to the van looking a whiter shade of pale.

"You okay?"

She nods. "Twice in twenty-four hours. Do you think they were related? Sorry. How idiotic." She laughs nervously.

Idiotic or not, I've probably been a bit hard on her.

"No worries," I say, opening the back of the van and grabbing her a bottle of water. "Plenty of people are scared of spiders."

She visibly shudders even at the word and drinks thirstily. I understand her phobia—I'm not too fond of them myself—but I've rarely seen someone react this strongly. Wayward strands of hair, just begging to be brushed aside have come loose and frame her heart-shaped face. My heart slows. The whole world microscopes to her perfect mouth and throat as she drinks.

What the hell is my problem? I don't know how or when exactly it happened, but the more I've gotten to know Alice, the more protective I feel about her. I don't like the idea of her traveling on alone without me, at all. Who will catch her spiders? As she hands the bottle back, our fingers touch and something hot flickers up my arm to my chest. She wipes her mouth with the back of her hand, and I cannot stop staring. We're standing very close, but she's not looking at me. At all. Meanwhile, I'm mesmerized by the light in her eyes and her flawless skin. I want to spend the day just drinking her in.

"We can go," says Alice.

But neither of us moves. The Earth has stopped spinning on its axis. There is only this moment. This girl and me. The heat of the sun on my face. The light dancing in her brown eyes. Music in her sweet smile. Nothing else matters. Nothing else exists.

"What about the rules?" I manage to say. "You were about to let me know . . . where I can touch you."

She sways like a leaf in a light breeze, and the gap between us closes. I take the bottle from her hand and put it down.

"What about your face?" I cup her cheek with my good hand, and Alice closes her eyes and leans into it.

A match is struck inside me.

"What about your lips?" I gently brush my thumb across her mouth. Her mouth opens and she licks her upper lip.

"You can't do that at the wedding," she whispers.

"Why not?"

"Because then, I might do this." She pulls me toward her and kisses me; I groan in fucking delight.

That's it. All my resolve goes up in flames. My mouth on hers is like being catapulted into a different universe: light scattering, heat burning, heart hammering. It is everything I remember from before and more. More sweet. More tender. More intense. More urgent.

Alice's arms wrap around my neck, her fingers thread into my hair, her body curves against mine.

Alice. I'm kissing Alice. Alice is my wonderland.

"Alice," I say.

Her lips smile against mine. We draw apart, staring at one another in awe.

"Guy?"

What the hell just happened?

"We need to work out our rules and you were about to, ah, give me some logistical parameters I believe," I say, kissing the curve of her neck.

A small sound escapes her. "Um, kissing me now and again might be negotiable."

"Thank fuck for that because I'm not sure I have the willpower to resist." I steal another kiss from her lips. "And fuck the wedding. If we're going to be late, we might as well be properly late." I kiss her more fiercely. She is the very definition of peaches and cream. Succulent and luscious. Sweeter than nectar. "Do you have any idea how badly I want to devour every inch of you?"

She looks genuinely surprised. "Then why didn't you come back to our room last night?"

"Because you told me you were knackered and not to wake you. I thought you made it pretty damn obvious you weren't interested."

"Oh. That wasn't the case."

"I want you so much, Alice."

"Honestly?"

"Far out, isn't it obvious? Yes! Even though you drive me fucking crazy. I am literally going insane trying not to kiss you mile after fucking mile." I grin and kiss her more tenderly. "I've wanted you since the moment I laid eyes on you in Sydney. I've hated myself from the second I called you the wrong name, but I think at the time my brain was already fried. You got in my head and I haven't been able to shift you since. And not for want of trying."

She laughs. "Seriously?"

I growl, "Do you need hard evidence?" My mouth crushes hers and I'm pretty sure she must be able to feel every inch of hard evidence. But when she whimpers, I force myself to pause and check she's okay.

"What about you? Are you okay with this?" I ask.

She chews her lower lip and a tangled sound escapes me.

"Alice, do you *not* want this?"

The silence terrifies me. I take a deep breath and hold myself in check.

"I'm more than okay. I want you too," she says, but she doesn't sound very certain.

"But?"

"But I think I'd also like to feel . . . um . . . you know . . . God, this isn't awkward. Much."

Have I taken it too fast? Pushed her too hard. I might have been more than a bit desperate in case she changed her mind.

She grimaces. "Okay, the truth is. I have this much experience"— She pinches the fingers on her left hand together—"and it would be nice to know how it really felt to be your girlfriend before the wedding. I mean, us." She blushes furiously. "It's a shame we don't have more time to explore this."

I'm dizzy with relief. "Fuck that. The wedding can wait. We have all the time in the world."

Although it's a cack-handed lopsided scramble, I lift her up and carry her into the van smacking my head on the roof in the process. Yeah, I may not be the smoothest operator, but I give myself full marks for eagerness and enthusiasm.

30

ALICE

He parks me on the table, pops the roof of the van and closes the blinds for which I am thankful: I've parked the van so *badly* and there's a steady stream of traffic passing by. After some more kissing, we both start tearing off our clothes. I do a better job at it than him and crack up laughing. Attempting to remove his t-shirt, he seems to have got stuck and for a moment, I'm torn between admiring the smooth muscled expanse of tanned chest and abs—They're a work of art—or helping him out.

"Hrrummph," he says, when I eventually pull his t-shirt over his head and chuck it over my shoulder.

He grins at me like a naughty school boy. "God, I love it when you get messy," he growls.

"I love it when you get naked," I say, feeling myself blush again at my own brazen words.

His grin broadens, but his eyes darken. "This is impossible," he says, and for a second my heart lurches. "I'm too big for this van. How do you feel about getting horizontal?" He searches my face for an answer. "But only if you're comfortable with that."

I love that he's being so considerate. "I'm very comfortable with that."

We roll out the bed. I can't resist running my hand across the muscles of his naked back. He sits on the bed and watches as I peel off my t-shirt and throw it aside.

He swallows. "And your bra."

"Is that an order?"

"Too right."

I unfasten my bra, sliding the straps down my arms.

"Alice, you're so so beautiful," he says, drawing me toward him so I'm standing between his thighs. With his large hands on my back, he kisses my breasts in turn, his tongue teasing and circling, his teeth grazing, his mouth undoing me completely.

Kissing my stomach, he slowly slips my underwear down my thighs to my ankles. "Tell me if you want to stop at any time. I'm happy just to gawk at you like an awkward teenager."

I laugh. "Talking of awkward, I don't really know how to do this."

"And I'm handicapped," he says, but then sits up. "Hold on. You have had sex before?"

I gulp. "Yes, but it wasn't exactly great. It was memorable for all the wrong reasons."

He smiles his roguish smile. "Let's see if we can make this memorable for all the right reasons. Improve your track record."

"You make it sound like an athletics event or a race."

He laughs. "Swap places. I'm aiming for the gold medal, even if it is one-handed and in the back of a van." Places reversed, he maneuvers me onto the bed while he kneels down on the hard floor between my thighs. For a moment he pauses again, looking concerned. "Do you mind? Us? Here? In the van like this?"

"Shut up!" I say. "I love this van."

Guy's smile does not begin to prepare me for the assault on my senses as he lowers his face between my legs. His tongue reduces me, legs trembling, to rubble. It's a good job I'm not standing up because I would have collapsed for sure.

Time ceases to mean anything. Sure, it goes by in another world, another dimension, with the swishing wave of passing cars, but in here there's only the soft shards of sunlight which chiaroscuro the interior of the van and his sculpted body. The memories imprint indelibly in my mind. Our hungry kisses. The hot leather smell of the van. His masterful fingers playing me like an instrument. My whole body singing as lines and limbs blur with tangled sheets and slick desire. His skin hot and torso hard. The tempo between us rising to a soaring crescendo. The van rocking . . .

And Guy breathing life into my heart.

31

GUY

"Shoulders and arms are fine," she says.

"Seriously?" She says this *now*. Afterward.

Alice still wants to clarify our 'terms of engagement', our rules for the day ahead, after I've had the most mind-blowing sex of my life. In the back of a van.

Because Alice, it seems, has an additional phobia as well as her fear of arachnids: an irrational fear of public displays of affection.

"Are you for real?" I demand.

"Do you need more?"

Fuck, yes. But what I need and what I want are two very different matters. And from the look on Alice's face that's a whole different yardstick to what I'm going to be allowed. Doubts creep in. "Am I permitted to put an arm around your waist?"

"Fine. But no touching my boobs or bum."

"Spoilsport," I say, and she flushes scarlet. "What about your neck?"

She shakes her head. No, neck either. From my recollection, her neck is a highly erogenous zone, but my mind is beginning to play tricks and it feels like she is holding me at bay.

"Face?" I demand.

"Do you have to?"

"Yes. It looks affectionate."

She groans. I almost make the mistake of asking her if I'm permitted to touch her legs, but I suspect that would be a hard no, so I say nothing. Better to say nothing because what she hasn't officially objected to . . . I'm already imagining running my hands up her long silky legs beneath the dinner table. What boyfriend in his right mind wouldn't?

"Anyway. We'll definitely need to kiss," I say. "Lots."

"In front of people?" she squeaks, and I have to grab the steering wheel again.

"Yes. It would seem odd if we didn't."

She is silent for the longest time. "How many times?" she eventually asks.

I have to laugh. "About a hundred," I say.

She rolls her eyes. "Maybe once or twice. Just to make the point."

"Oh, come on! Do we even like one another?"

"At this point, not much." She giggles.

"Fine. Ten times. Per hour."

She cracks up some more. I fucking love the sound of her laughter. It does something wild to me. Brightens my whole day. Ignites me inside.

"No, Guy. Three at most."

This response, however, does not brighten my day.

"Not good enough. I would kiss my girl way more than that."

"You're forgetting I'm not your girl."

"You're forgetting you *are* my slave and my hot date at that, so I'm not accepting less than five times an hour."

She bites her lip, and I want to order her to stop the van immediately so I can ravish her again already. Fuck, who gives a shit about being later than we already are?

She holds up her hand. "Five," she says. "Five kisses maximum and no tongues."

"Far out! You are no fun at all, Alice Havoc. I would *not* want you as my girlfriend for real," I lie, but I can't help smiling. "Come on! You can't blame me if my tongue slips—"

"It had better not!"

I roar with laughter. I'm looking forward to kissing Alice again a little too much. I would like to spend forever kissing her. "Okay, would you rather six kisses with no tongues or five kisses with." This is fun, but there is absolutely NO way I am sticking to these kissing quotas of hers.

A nervous giggle escapes her. She glances my way and bites her lip. "Six kisses without, I guess."

I sigh. "Seriously? Am I that bad at kissing?"

She grins. "You know you're not, so stop fishing for compliments you don't deserve."

"And you can forget about a kiss quota. You're my slave remember? Besides, I think we're beyond that."

She blushes. I swear Alice is the *color* of Love.

I put on the radio and we sing along together. This could possibly turn out to be one of the very best days of my life. I am so in harmony with her. In harmony with the world. Fuck, apart from the looming wedding, life is dope.

We're still a couple of hours from the venue, when Alice turns to me and says, "Oh, fuck!" She looks horrified.

My eyebrows shoot up and I smirk. "Okay, if you insist, but you'd better pull over."

"No, you great schmuck. What the hell am I going to wear? I have absolutely nothing whatsoever appropriate for a wedding." Her voice rises to a squeak.

"I may have bought you a little something," I say, sheepishly.

"Shut. Up. You have not!" She glances my way. "What really?"

"Yes, really, but if you'd rather go in your dungarees, I don't mind."

"But I do! What'll your family say?" she whimpers.

I fiddle with the cast on my hand. "Who cares what they say or think?"

"You must care what they think otherwise why would you put us through this whole rigmarole!"

"Good point." How do I explain this and make it sound convincing? Right now, I just want to be with her, period. "Let's not forget I told Mum I had a girl and everyone's expecting Tilly to be with me even the RiffRaff lads."

That keeps slipping my mind. There's a certain irony in the fact that today I need to make sure I call her Tilly today, not Alice.

"Ta for the reminder," she says. "Okay, I just might be desperate enough to take whatever you've got on offer."

I smile. "And as my slave, you don't have much choice."

"We're still doing that?" she asks.

"Of course. It'll add a certain frisson to the day, don't you think?"

"I think my day has already been frissoned enough, thank you, you git," she says, smiling.

I grin. "Hmmm. I don't think you should call me that today. I think *darling* will suffice."

Alice starts giggling. "You're a big knob."

A bark of laughter escapes me. "Me and my knob'll take that as a compliment too."

"It wasn't meant to be a compliment."

"But out of the mouths of babes . . . I'm beginning to think, if we ever actually make it to this wedding, we might have a laugh."

"Yeah, or it might be the death of either one of us."

We both start laughing. I don't know what gets into us. It might be the nerves or the fact that we're going to be lucky if we make it before the bride arrives, but we laugh until the tears are pouring down our faces and my stomach hurts. I take Alice's hand in mine and kiss her knuckles. "At least we're this together."

"So, um, is there anything else I should know if I'm going to pass off as your girlfriend at the wedding?" she asks.

I fill her in on some more of the family history. It takes my mind off the shitstorm I'm about to face, and it really does make me feel more secure knowing Alice's going to be with me, but the closer we get to home, the more my anxiety rises like an incoming tide. Should I give her more honest details? No. That would only worry her more. She might duck out of our arrangement altogether.

"Tell me about previous girlfriends. Any of them likely to be there? Any childhood sweethearts I should know about?" she asks.

Sweethearts? When have I ever been sweet? "No. I wasn't that kind of teenager. I was pretty geeky. Only into music and surfing. No girlfriends."

She gives me one of her reproving looks. "So you just have lots of casual sex, but you've never had a real relationship. This is going to be just as difficult for you as it is for me."

She has no idea. Alice wears her heart on her sleeve. She would be even more horrified if I told her the truth.

I do not do relationships because I don't believe in them. I had a massive argument with my dad about this very subject. And that's when he had his heart attack. There is so much guilt and disgust and resentment burning inside me that going home always feels like braving a battlefield. And I'm such a fucking coward.

Fuck, even with Alice at my side, this afternoon is going to test my nerves.

32

ALICE

By the time we reach the Mornington Peninsula it's 2pm, the sun blazing over the sweeping coastline and opaline waters.

The Peninsula, or the Ninch, as Guy calls it, reminds me a little of the Amalfi coast of Italy. Apparently, there's even a town somewhere near here called Sorrento.

Despite all the scenic loveliness, I'm fraught with nerves when fifteen minutes later Guy tells me we're almost there and we may just make it before the bride as he unclips his seatbelt.

"Don't stop driving. I'm going to get changed," he says, and clambers through to the back of the van.

I check the clock. By my estimation, we're half an hour from our destination and ten minutes late for the wedding.

As much as I try not to peek, one has to check the rearview mirror occasionally. I get flashes of Guy stripping down to his boxer shorts while talking to someone on the phone. "That was Electra. She says you can change in her room."

"Into what?" I ask, my stomach swooping.

"This," he says, holding up a bag.

"You want me to wear a bag?"

He smiles. "The dress is inside and a pair of shoes—"

"But—"

"If you keep arguing with me, I might need to kiss you just to shut you up and that would be a bit dangerous while you're driving."

My jaw snaps shut. "If you're *commanding* me, then okay, I suppose, your bloody highness," I say, as I watch him thrusting his legs into a pair of tailored black trousers and struggle with the button.

"Shit. You might have to help me out here," he says.

I blink a few times. What a delight. Help Guy to *do up* his trousers. He shrugs into a crumpled white shirt. He shoves his feet into shoes without any socks. Then he clambers back into the front seat. "You're going to have to help me with my bowtie when we get there as well. Fuck, is it hot in here or what?"

"Hot," I say. Fucking hot. Who needs buttons when instead you can have an eyeful of Guy's toned abs.

"Fuck, I hate weddings, especially family ones!" He opens the window and sticks his head out like a dog.

If I could capture this—Guy sticking his tongue out, his hair ruined by the wind, half dressed, his white shirt flapping in the breeze. Guy effortlessly rendering me speechless and trying to suppress the crazy Pavlovian reaction I appear to always have to him —imagine the meltdown his adoring fans would have if they could see him now.

We drive up a narrow stretch of road beneath a canopy of ancient trees, cars parked on the grass verge on either side of the road and massive gates festooned with white flowers. A sign welcomes us to Balcombe Brothers' Estate Winery.

"Oh. My. God!"

"Don't be nervous," says Guy.

"Who says I'm nervous?" I'm bloody terrified. This is way beyond what my paltry imagination had come up with.

Ornate wrought-iron gates open to a drive of stately silver gums, the girth of each tied with a gold bow. More cars line either side of the driveway, and row upon row of green vines march toward the horizon where the jeweled sea sparkles and dances under the sun. I am dumbstruck. How can he possibly bear to leave all this behind?

"That's the restaurant and cellar door," says Guy, nodding toward the building ahead of us. It would be right at home in Italy or France with its terracotta roof tiles, arched walkways and shuttered windows. "Keep left." He directs me along an adjacent driveway lined with white agapanthus. We pass an orchard of apple trees and a high hedge which eventually opens to reveal a farmhouse with a deep veranda running around it. I get a glimpse of front lawn, overlooking more vines and the sea, and guests already assembled.

I park and an old dog shuffles down the front steps of the farmhouse, barking.

"Bonno!" shouts Guy out the window.

A flock of geese come hurtling toward us, squawking in protest. Ignoring them, Guy jumps out and scratches the dog behind the ears.

I'm glued in my seat, jittery as hell. This is it. I'm about to assume my role as Guy's girlfriend.

He comes and opens the door to my side of the van. "You ready for this, babe?"

Babe?

Dry-mouthed, I nod. Before I can clamber out, unexpectedly, Guy cups the back of my head and kisses me. It is reassuring and tender and not at all what I was expecting.

I hold up two fingers. Kiss number two.

Smirking, he sets me down on my feet. "We're going to ace this," he says. "Could you do up my pants?"

My hands shake. Hideous torture. Beautiful skin. Faint downy hair.

"Don't take too long. People will talk," says Guy.

"Shut. Up!" I hiss.

He lifts my chin with his broken hand, his eyes hot on my face. "Breathe, Alice. You'll be fine. Not sure I can say the same for me, though," he says, readjusting himself down below. "Not really the done thing to greet family with a stiffy."

Cheeks burning, I focus on doing up the buttons of his shirt and silently saying goodbye to his sun-kissed torso. It's not an easy task. "Done." My voice quavers.

Taking my hand, Guy draws me toward the house. I have a moment to take in the enormous pots of flowers, before the door is flung wide and a figure in a flamingo pink trouser suit comes hurtling out.

"Guy!" She launches herself at him.

"Sparky! This is Electra," he says, grinning over her shoulder as he swings her around. "Electra, meet Al . . ." My eyes lock with Guy's. "A lovely friend of mine, Tilly."

"Nice to meet you," says Electra. "You must have several screws loose to put up with this jackass!"

I can't help laughing. "Well, the road-trip here was quite enlightening."

"I bet. Take a few detours, did you?" Electra punches her brother in the shoulder and slides to the ground.

"I've been waiting for you for days," continues Electra. "Why didn't you contact me? Why haven't you answered any of my calls?"

"I've been kind of preoccupied," he says, his warm gaze sliding my way again.

"Oh, like that is it. Well, all I can says is you're fucking hopeless at keeping in touch."

"Electra, really!" says a voice behind us.

Wow. There's an incredibly glamorous woman in a fitted off-white lace dress with her hands on her hips. Guy's face breaks into a huge smile. He sweeps the woman into an enormous hug. "Mum, I've missed you." He kisses her cheeks. He cups her face and looks at her with such affection, my heart squeezes. This is a Guy I've never seen before. This does not seem like a man who dislikes being at home.

"Well, whose fault is that? You know where we are. Now put me down. You'll crease my dress!"

When he sets her down, she only comes up to his shoulder. Her face is clouded with emotions: relief, joy, the hint of sadness.

"And you must be Tilly. I'm Lisa, Guy's mother. Welcome," she says to me. "Now, we're going to have to do our introductions properly later. The bride is already on her way, so you have about ten minutes to change. Electra, show Tilly to your room. Come on. Hustle. Quick sharp."

Guy slings a black tuxedo over one shoulder, hands me my mystery 'bag' from the van.

"Stop gawping at one another and get moving," says his mum, clapping her hands.

Upstairs on the landing, Guy deposits my belongings in what I presume is Electra's bedroom. "See you at the wedding," he says, kissing me again.

"That's three already," I murmur.

"Bleurrkk!" says Electra.

He rolls his eyes. "You're not seriously going to count?"

"Count what?" says Electra.

"Count how many times I kiss her today because she can't get enough of me," says Guy, grinning.

Yes, he's mouthwateringly, knee-bucklingly handsome, but this is all a farce. I need to keep my head on straight. And not forget I'm Tilly. And act like I'm used to Guy putting his hands and lips all over me . . . if only.

"See you outside," he says and disappears.

"Talk about cutting things fine," says Electra. "This is so typical of Guy." She helpfully starts to catalogue all of Guy's flaws. He's rubbish at keeping in touch. He's a heartbreaker as several of the women at the wedding could confirm. He's so messy, but that's their mother's fault for pandering to his every whim. "You mustn't pander to him, ever!" she instructs me.

"No, of course, not . . ." I say, my wilting ego distracted by the dress I pull from the bag. "Oh. My. God." I hold it up. The dress is firecracker red and little better than a Band-aid. What sort of hellish apparition is this? Where the heck is the rest of it?

"Wow. Is that all what you're wearing?" says Electra. "I wish Mum would let me wear something like that. She's so old fashioned and wouldn't let me buy anything quite so . . ."

"Slutty?" I say.

"Nooooooo! You're not going to look slutty," she adds hastily, "but Mum hates it when I so much as show a bra strap. You're going to look . . ."

"Slutty," I say again.

She giggles.

"You'll look amazing . . . But you'd better hurry up. Shower's in there. Help yourself to anything you need."

I peer into the bag to see if there is any more material. A belt? A jacket? A spud sack? Nada. Only a pair of ankle-breaking red patent heels. Oh, dear God, as if today wasn't already challenging enough.

"Oh shit! She's already here." Electra, kneeling on a window seat, beckons me over.

Down below in the courtyard, a midnight blue Daimler has just pulled up. The chauffeur jumps out and opens the door. One elegantly shod foot appears, then another. The hem of a white dress. And then the bride complete with bouquet.

"Ahhhhh." Electra and I sigh simultaneously.

A flurry of little bridesmaids appear, fluttering around her, before being ordered into formation behind her.

"Electra sticks her head out the window. "Hold on, Xanthe. Give us five minutes!" she hollers.

The bride looks up. Wow. She is beautiful. Beautiful and elegant. Her smile is radiant. "Get a move on, Electra. I'm impatient to marry your brother!"

"I'm just coming. Do you mind if I go down?" says Electra, already at the door.

"No, of course not. Go ahead. I'll be down in a second."

In a panic, I text Twister.

You awake?

Just about. You make it to the wedding on
time?

Yes, but late. And look what I have to wear!

I take a quick photo of myself in the camera and send it to her.

Wow! You look hot.

I look like trash.

You do not. Go out there and sing your
heart out.

33

GUY

The sky is blue. The birds are tweeting. White wooden seats festooned with gold ribbons are set out in rows on the geometrically mown terrace, overlooking the legions of vines below. A wedding arch draped with white and gold tulle and what looks like wisteria frames the sea view in the distance, and marks the spot where my brother, Ben, and Xanthe will make their vows. It's about as idyllic a setting for a wedding as you could imagine. But no matter how you dress it up, I still can't imagine why anyone would put themselves through this rigmarole.

"You done good," says Sparky, reappearing and grabbing my arm with a cheeky grin. "I like Tilly already."

It takes a moment for me to recall she's talking about Alice, and another to remind myself to call Alice Tilly, and reassure Tilly with a text that Alice and I have arrived safely. Jeez. My head is spinning already.

"Yeah, she's alright," I say.

"Wow. With flattery like that, I'm amazed she even looked at you," says Sparky.

Alice is more than *alright*, but as my feelings aren't reciprocated, I need to keep a lid on them. The last thing I want is Electra getting her hopes up that there's going to be another wedding on the horizon.

We make our way down the steps and along the aisle to the front, murmuring greetings to family and friends. I spot Brum, Scooter and Fin, the other members of my band, and quickly shake their hands. "Looking sharp!" I say, grinning.

Electra peels off to sit next to Mum, and I head toward Ben and the groomsmen lined up at the front. After the usual handshaking and back thumping with the other groomsmen, Ben pulls me in for a hug. He holds on to me for a moment too long, and I can feel the nervous tension vibrating off him in waves. "Wish Dad were here," he grunts.

"Yeah," I say, choking on the thought. Dad should be here. If my timing hadn't sucked, if I hadn't argued with him, he would be.

Beads of sweat have sprung up on Ben's brow, and I can't say I blame him.

The best man hands Ben a handkerchief to wipe his brow. Of course, he does. Marcus is always prepared. Always immaculate. Always an aloof French asshole.

"Marcus!" I thump him on the arm and shake his hand, perhaps a little over enthusiastically.

"*Guillaume.*" Ugh. It always bugs me how he Frenchifies my name. We seem to be in a silent battle to see who can irritate each other more and squeeze the shit out of each other's hand.

"Good to see you made it," he says, although his eyes are scouring the congregation. Dickwad.

"You alright?" I ask Ben, making sure to stand the other side of him to Marcus.

He nods. "Course," he squeaks. "How's the van?"

I grin. Poor sod. "Good to go. It's not too late to change your mind," I add.

Despite his obvious nerves, looking straight ahead, he whispers out of the corner of his mouth. "Today is not the day for your brand of cynicism. I love Xanthe."

"Of course, you do. I was talking about if you wanted to sell the van."

The music starts up and we take our positions.

My stomach free-falls and my toes curl in my shoes as Tina O'Sullivan and I clash eyes. I look away pretending not to have noticed, but the after-image of her predatory smile is scored on my retinas. She might look great for her age, her abundance of chestnut curls framing her face, her tight blue dress showing off all her curves, but her attention makes my skin crawl.

Where the hell is Alice?

A murmur goes through the congregation, as Xanthe appears on the terrace holding her, no doubt, long-suffering father's arm. Poor fucking James, how he puts up with Toots I can't imagine.

Xanthe and her father sedately progress up the central aisle toward the front.

Xanthe looks beautiful and her father so proud. Beaming.

Glancing in Tina's direction again, I want to kick myself. She's not looking at either her daughter or husband. Her eyes are fixed on me and it makes the contents of my stomach curdle. This is the reason I wanted to make sure I had a girlfriend today. Anything to keep Tina at bay.

Behind them, Alice tries to sneak into the back row, squeezing past other guests, apologizing, tugging at the hem of her dress. She looks sensational, if a little flustered. I alter my position so I can watch her out of the corner of my eye without it being obvious. Hell, has she got ants in her pants? She's as fidgety as I feel, one second pulling at the hem of her dress and the next adjusting the neckline, nearly giving the man next to her a black eye in the process.

I can't help smiling. That's my girl! The havoc she has created in my head is beyond comprehension. It's like all of a sudden, I want to do the right thing, once I've figured out what that is. I know one thing: she's got me riveted.

And unfortunately, I notice, fucking Marcus is too.

A muscle ticks in his jaw and he's staring at Alice's little red dress like a goddamn matador ready to go into the arena.

Alice blushes bright pink when she realizes she's being watched by the pair of us. A snort escapes me, and I have to make out it's a cough, watching her concerted efforts to look composed. With a straight face, I glance in her direction and have to smother my laughter as she glares back at me and runs a finger across her throat as if she would like to see me decapitated. Classic Alice.

The ceremony passes in a blur. I spend most of it watching Alice watching me. A warm glow spreads in my chest. With her by my side today, everything is going to be sweet. I stand a little taller.

Ben and Xanthe's vows are so damn earnest it brings tears to my eyes, mostly because I have little faith it will last. If Xanthe is anything like her mother, it doesn't bear thinking about.

After the ceremony, I make my way toward Alice, but a manicured hand on my arm stops me in my tracks. "Guy, I hope you're not going to walk straight past. How lovely to see you again."

"Tina," I say, dutifully kissing her cheek, inhaling the heady rush of her perfume. Like I've just stuck my face too close to deadly nightshade.

"Looking as handsome as ever," she purrs, patting my chest.

"Excuse me," I say. "I think my *girlfriend* may need a hand." I walk off, but I've already broken out into a sweat. I shouldn't enjoy the way Tina's expression clouds as I rudely turn my back on her, but I do. I've nothing whatsoever pleasant to say to the woman.

Walking toward Alice feels like stepping from shade into sunshine. Despite her frown, despite her melodramatic eye-rolling, I can't help grinning.

"Guy, I cannot believe you thought I'd fi—"

Without thinking, I interrupt, wrapping an arm around her and kissing her. Thoroughly. Maybe it's to send a message loud and clear to everyone. *See me? This girl is mine. And I am hers.* At least for today. Suddenly, I am overwhelmingly grateful that Alice is here with me. Even if she would rather be anywhere else. I will make it up to her, and I will do my utmost to make sure she has the best day ever.

Head in the clouds, my tongue tastes her lips. They part in surprise, and I can't help myself. I take advantage. I couldn't give a fuck about everyone else here, she tastes like honey and blossom and—

I growl in my throat as she gently pushes against my chest.

Alice teeters, blinking, clutching onto my lapels.

I feel much the same as she looks. Momentarily spaced out. I would quite happily forego this entire event and spend the day lavishing my attention on Alice. She makes me feel good about myself. And happy. And admittedly, as horny as hell . . .

"I think that's—"

"You look . . . so incredibly beautiful," I say, before she can tell me I've overstepped the mark or my kissing quota is all used up.

A frown puckers between her brows like she doesn't believe me. "It's a shame you didn't buy me a dress that actually fits. Give me your jacket," she hisses.

"What? Why?"

"Why do you think? To cover up."

Grinning unashamedly, I look her over. "You really don't need to. You should wear less more often. It suits you."

She blushes a deeper shade of red and thumps my stomach.

"Ooof!"

"*Mathilde*?" A voice like a hatchet makes her spin around.

Marcus has materialized behind us and for a change, the look on his face is not his usual deadpan. He has a crooked smile on his lips and a muscle ticks in his chiseled jaw and he . . . almost looks human. He's paying Alice and her little dress far too much attention for my liking.

I sling my jacket around her shoulders.

"Um . . . hi." Alice looks stricken as she shrugs into my jacket.

Shit. Fuck. Bollocks.

How could I have forgotten Marcus met Tilly and the rest of Riff-Raff in Sydney months ago? Back in September, we'd met up with my brother and Marcus after a music gig, purportedly to discuss Ben's potential bucks' weekend. I'd been forced to introduce Tilly as the newest member of our band. Marcus had offered us dinner at his Michelin-starred restaurant. But Alice has no memory of him, which is both fucking delightful and exactly how I'd like it to remain.

"You remember Marcus Sauvage from our gig a few months back, don't you, babe?" I say reluctantly.

Alice's eyes are huge. "Of course!" She laughs nervously. "So nice to see you again ... um ... Mark."

"Marcus," I whisper in her ear.

"Marcus. So you're a fan of RiffRaff's?"

I cannot help but laugh. I'm pretty sure Marcus is a fan of no-one other than himself, and her polite act is fooling no-one, but seeing him with his nose out of joint is a rare pleasure. With his celebrity-chef-bad-boy reputation, I doubt there are many women here who wouldn't recognize his face, and because Alice doesn't realize who he is, she's yanked his ego several rungs down the ladder. It's all I can do to stop myself from high-fiving her.

"Would you excuse us? I need to talk to my boyfriend in private." Alice gives my sleeve a yank before teetering off around the side of a high hedge, beckoning frantically for me to follow.

Marcus's eyes trail after her. Admittedly, she has a great set of pins ... and the hem of my jacket is barely covering her ass.

"What 'appened with *Mathilde*?" says Marcus.

Only a pompous ass like Marcus would call Tilly *Mathilde*. "Tilly's happy." An emotion I imagine he's unfamiliar with. I grab a couple of glasses of champagne from a nearby waiter, stoked to leave Marcus looking more constipated than ever.

I hand Alice her glass and she knocks it back like it's water.

"Woah. Slow down."

"This is not going to work, Guy. Who was that French man? How did he know me?" She holds the back of her neck as she paces back and forth, chugging back her champagne to punctuate each about-turn.

"Ben's best man. You mean you don't recognize the famous Marcus Sauvage?"

She frowns. "Should I?"

"He's a celebrity chef and restaurateur."

"Oh. Of course. Like I dine out at posh restaurants *all* the time."

"He's also on tv."

"Must have missed that one. More to the point, how does he know me?"

"Tilly met him once in Sydney, but you don't need to worry about him."

"Are you kidding me? She met him and you didn't think it was important to tell me? Thanks for the warning. We're barely five minutes into the wedding and I'm already this close to . . . messing everything up. Did you see the look on his face?"

"Mmmm, he can't help it. Ugly bastard."

"Ha! You need your eyesight checking. That man is *far* from ugly! Is anyone else likely to throw a spanner in my direction?" she demands, eyes flashing. "Is there anyone else I'm supposed to know?"

For some reason, the fact she thinks Marcus is *far from ugly* bothers me. I scratch my head. "Actually, now you mention it, my brother, Ben, also met Tilly."

Alice groans. "Guy! No! I can't do this!"

I take her hands in mine. "Of course, you can. You'll be fine. I won't leave your side. I swear."

"You'd better not." She thumps my shoulder, and I can't help grinning.

"Jesus! Anything else you've failed to mention?"

"No," I say, taking a slug of my champagne. "Out of interest, if I'd just asked you nicely, would you have sung with us today?"

She takes another slug of champagne. "Maybe. Maybe not. We have a bit of a problem by the way. I only know the numbers we sang in Sydney on that boat on New Year's Eve and we haven't even discussed what we're supposed to be singing." She looks like she might pass out at any moment.

I pull her close and wrap my arm around her waist, whispering into her ear, "As my slave for the day I command you to stop worrying. Any songs you don't know, you can mime, um and ah to your heart's content."

"Oh ta. Really bloody professional. Mime like this?" she says, wrenching away from me and flipping me the bird. She paces back and forth.

"Calm down. You'll be awesome." *I* need to calm down. Her nervousness is making me twitchy.

"Don't tell me to calm down, Guy! There's nothing awesome about this situation whatsoever. This wedding is . . . fucking horrendous!" she hisses. I know I'm in trouble now she's using the f-word, but she's irresistibly cute even when she's angry and swearing. "This is the stupidest idea ever. Almost as stupid as New Year's Eve and my stupid sister's bloody game."

She glances at me like she's said something wrong. I suspect it has nothing to do with the wedding.

"What game would that be?" I ask, remembering her journal.

"Nowt. I need another drink," she says, skulling her glass.

Now I'm even more curious. What is her and her sister's IT game? I neck the remainder of my champagne.

"God almighty, this is nerve-wracking. Promise you won't leave me alone for a second," she says.

"I promise." That suits me just fine. I take her hand and tuck it into the crook of my elbow.

"Although you could fetch me another drink," she says.

I thought she was supposed to be *my* slave for the day, but she seems to have the upper hand already.

"Wait here. I'll be back," I say, doing a terrible Schwarzenegger impression.

"No way. I'm coming with you."

"Do I have any say in the matter?"

"Zero!"

Yeah, like she's my slave. As if I have any authority over Alice whatsoever.

34

ALICE

Guy has just placed another glass of champagne in my hand when an older woman accosts us.

"Guy, there you are! Why do I get the feeling you're avoiding me and who's this delightful little morsel?" She looks me over like a bird might eye a worm. I'd guess she's in her late forties or early fifties, but she looks like she works out. Carrying all those jewels on her fingers must make every move of her arm like a power weight session.

"I'm—"

"This is my girlfriend, Tilly," interjects Guy. "Tilly, Tina. Xanthe's mother."

"Less of the formality. Call me Toots. So this is the mysterious girlfriend keeping you away from home over Christmas. I wouldn't have believed it if I hadn't seen her with my own eyes." Her laugh is guttural and her hand on Guy's arm makes me want to swat it like a mosquito. "I've so much I could tell you about our dear boy," she says, practically devouring him with her eyes.

Guy has high spots of color on his cheeks. I've never seen him look this uncomfortable. His good hand slides into mine and he kisses my wrist.

"Didn't Ben and Xanthe look wonderful!" she says. "They made getting married look so easy, didn't they?"

Why does she keep checking Guy over like that?

"Getting married is easy. Staying married is more of a challenge, I imagine. What's the secret?" Guy asks Tina.

"Alcohol, and a lot of it I imagine," I say, without thinking.

Guy snorts his drink, and Tina steps back in a hurry. "Excuse us, Tina, we really need to go and talk to the band," he says, laughing.

"What was that all about?" I ask once we're out of earshot.

"All what?" says Guy.

"Whatever was going on between you and Tina," I say.

Guy stops in his tracks, frowning. "There is nothing going on between us" he snaps.

"Okay. If you say so. I just thought she seemed bizarrely possessive," I say.

"You have no idea what you're talking about. You've got totally the wrong end of the stick," says Guy.

And he's doing an awful lot of protesting for an innocent man, I think.

Thankfully, we're waylaid by a dozen more people on the way over to RiffRaff at the far end of the lawn, sitting on the stage and chatting, and the matter is forgotten.

"Tilly!" shouts Brum, pointing at me with one of his drumsticks. "Look at you. You look hot as." He wraps his arm around my shoulder and pulls me in for a squeeze.

"As what, a hot dog?" I extricate myself.

I do the rounds, hugging and chatting with Scooter, the saxophonist, and Fin, the bass player. It's great to see them again. At least there are some friendly familiar faces.

"So what's the plan?" I say and immediately want to kick myself. I should know the plan. Thankfully, Guy picks up my gauntlet. He explains they are going to do some of the numbers we sang on New

Year's Eve as they were such a success, and his brother and Xanthe saw a video of the event and have requested some of the same.

With the lads in the band, Guy looks relaxed and unperturbed, somehow outshining everyone with his boyish laughter. But there's a strained quality to his eyes I've never noticed before. Almost as if he's having to put on as much of a performance as I am.

I have to be honest. I spend most of the next half hour secretly studying Guy, his thick hair curling over the collar of his shirt, just begging for someone to run their fingers through it. His twinkling eyes and flashing dimples. Jesus, he is so divine it's little wonder women are falling over one another to talk to him, even the old matrons like Tina O' Sullivan.

How am I going to get this lot to agree to Diva Alice performing opera tonight?

A bell tinkles, and the French bloke announces that it's time to sit down for dinner.

"I really think Marcus suspects something. He keeps glowering at me," I murmur to Guy quietly, as we all head over toward the marquee.

"I don't think that's glowering," Guy says, studying the seating plan. "That's just his face for you—What the fuck is this?"

"Dude, it's the seating plan," says Brum.

My stomach sinks. I'm nowhere near Guy.

"Thanks mate, I can see that. But why have they put you guys on the table with the fucking kids and meanwhile I'm seated next to. . ."

"Oh, delightful," says a voice behind us. "We're seated next to one another on the top table, Guy. You can escort me."

"I'll be right there. I'm sure you can find your own way, Tina."

I've no idea what possesses me, but I step forward, take Guy's face between my palms and kiss him. He stares into my eyes, shock written all over his face. We part and his slow smile nearly knocks me backwards.

"Don't worry about me, I'll be fine," I say. Tina is smiling, but her expression has the frozen quality of someone overloaded with Botox.

"Come on, Guy. Don't keep everyone waiting. You can catch up with your band later," she says.

"We'll look after Tilly," says Brum, putting an arm around my shoulders.

I force myself not to look back as I head toward the noisy corner. It looks like RiffRaff and the kids are already getting on like a house on fire . . . Hopefully there are no candles on our table.

I swipe another fortifying glass of champagne from a waiter *en route* and introduce myself to my new friends. They rattle off their names, along with their roles and responsibilities for the day, as if being a page boy or flower girl or rose-petal thrower is something they could put on a resumé.

There are definite bonuses to being seated on the children's table. One, we get our very own goody bags, and there are also coloring table mats and tubs of crayons for drawing. Two, the children are a great distraction from Guy, and worries about Tilly and my performance later. And three, we get our food first, because little people cannot wait. Yay. Because who wants the mouth-watering plates of French delicacies and fillet mignon when you can have chicken nuggets and chips? But at least they make less mess when hurled across the table.

One of the flower girls, Jessie, asks me why I'm not married.

"I'm far too young," I say.

"Yes, me too!" she replies emphatically, which is probably about right, as Jessie looks to be about eight years old.

"How old do you think I am?" asks Brum. Not the best question to ask a child if you want your ego pampered.

"Maybe fifty," says Jessie.

"I'm thirty!" he says, looking outraged and making us all laugh.

"Sorry, but you look older. You have a seedy hairline," she says.

"Seedy?"

I snort. "Receding."

"I don't have a receding hairline, do I?" Brum asks Fin, clearly mortified.

"I'm not getting married in a million years! Errkkk!" pipes up another of the kids. The giggles take over as all the boys around the table, including Brum, Scooter and Fin, start making gagging noises and sticking their fingers down their throats.

"I might get married, so long as I never have to marry a boy!" says one of the girls, wide-eyed with horror.

"Well, no, you don't have to. You could marry a girl if you prefer," I reassure her.

"Or your pet dog. I'd like to be a dog. It'd be cool being able to lick my own nuts," says one of the boys.

"Ewwww!" All the kids squeal.

"I'm allergic to nuts," comments Jessie primly.

Fin and Scooter are laughing so hard, they hold on to one another to prop themselves up.

"I want a fucken' knife!" shouts Lucien, the smallest child at the table sitting opposite me. He must be all of three. He bashes the table with his plastic spoon, his face turning an alarming shade of puce.

"Lucien. Shh!" I say, trying to control my giggles. "That sort of language isn't good. Your parents wouldn't be happy." Though to be fair, it's likely he's got it from them in the first place.

He ignores me and keeps right on yelling, his face turning beet-root. "I'm a big boy an' I want a fucken' knife!"

A woman appears at his side. "Lucien, if you keep on like that you'll have to come and sit with me. Wouldn't you rather stay here with the big children?"

"No, I want a fucken' knife! It's not fair!"

Lucien would have been more appropriately christened Lucifer. I wait for his mother to try to calm him down.

She sighs. "Manners, Lucien. *Please*," she says.

Not the response I was expecting.

"I want a fucken' knife, *please!*" he shouts at the top of his lungs.

His mother rummages through her bag and produces some plastic cutlery. Realization dawns: Lucien wanted a fork and knife, not a *fucken* knife.

Or not—Lucien immediately hurls his cutlery across the table and I duck narrowly escaping losing an eye. They sail over my shoulder and hit the man approaching our table.

Oh, God. It's Marcus, and he looks furious.

"*Ça suffit, Lucien!*" he snaps, picking him up. "I apologize. Come on, I think it's time you had a rest."

Marcus, the wife and Lucien exit the marquee, Lucien screaming and kicking.

"I wish I had curly dark hair like yours, Ocean," says Jessie, as if nothing whatsoever has happened.

Brum, Scooter, Fin and I snort with laughter again. I'm happy I'm not on the top table. Guy looks like he is having no fun at all. I will him to look my way, but he doesn't.

Marcus reappears some time later, returning to the head table just in time to give his best man's speech. I have to admit, even though he's a little dour, I could listen to his French accent all day. He recounts a hair-raising tale about how he met Ben during opening week in his Melbourne restaurant. Guy was the first Balcombe he met because the woman he was with had the audacity to complain about the food. There is muffled laughter. This resulted in Marcus asking Guy to leave, the story continues. Guy was *un peu* drunk and there was an expensive scuffle. More laughter. The end result was Marcus locking Guy in the cool room until a very apologetic and concerned Ben arriving on the scene and insisting on paying for the damages. Now there are guffaws around the room as Marcus describes with a deadpan expression how he had refused to release Guy until Ben had signed a written declaration that he would return to the restaurant to eat with friends who had better taste in women and food and who didn't demand ketchup with bloody everything.

Guy catches me grinning, rolls his eyes and almost smiles.

The children are getting impatient, so as soon as speeches are finished, we usher them outside.

Scooter, Brum and Fin amble off while I do my best to entertain the kids—the girls hold hands and dance, while the boys get grass stains on their knees trying to skid through the gaps.

My phone pings with a text message. It's Twister. Aka Tilly. Aka the pain in my day.

> Have you sung your diva heart out yet?

> Give me a chance! We've only just finished eating. And dealing with demonic kids. Who'd want to be a mother?

The dots scroll for a while. Stop and scroll some more. Disappear altogether.

> You still there?

> Don't forget to send me the recording

"Yay, we're going to watch a Dizzey fil-um!" Lucien yells, reappearing with Marcus's wife.

"First, what did Papa say you must do?" says the harassed-looking mother.

"I'm very sorry!" says Lucien to me in a very unapologetic tone, twisting out of his mother's grip like a whirling dervish, grinning impishly and running away.

"Would you like to join us in the games room to watch the movie?" Lucien's mother asks me, looking hopeful.

"I . . . uh . . ." I feel sorry for her, but also, no bloody thanks. I do not want to be any more involved than I need to be. "Unfortunately, I'm supposed to be . . ." I look around for Guy. Where the hell has he gone?

Marcus appears with Lucien tucked under his arm. "You're on your own. Tilly's part of the after-dinner entertainment."

"True. I'm with the band," I explain lamely to Marcus's unfortunate wife. "Good luck." With the rest of your life.

"No worries. We'll be fine," she says, looking harassed.

"For sure, you will. See you later," says Marcus, handing over Lucien.

I make a swift exit, but Marcus catches me up. "Mathilde, 'ave I said something to offend you?"

"No." I bite my tongue. I turn on my heel and walk away before I say something I might regret.

What an asshole, treating his wife so dismissively. Why do women put up with men like that? Why weren't they even sitting together? Little wonder his son is such a bloody handful.

I find Guy and the rest of RiffRaff setting up on the stage and judging from the aroma in the air, sharing an illicit after-dinner joint, which I suppose seems suitably rock 'n' roll. Fairy lights glitter in the surrounding gum trees.

Xanthe and Ben walk over. Xanthe removes her shoes.

"We're ready for the first dance, if you're ready," says Ben.

Not really.

But Guy beckons me up onto the set and takes my hand. "You'll be fine. Remember *Perfect*? Just follow my lead," he says, the smile in his eyes flickering like hot flame over my skin.

Ben and Xanthe take to the middle of the dance floor.

Somehow, singing with Guy, I always forget my nerves. It feels more than intimate as his eyes hold mine. He could be singing this song just for me. I forget we even have an audience. People are too busy dancing to pay us much attention. Singing with Guy again is all-consuming. His smiles tender and heart-warming. His eyes burn with such an intensity that it would be too easy to believe this is all real. And as the evening unfolds, and the sun sets, like a flower, I open up. I sing my heart out for him. I forget myself and my worries about Twister. I simply exist for the moment. I finally understand why Twister got so caught up with this band. I love being here and being a part of this. I've never experienced anything like it and as far as grand adventures go, this couldn't be surpassed.

There is nothing like this feeling. I never want it to end.

35

GUY

My fingers twitch without my guitar and stray to Alice's hand. Alice snares me with her soulful gaze and I have to keep reminding myself that this is a performance. But my body doesn't seem willing to listen. The music thrums in my core and Alice's voice brings my skin out in tingles feathering down my spine, my bones turned to liquid gold. Fuck, I defy anyone listening to Alice not to fall in love with her. I sing *Perfect* and I mean every damn word. She is so perfect.

Too perfect for me, I tell myself more than once. You can't fall in love with someone in less than a week. Whatever I'm feeling for Alice is strong, but it can't be love . . . But the next minute, my head is telling me to tell her how I truly feel. Tell her I want to go on an extended road-trip with just her and my guitar. Tell everyone here the way I feel about her. I never responded this intensely to anyone. This is something else again. A whole other level. It's almost impossible to remain levelheaded. I want nothing more than to keep Alice here, by my side, singing in the band. I want to ride this wave and never come down. And selfishly, I want to do whatever it takes to keep her here.

If she were here in Australia for good, I would reform myself. Become a better person. I could change for her. She makes me want to clean up my act. I would treat her so right.

Before I know it, we're breaking for half time. Reluctantly, I let go of her hand to put on the Spotify list.

"Be right back," says Alice, jumping down off the stage and disappearing without a backward glance.

Bugger. I wanted to talk to her. I fully intend to go after her, but Tina steps into my path.

"Isn't it about time we had a word in private," she says huskily.

I can think of a lot of words I'd like to call Tina, but I don't want to make a scene.

"Sure. Let's take a walk," I suggest, so we haven't got an audience.

She takes the lead and like a fucking idiot, I follow.

36

ALICE

I take the scenic route on my way to the bathroom to avoid Marcus. He's on his phone, but the way his eyes follow me across the lawn makes me uneasy.

In the quiet of the bathroom, I check my phone. There's another text from Tilly.

> Have you sung the song yet?

God. And she calls me a nag! Part of me is irritated, but if I'm being completely honest, it had slipped my mind. I've had other things to think about like how maybe Guy genuinely likes me . . . and stuff my principles, perhaps it wouldn't be the end of the world to have a holiday fling.

I smile at my reflection in the mirror and drag my fingers through my hair. For once, I don't look too bad. My skin is sun kissed and okay, the dress is a little extreme, *little* being the key word, but all the attention I'm getting from Guy has boosted my confidence. I think I'm actually pulling this off and, apart from the first thirty seconds, I haven't been nervous at all. I'd even go so far as to say I'm enjoying myself. Dare I say it, I could even see myself doing this again. I don't see why singing in a band should be Twister's remit. It's not like she 'owns' having fun.

Taking a deep breath, I ring her. Typical. Her phone is engaged, so I send her a quick text.

> Not forgotten. It will happen. Looking forward to being done with these stupid ITs!

There's no response.

I've got about ten minutes before we resume playing. Rather than risk running into anyone I don't want to talk to, I take the scenic roundabout route back to the stage.

I'm half way there when I hear Guy's unmistakable voice coming from behind the hedge. He's talking to a woman, their voices low and intense. What are they doing back there? Unless they're trying to avoid being seen.

My feet slow and I can't help myself: I peer through a gap in the hedge.

At first I'm confused, but as my brain makes sense of what I'm seeing, my stomach plummets: Guy's back and broad shoulders, and between him and the tree, a woman. Her throaty laugh makes my blood chill. A glimpse of blue. A sky-blue dress. The same blue as Xanthe's mother was wearing.

"Do you have any idea what it would do to Mum if she found out?" says Guy, sounding strangely mechanical and unemotional.

"But you're not going to tell her . . . are you?"

"I should, but it would destroy her. She's already suffered enough."

"I know, sweets, so true. But what can I say? These things happen all the time between perfectly nice people. I'm human. I have needs. James is so seldom interested in sex these days and well . . . it's only sex. I thought so long as Lisa never found out, there was no harm done."

I feel sick.

"No harm? She's supposed to be your friend for God's sake. You're supposed to be my godmother. But because of you, I can't even come home anymore."

"Because of me?" she laughs. "Dear boy. It's not entirely my fault. It takes two to tango."

I don't hang around to hear any more.

I'm such a fool. Such a blind stupid idiot and I think I'm going to throw up. I tear around the side of the building and crash straight into Marcus coming in the other direction.

"*Bouf!*" He catches hold of my shoulders. "Are you okay?"

"I-I . . ." I can't speak.

"What's 'appened?"

I can't hold it in any longer. "G-Guy happened!" A sob escapes me and as fast as I try to wipe them away, tears leak from my eyes.

Surprisingly gentle, Marcus shepherds me into the kitchen. "*Merde*. That idiot. He's a fool. You may have noticed, men, we can be selfish and also fools, *non*?"

"He's not a fool!" *Why the hell am I defending him after what I've just seen?* "I am!"

He raises my chin and passes me some kitchen roll. I blow my nose. "Would you like me to deal with him?"

"No! Don't you dare. He's . . . otherwise occupied. And I can deal with this myself," I say, somehow pulling myself together.

I splash water on my face. God, I bet I look a real mess. I bet you can tell I've been crying. "How do I look?"

He stares at me for a long time, saying nothing. He brushes a strand of hair away from my face and sighs. "So much like Mathilde, you almost had me fooled. But also, not her. Very different."

Shit. "Sorry, I-I'd better get back out there. They'll be waiting for me." I take a huge breath and do my best to smile.

"*Pah!* Let them wait," says Marcus, studying me a little too closely for comfort.

"Ha! Thank you, and . . . I'm sorry about everything . . . especially your shirt."

"It's just a shirt."

I take a step away then turn back again. "Marcus, I'm sorry. I think because of Guy, um, maybe I may have misjudged you."

He shrugs. "I doubt it."

Marcus holds the door open for me and we step outside. He's kind of old-fashioned, which right now, I appreciate. Nothing at all like Guy. The less like Guy the better.

The band has started up again, but Guy is still markedly absent.

A surge of homesickness hits me. On the spur of the moment, I nip behind the stage and call Mum.

"Hello, love." My heart lifts at the sound of her voice on the phone.

"Mum! How are you? I miss you!"

"Are you alright, dear?"

There's a pause—perhaps some lag—on the line. "I'm fine. What about you and Dad . . . and Tilly.

"We're all good, but . . . Are you still in Australia?"

The *but* lifts the hairs on the back of my neck.

"Yes, I'm still here. What's happened? What's Tilly up to? I can't get hold of her. Is she with you?"

"Oh, love," says Mum, her voice a bit muffled. "We're at the hospital with her."

My heart stops. "What do you mean you're at the hospital?" My voice rises in panic. "Where? What's happened?"

"I thought you knew, love."

Clearly, I know nothing. "Knew what?"

"Nothing to fret about . . . but Tilly's pregnant."

37

ALICE

Nothing to worry about? I can't stop worrying. I want to go home *now!* But I have one last thing to do before I leave: my final IT. As it's for Tilly, it feels right to do it somehow.

I only have to believe I can do this right.

I climb the steps off the stage just as Guy *finally* reappears attempting to tuck his shirt into his trousers with one hand, his bowtie slung about his neck.

Tina is hot on his heels.

Cold fury slices through me. When is enough enough? He swore Tilly and he were not involved, and stupidly I believed him. He acts like he's genuinely interested in me, and now there's fucking Tina too. Who next? I haven't been able to talk to Tilly yet because she was with the doctor, some complications that Mum reassures me I shouldn't worry about, but I can't help want to scream at him.

Is there a reason behind Twister's choice of song she wants me to sing? Is she trying to send him the message that she doesn't care?

Because if I know Twister, she would hate for anyone to know she was hurting, but she absolutely cares. Sometimes, she has a strange way of showing it. In my bones, I know she's in pain. As I am. And I can't help but wonder if despite their denials, this is her attempt to let him go.

As he crosses the lawn, looking oh-so handsome, smiling apologetically for his tardiness, it takes a second for the gray cells in my brain to shuffle, recalibrate and reality come into hard focus. Guy and my sister. Guy and Tina. Guy and me. Me, only because he needs me in the band and I'm useful as a decoy to distract people from whatever else is going on behind the scenes . . . with Xanthe's mother. I feel so angry I could commit murder on my sister's behalf.

How could I be so stupid? So blind? So gullible?

In large steps he lopes up onto the stage. "Let's do this!"

For the love of God, he has lipstick on his shirt collar, which I'm pretty sure you don't need to call a team of forensics to identify the matching shade that Tina's wearing.

"Let's not." I put up a hand to block him stepping closer, surprised to feel a beating heart beneath his shirt. He is still his familiar, warm-blooded self. Hot blooded. Hot headed. Too hot to handle.

For a second, he looks disconcerted.

"Before we get started again, I hope you don't mind, but I'd like to sing a solo," I say, the ice in my veins giving me the confidence to look him in the eye, "for Tilly's sake."

Maybe for the first time in my life, I see this song in a whole new light. I sympathize with my sister and countless other women who've been wronged and had to put on a show. Already damaged.

"That alright, lads?" asks Guy, looking surprised, but doing his damnedest to look magnanimous. "Go ahead, Tilly. The stage is yours."

"I don't need any accompaniment," I say, managing a smile for the other members of the band. "I'll take this à cappella."

I am consumed with contempt. My mouth is dust, and I help myself to a swig of Scooter's beer before stepping up to the microphone. I close my eyes and take a deep breath. I can do this. For Tilly. And for me.

I need to show Guy he means nothing to me.

Nothing but tumbleweed passing through.

38

GUY

"Evening, everyone. I hope . . ." Her voice quavers and I pray she doesn't lose her nerve now. "I hope you don't m-mind me singing something a little . . . um . . . *wild* . . . ha . . . So, um . . . Th-this s-song is for my sister . . ."

Thankfully, Alice launches into song. And not just any song. Bloody opera! I'm too stunned to move. And judging from the expression on the rest of the faces in the audience, especially Marcus, everyone else is as shocked as I am. Electrified.

For a moment, I fool myself that she's singing for me because she holds me in her fierce gaze before shrugging out of my jacket and dropping it at my feet. She cups my jaw with her hand, tugs on my shirt collar, pulling me off-balance and her fractured smile lights embers in my chest.

I am so fucking confused.

What is she doing?

Her voice slays me. There's no other way to put it. But there's a diamond quality to her usually tender voice that has me thinking of an avenging angel.

Goosebumps pepper my arms.

The night is sultry and like a storm brewing beyond on the horizon. I have no idea what the fuck Alice is singing about, her voice soars, but it feels dark and ominous, a bird of prey about to strike. Still, I'm spellbound. I could listen to her all night.

Thunder, lightning, and Alice. Nature's miracles.

Her hand lingers on my chest, but the look on her face is one of . . . utter contempt. My face burns with the sting of it. She's composed. And icy. And like a temptress, still singing, she struts away from me looking so damn . . . fine.

Flashing a siren smile over her shoulder, she flirts with the next man, and the next, and I tell myself to cool the fuck down because it's just an act. Until she gets to Marcus. Who I want to kill because she pays him more attention than anyone else and clearly, he's transfixed, his eyes bright with tears, his jaw rigid. I'm sure he'll feel a whole lot better when I knock his front teeth out of it.

It's clear Alice is toying with us, but that doesn't make it any easier to bear. It makes me angry to think I'm included. It makes me question whether she's been playing me all along. Are all women like this? Is she just another Tina?

I honestly have to blink to stop myself from crying. She has the voice of an angel, and I'm stuck here in hell. It's like my worst nightmare. I can do nothing but watch and burn and hurt and yearn.

What the fuck? What is happening? She's supposed to be *my* girl tonight. And yet here she is, fawning all over Marcus. This was not the fucking deal . . .

Not that she ever willingly agreed.

Every exquisite note she sings is torture. Another twist of the knife. I cannot breathe air enough into my lungs.

At the end, there's a moment of ragged silence before the audience erupts into applause as if woken from a spell. If I thought Alice had talent on the boat on New Year's Eve, this surpassed it a thousandfold. She reverts to shy Alice, head down, smiles left and right, coy beneath her long lashes like she hasn't just slain a hundred souls.

The guys in the band are grinning and nodding and clapping like buffoons. But I just cannot. My head is a mess. I want to punch Marcus's fucking lights out because now she is talking to him—*Again!*—their heads bent together. It's obscenely intimate.

"Wow. Just fucking wow!" raves Brum.

"Man, the pipes on her. I had no idea she could sing like that," says Scooter, shaking his head.

"She's fucking something else," says Fin.

"Fucking someone else more like," I mutter, my head reeling. I turn to eyeball Alice as she steps back on the stage and places the microphone into its stand.

Who even is this woman? Confident, strong, dazzling...

Holding onto the microphone stand, I grit my teeth, not sure I have enough strength to pull myself through this...act.

"How do you f-follow a performance like that?" I say into my microphone without looking at her. I feel amateur. I feel played. I feel bereft. I cannot sing anymore. How can I sing when my heart has been ripped out in front of an applauding audience and dumped at my feet? "Give it up once again for the astounding, impossibly talented Alice Havoc."

Alice's smile is tight. Her head bobs toward the microphone. "I think Guy may have had one too many drinks. You mean Tilly. Alice is my twin sister."

I look at her. And take a breath. "Oh yeah? Credit where credit is due, Alice."

All at once, Alice looks vulnerable. Exposed. "Tilly. Sorry, I know that wasn't on the song list tonight. I was just feeling a little, uh, spontaneous."

"Spontaneous?" I laugh bitterly. "That seemed very well *rehearsed* to me. Your performance was masterful." My voice is laced with bitterness. I think my mind is officially blown. I never knew love could feel this bad. Not love, but you know, this temporary crush I seem to have been cursed with. It's mortifying. Corrosive. Literally eating me from the inside out. "But not quite what we had in mind for this evening's entertainment."

I am a cruel bastard, but if I expected Alice to shrink back into her shoes with embarrassment, I'm sorely mistaken. She flicks her hair over her shoulder, smiling out at the audience back in performance mode. "I don't think we want to know what *you* had in mind this evening."

Did I hear that correctly? "You what?"

"Nothing," she singsongs. "How about we sing *You're So Vain?*"

My eyes narrow to slits. "How about we sing *Wicked Games*. It might be more appropriate as you like playing them so very much."

"How dare you preach to me about games!"

I don't know what comes over me, but I scrub a hand across my mouth and words spew from my mouth. "Oh I dare. Just because you can hold a note, darl, doesn't mean everyone has to like your vibe. That was not *ever* a wedding vibe. *That* was certainly not my vibe." Such a fucking lie. She could read the weather report and it would be my vibe. But singing opera kind of confirms my worst fears. We are two people from two entirely different worlds. Better to rip off the Band-aid fast.

"Uh, you guys . . ."

I'm not listening to anyone else in the band. My target is Alice and she is white knuckled, holding onto the microphone like the plane is going down and the mike holds her oxygen supply. "Not your vibe? I thought anything in a skirt was your vibe, Guy, but what, just because I'm not serenading you, you're upset?"

I scoff. "I'm not upset. I'm indifferent. There's a big fucking difference, sweetheart."

"I know the diff—"

"But what, you're so smart because you can sing a song in Italian? I couldn't give a rat's ass scholarship girl. I've heard better ice-cream adverts."

She walks over to me bristling. "That was French, you moron. And you're the rat. And you owe me for driving you here and pretending to be your girlfriend while you were playing *your games* in the bushes!"

"Me play games?" I snarl. "Your *game* with your sister is the reason I ended up in hospital with a broken hand."

That stops her.

"Yeah, baby, I know all about your Impossible Games, so you can drop the high and mighty act—"

"Well, at least I didn't suck the face off Xanthe's mother!" She's as fierce as she is breathtaking.

We glare at one another. And then in the deathly hush she stalks off stage.

Marcus is waiting for her. With a protective arm about her shoulders, he whisks Alice away through the guests who part like the Red Sea before them . . . which is about when I come to my senses and realize our argument has been broadcast to all the wedding guests and I just made the worst mistake in my life.

Fuck.

What have I done?

Ben glares at me, Xanthe with a hand over her mouth looks like she might throw up on her own wedding dress, Mum has her eyes closed, a hand on Electra's arm, Electra is looking at me like *I'm* the prick, and Tina, the old trout, has an expression on her face which could be interpreted as astonishment . . . or gloating.

"On that note, I think the band might wrap up for the night," says Brum, snatching the microphone.

I snatch it back. "Hold on. Before I go anywhere, I just want to assert, I have not *ever*, nor am I interested in *ever* sucking the face off Tina O'Sullivan."

Though it was not for *her* want of trying.

It was my dad who made that mistake.

39

ALICE

It takes me seconds to rip off the dress Guy bought me, throw on my t-shirt and dungarees and grab my backpack. When I hurtle back down the stairs, Marcus is waiting at the bottom, thank God.

He guides me toward a Mercedes with darkened windows. I'm so desperate to get away from there, I don't even consider why Marcus is being so nice or if he has ulterior motives like chucking me off a cliff somewhere.

He opens the car door and I hesitate. "Where are your wife and son?"

"Lucien is being looked after by my *sister*."

Sister? "That woman wasn't your wife?"

"If you were Tilly, you'd know Sasha, my ex-wife, died a couple of years ago. Do you want to get in the car, or would you rather stay?"

"Oh, Marcus. I'm so sorry."

Marcus looks understandably pained. "Get in." I'm pretty certain he could rip open my ribcage with just his eyeballs. But I would rather face him than Guy or his family ever again.

On legs like jelly, I stumble into the car.

As we pull out of the Balcombe Brothers' Estate Winery gates in Marcus's fancy chauffeur-driven car, I do my best to stifle my tears and fail miserably. What's the point? Marcus is far too busy reeling off commands in French to his driver like a mafia boss at a street fight to notice. I stare out the window and bite my lip. A glorious display of fireworks lights up the night sky behind the winery. Tears blur my vision.

Blinking furiously, I text Twister.

> IT#6 done and dusted. Now tell me what's going on.

I wait for Twister to respond, but only get silence.

> Twister, this isn't fair. I've done all your sodding ITs. I know you're there, so why won't you answer me? Why won't you tell me anything?

Nothing.

What has this whole thing been for? I've kept to my side of the deal, done her ridiculously childish pranks, and where has it got me? Nowhere. Talk about jumping out of the frying pan into the fire: I'm now seated in another car with an angry Frenchman—and an intimidating one at that.

Marcus slides the window partition closed between us and the driver. I try to sit up and put a bit more space between us, not that he seems inclined to close the gap at all.

He folds his arms across his chest. "That was quite some performance. You were magnificent . . . But where is Mathilde? She said she'd be here." He passes me a handkerchief. Hooded eyes regard me curiously.

"She did?" I gulp back my tears, happy to be distracted by other matters. "What's my sister to you?"

"We . . . We are . . . friends."

"As in friends with benefits?" I rasp. Talk about poking the bear.

His eyebrow cocks. He sighs. "Perhaps, though, I would not put it so crudely."

"How would you put it?"

A muscle ticks in his jaw. "Mathilde means a great deal to me. I took her to see Carmen at the Sydney Opera House. I presume that is why you chose to sing that song."

"Oh." Oh hell. I close my eyes and screw up my face. I am struggling to think straight.

Hell and bloody damnation.

Could I have got this all wrong? What if Guy and Twister were never involved in any sort of relationship . . . like they'd both assured me? What if I'd misread the whole Tina scenario? But I couldn't have. There was no mistaking how intimate they'd looked. Was there?

"Could you . . . could you stop the car?"

Marcus orders his chauffeur to pull over and I stumble out retching. Normally, when Twister or I are sick, we have each other's back. Now it's Marcus of all people holding my hair out of my face and watching me empty the contents of my stomach at the side of the road. I can't help myself, I start sobbing. He hands me a bottle of water and a box of tissues.

Back in the car, the tears keep coming, but so do the images. There's no retracting the wrecking ball maneuver I just pulled on stage at the wedding. Paparazzi flashes of the scene reel through my head like a breaking newsreel . . . of a high-rise tower collapsing in on itself in a cloud of dust and rubble. There's no going back. It could not be more over. "I've ruined everything!" I groan.

"Welcome to my world," says Marcus. "Now do you think you could tell me where to find your sister?"

What is Marcus to my sister? Is he someone special? Or just another one of her flings?

"Are you, could you be . . . the reason she skipped the country?" I ask.

"Excuse me? She's not in Australia?" He looks grim-faced. As if he could be in pain.

"No. She's in England."

"*Putain!*" He puts a fist to his mouth.

"And she's pregnant."

His head hits the back of the seat. "Fuck. No, no, no!" He says and presses his fists into his eye sockets.

"Something you'd like to share?" I ask him quietly. "Are you the dad?"

"I don't know. *Merde*. But I do know, I told her I didn't want any more kids. I told her all sorts of shit..."

ENGLAND

Dreaming as the days go by,
Dreaming as the summers die:
Ever drifting down the stream—
Lingering in the golden gleam—
Life, what is it, but a dream?

Lewis Carroll,
Alice Through the Looking Glass

40

ALICE

England is horribly cold and miserably gray; it matches my mood. On the train north, a phone call from Mum stops me feeling quite so sorry for myself. It's the worst sort of news. Tilly has had a miscarriage . . .

I can't begin to imagine how she's feeling. Even if she never wanted to have the baby, it still must be devastating.

"But I was just ringing to let you know we've got Tilly back home," says Mum.

I swallow the lump in my throat. "How is she?"

"Acting like she's perfectly fine, of course. Acting like she's relieved, which only makes me all the more worried."

It would be typical of Twister to hide how she's really feeling, even to Mum and Dad. I feel sick. Heartbroken for Tilly's sake. I'm not sure what to say, even to Mum.

"I'm so glad you're on your way home, duck. If anyone can help to pull her through this, it's you."

I'm not so confident. "Oh, Mum. I'm not sure what I can do to help the situation." I might make matters worse. I feel like I'm on a downward spiral, bad luck following me, fucking things up left, right and center. I'm not sure how Twister feels about me at the moment, but I suspect our special connection has frayed, possibly beyond redemption. Meanwhile, I'm trying to conceal all this from Mum. Talk about pressure.

"So where are you now?" Mum asks.

I look out the window. "I'm not sure. Somewhere between Doncaster and York." Somewhere in Dismal Damp Depressionshire. Rain streams down the glass pane of the train window. The buildings outside look gray and bleak. England is like a bad watercolor painting, the colors a mishmash of indiscriminate sludge.

"Oh, my goodness! Look at the time. I'd better set off immediately then or I won't be at the station to meet you," says Mum.

"Mum, really, no need to worry about me. You've enough on your plate with looking after Tilly. I can get the bus."

"Nonsense. Dad's here if Tilly needs someone. I'll be there . . . Unless I'm not. In which case, I'll call you. I can't wait to see you, love. So glad you're on your way home. I'm looking forward to hearing all about your adventure Down Under."

My breath hitches in my throat. I can't reply. The man sitting opposite me on the train shoots me an anxious look.

"Are you there, love?" Mum asks.

"Poor reception. Talk soon. Bye Mum." My voice teeters on a knife edge. I'm so far from fine I might as well be lying on the train track, but my problems, my heartache, are nothing compared to my sister's.

I end the call. I can't help but notice I have eight missed calls from Guy. I hate to think what more he wants to say to me.

Determined not to be such a wet blanket, I delete Guy's contact details, surreptitiously wiping my eyes.

I'd have thought I'd have run out of tears by now, but evidently not. I could never have imagined coming home under these circumstances. It crushes me that I never for a moment sensed Twister was pregnant, and no sooner do I find out, than she loses her baby. It feels like the world has spun at warp speed ever since I left Australia.

God, how pathetic am I? Crying when I'm perfectly fine and healthy. Crying because my sister has lost her baby. I wipe my eyes on my sleeve. At the rate I'm going, I'll look like I've pulled my sweater straight out the washing machine by the time we pull into York Station.

"Here," says the man opposite, offering me a packet of tissues.

"Th-thank you," I sob. "S-sorry . . . I'm n-not n-normally . . . like this . . . b-but I had . . . some b-bad n-news."

"Aye, luv. I gathered."

Thankfully, when the train draws beneath the huge domed ceiling of York Station, I have myself under some semblance of control. I probably look much like any other inhabitant of Yorkshire with my red nose and watery eyes, and at least I can blame it on the weather which is minus minus minus degrees.

It's so biting cold, I have to grit my teeth as I step onto the platform. Head down, hands in my pockets, I charge along until I spot Mum standing like a human oasis, arms outstretched.

I walk into her hug and start bawling all over again.

"There, there, pet, you're home now," she says, rubbing my back. She's probably had to do a lot of comforting lately. "Get it all out of your system. Here. Maybe best not to break down in front of Tilly. We don't want to make the situation any more dire than it already is, do we?"

"Of course not." I gulp and sniffle and inhale a few juddering breaths before blowing my nose.

She puts an arm around my shoulders and ushers me out of the station toward the car park. "Welcome back home, pet," she says. "Home sweet home."

Who's she trying to convince? Me or her? I can't help but wish I was on a sunny beach somewhere . . . or in the van, even with Guy with his big feet on the dashboard.

In the car, listening to Mum rattle on is like having an extra heater on full blast, but at least it takes my mind off things. She chatters on about how quiet Christmas and New Year were without us girls, the problems at school with the Board and finances—The school and its land are being sold in order to raise funds to make improvements to the school and drag it into the 21st century, and Harry and his antics at university, before she finally gets onto the subject of Tilly.

"We were worried sick when she turned up without you. She wouldn't tell us a thing. I should've known she was fibbing when she said she was just homesick. The first thing we knew about it was when Judy rang from the hospital." Judy's the local GP and a close friend of Mum's. "So, what happened in Sydney, love?"

"I wish I knew." I've only had potted recounts from Twister and Marcus, and I've still felt like both were being evasive, keeping critical information from me. I've never felt on the outside like this with Twister before and it hurts more than I care to admit. "Besides, I think that's probably Tilly's story to tell, not mine."

Mum buttons her lip, looking disappointed in me. I'm disappointed in me.

I take her hand. "Mum, she didn't tell me anything. We've been kind of living separate lives."

"Oh dear." Mum shakes her head. "Dear, dear, dear . . ." It's horrible seeing my mother on the brink of tears. I always think of her as being such a tower of strength. It makes me simultaneously want to throw my arms around her to give her the support she always gives the rest of us, but also, just bawl my eyes out.

The house is as quiet as a tomb when we get back. Dad comes out of his study and pulls me into a hard hug. He smells of his usual combination of Old Spice and musty old books. "Good to have you home, love."

"Good to be here. I missed you so much." I finally manage to extract myself from his arms. "I might just go and check on Tilly."

"Absolutely. Absolutely."

Upstairs, I pause on the landing outside her door. Should I knock? I've never done that before. Taking a deep breath, I open the door.

The room is in darkness.

Twister is huddled on her side, facing the wall.

"Twister," I whisper. There's no answer, but she's awake. I know she is. I sit down on the edge of her bed and put my hand on her arm. It feels reassuring to have physical contact with her again, and I hope she's feeling the same surge of energy that I do. "I'm so flipping sorry. I wish there was something I could do to make it better."

Twister rolls onto her back and stares at me defiantly.

"I'm sorry I wasn't there for you. I'm sorry I wasn't a better sister in Sydney, and you felt you couldn't tell me. I'm so sorry you lost . . . your baby."

That one word seems to unlock something. She sits up and flings her arms around my shoulders. "I wanted so badly to keep her . . . I didn't think I did . . . until it was too late." A keening noise escapes her, and I hold her tighter, both of us crying.

I'm not sure how long we stay like that with me rubbing her back and her sobbing against my shoulder . . . but eventually, as in the way of all things, it passes.

41

ALICE

Usually, Twister put's on a brave face, but this pregnancy and miscarriage seem to have knocked her sideways. She tells us she's fine, but then hibernates for the rest of the month. Mum, Dad and I take meals to her on trays and cajole her into the bathroom. She's quieter than I've ever known her, not interested in seeing any of her schoolmates. We walk and talk, but I know she's holding stuff back. Holding so much pain and anguish inside.

If I'm being honest, I'm scared if I broach the subject of the baby and she starts crying again, she might set me off. I'm not sure how much more I can take. I feel responsible. I ache all the time. The physical pressure of not crying is like being slowly suffocated. But I have to be strong for her. And I try not to think about Guy . . . more than a million times a day.

We spend hours skirting around the subject of the baby and Marcus and Guy, and instead, most of the time, we talk about mundane gossip from the village and Colin the Colon and what the hell we're going to do with the rest of our lives.

"You'll be at university before you know it," says Twister.

"Yeah," I reply, "I don't know about that." Studying Law at Oxford has about as much appeal as studying my toenail clippings. Probably less.

"I feel like I'm going mad. I need to do something," says Twister. She even mentions applying for university, which is a complete reversal on her stance last year.

Perhaps we've swapped places; the coin flipped.

Twister finally emerges from her cocoon like a beautiful fragile butterfly on Valentine's Day when Marcus rocks up in Little Pickering and knocks on our door.

The house sounds as quiet as a morgue after the pair of them drive off in another of his swanky cars.

When she returns later that afternoon, she looks perkier than I've seen her in weeks.

"I've decided," she announces to Mum, Dad and me, "I'm going to spend some time with Marcus in Paris."

"Paris?" yelp Mum, Dad and I simultaneously.

"Yes, Paris. It's not like it's the other side of the world. You could come and visit."

I think Mum and Dad are as shocked as I am, but it's encouraging that she wants to do *anything*.

While Twister packs, Dad beckons Marcus for a 'quiet word' in his study, but fails to shut the door, so Mum and I shamelessly eavesdrop. An open door is an open invitation to our family.

"What are your intentions?" Dad asks. *Good on you, Dad, straight in there with a cudgel!*

"I have a restaurant and an apartment in Paris, and I own a vineyard in the south of France." *Of course he does.* "I think France will do Tilly some good."

"Oh," says Dad, sounding puzzled. "Right. But um, staying together? Under the same roof?"

"You'd like her chaperoned?" says Marcus, sounding amused.

Mum bustles in. "Don't be daft. What a grand idea. It's exactly what she needs. A change of scenery. Some wonderful French food. I wouldn't mind being cooked for. It sounds delightful. What sort of things will you be doing together?"

Marcus clears his throat. "Unfortunately, for the most part, I'll be working, running my businesses and—"

"And I'm going to help in the Paris restaurant and work on my French," says Twister, dumping her suitcases in the hall and pushing past.

"Right," says Dad. "Well, it sounds like your mind is made up."

"One hundred percent," says Twister.

And that seems to be that.

"Oh, congratulations on the song," Marcus says to me, as he puts Twister's things in the trunk of the car.

"What?" I say.

"Oh yes, I nearly forgot." Twister laughs joyfully. "Marcus showed me at lunch. RiffRaff has had a massive hit. It's gone viral . . . *Vanessa*, I think it's called." Temporarily, the smile leaves her face. "And guess what? Your opera singing is stitched onto the beginning . . . If it's any consolation, you're famous!"

Consolation? When my sister is leaving and all I have to console me is news of Guy's latest woman—*Vanessa!*

"Marvelous!" Just fucking marvelous.

"Didn't he contact you?" asks Marcus, as he gets behind the steering wheel.

I wouldn't know. I've deleted him from my life. "Why would he?" I ask.

"Because you're in the video that went viral? You have certain rights, you know, if he hasn't asked permission . . . *Pah!* You should contact Guy."

"Guy who?" asks Mum, looking as perturbed as I am.

"Guy Balcombe," say Twister and Marcus at the exact same time I say, "No-one."

I glare at them. "He's no-one Mum. Just someone I met but haven't kept in touch with. He's a passing . . . acquaintance . . . at most."

"A passing acquaintance and a massive hit!" shouts Twister, waving out the window as the car pulls away.

I spend the rest of the day fretting and feeling lost. Last time we left home, Twister and I were buzzing with excitement about our impending trip around the world. Life seemed like one big adventure playground. But in the end, it all came crashing down around our ears. Although Twister, in the way she always does, seems to be rising again like a phoenix from the ashes.

But strangely enough, it's Guy I can't stop thinking about. I can't help but wonder where he is now and how he's doing. I can't help but wonder about this song and his new woman. I wonder if he thinks about me at all these days. Probably not. Or only to curse me and thank his lucky stars he escaped with only a broken hand.

If Twister is now back on her feet and off elsewhere, where does that leave me? Stuck in the same Little Pickering rut I was so desperate to get away from in the first place. I lie on my bed staring at the stars painted on the ceiling.

How much longer can I do this for? Stay at home with my parents and not go insane? As much as I love them, I need to do something to take my mind off being here. I could be doing some preparatory reading for Oxford, but the thought of university at all makes me want to throw up. What on earth made me think I wanted to spend the rest of my life studying litigation? There are about a million other things I'd rather do. Such as . . .

I can't resist. I download TikTok . . . and there are RiffRaff in all their hunky glory. Guy looks eyeball-achingly handsome. And, oh God, me, singing opera like the Queen of blinking Sheba. I can't watch any more. I delete the app, but it's too late. Everything comes hurtling back in a rush: the joy and the pain, the hitchhiking, the brush turkeys, driving the van and our unplanned 'diversion', skinny dipping, dancing with some builder whose name I can't for the life of me remember, and Guy. Dancing with Guy. Singing with Guy. Playing chess with Guy. Having sex with Guy. He's there behind my eyelids.

My feet take me into Harry's room, where his neglected guitar hangs on the wall. One of the strings is bust, but I still spend the rest of the evening strumming, memories of Australia flitting like fireflies through my head. It's about as close as I'm going to get to happy in Little Pickering.

The next morning, I take the bus into Burtonbridge to get the guitar string fixed at the music shop.

"Alice, right?" says Angus Dalton the shop owner.

"Right."

"Not seen you in here for a while."

"Been traveling around Australia. Would you be able to put a new string on this guitar for me?"

"Aye, luv, in a jiffy. D'you want to wait?"

It's not like I have anything else to do. "Sure," I say, wishing my heart could be restrung as easily as replacing a guitar string. Not that I have a broken heart. That's me just being melodramatic and feeling sorry for myself.

I'll be champion. Life goes on. Even when one of your strings is broken.

42

GUY

The two weeks after Alice leaves are the most exciting and the most excruciating weeks ever. My family gives me the silent treatment. Their disappointment because of my behavior at the wedding is worse than any ear-bashing. I still can't play guitar because of my frigging hand. And worst of all, I'm unable to dislodge Alice from my brain, so I throw everything into writing songs in a crazy-ass effort to expunge her.

I've never been so miserable in my life and most of the time I have pain in my chest that makes me scared I might be having a heart attack like Dad—it's no less than I deserve. But at least I'm writing and recording songs at record speed, barely sleeping, waking up before it's light invariably woken by Alice's voice whispering in my ear.

I force myself out of bed to write down the lyrics and tunes in the hope that if I can get this pent-up frustration out of me, with time I'll find relief, and get some goddamn rest from whatever the fuck this is I'm feeling . . . Not normal, that's for fucking certain.

And then one of our songs goes viral: *Vanessa.*

It's a song I started on the road-trip with Alice. In a drunken moment, I even sung it to her over the phone after she left, for fuck's sake . . . but of course, she never responded. God knows if she's listened to it at all. She hasn't answered any of my texts or calls and hasn't mentioned the money I've transferred to her bank account. She's ghosted me so comprehensively, it's messing with my head; I'm beginning to think I imagined there was chemistry between us.

Not me, but some other twat on TikTok stitched footage of Alice singing her frigging opera at the wedding with the start of the *Vanessa* song. God knows where it started, but I guess I'm thankful because that's the version that goes viral and overnight RiffRaff is famous. Everyone asks, where's *the girl?* Our line is, *she'll be back*, like a bad rehash of *The Terminator.* The lads give me a hard time about scaring Tilly and Alice off, and I promise to rectify the situation . . . Just as soon as I have time to shit, shower and think straight.

What a fucking mess.

All at once, it's like I have no control over anything; I can't eliminate her from my life, even if I wanted to. Alice is woven into my fabric. My song has an *overlay* of Alice, I have an *underlay* of Alice, and unfortunately, that's about as close as I'm ever going to get to *laying* anywhere near Alice again. Metaphorically-speaking, of course. She would burn my house down if she thought I was even thinking of her.

Some days, even though she's miles away, it's like she's still here, her head resting on my chest, her hair silky beneath my fingertips, her warm breath on my skin. It's so real it guts me every time.

One morning, I wake up in a tangle of sheets realizing we're making all this money, but we never got permission to use her voice; she might sue the shit out of us. She's going to study Law at Oxford, isn't she? She's likely to sue my ass just for the joy of it.

I kind of hope so, just to hear from her.

But nothing. Radio silence from Alice.

"Jeez, mate, you look like something the cat coughed up," says Brum, one day.

"Cheers, mate. You're not exactly a ballet dancer yourself." But he's en pointe. When I look in the mirror, my eyes are red rimmed from lack of sleep and I could've been dragged from a coffin. But the show must go on . . . and suddenly, RiffRaff is a fucking *sensation*.

Our success is as huge as it is unexpected. I'm terrified the interest will vanish as suddenly as it appeared, but it goes on . . . and on . . . and on. I'm reminded of Alice telling me that the only way to achieve the impossible was to believe in it; the more our luck lasts, the more I start to believe.

And man, we work our asses off: schmoozing, promoting, yelling our heads off about all our other songs. We're no longer just a cover band.

The phone is clogged with offers and opportunities, agents and record companies, fans and bullshitters.

But still not Alice.

Will she ever forgive me for all the crap I put her through? My slave?—What was I even thinking? What a wanker!

One night I dream I'm on a sinking boat, Alice laughing so hard, it's fucking delightful, but I can't bail water fast enough and I know we're going down . . . When I wake up the sensation of drowning won't leave me.

Weeks pass.

We play more gigs.

And there's always Alice, Alice, Alice in my head. She's ruined me in so many ways. Every day I'm reminded of her. Every day, I'm grateful and resentful in equal measure. Every day, the bigger the hole inside me seems to fray.

Even though I'm the front man of the band, it's the lads who drag me through. I bellyache about Alice until even I'm bored of my own voice. I drink a skinful every day and take whatever shit is on offer. The lads hold me up in what is increasingly feeling like waiting out a sandstorm in a desert.

The shit-storm of oblivion.

I'm alive, but it seems to me like when Alice up and left, she took my oxygen supply with her. It's like I have to write and perform before I run out of breath. I wake up morning after morning gasping for air, sweating, my arms empty. I have to remind myself where I am and what I want and that I owe these dudes—Brum, Scooter, Fin—fucking everything. This is the sort of mad success we've all dreamed about for years. Success is a blessing and a curse.

A month after Alice walked out, on Valentine's Day to be exact, I receive a sack load of cards (and other unmentionables) from fans, but nothing from Alice (Why would I even begin to think she might . . . ? She's right, I am a moron).

That night, made bold by several too many tequila shots, I call Tilly.

Big awkward mistake. Reception is bad. We bitch about the weather (too hot in Sydney, too cold in Paris).

"I guess this means you're not coming back," I say.

"Um, no, in fact, I'm on the way to Paris with Marcus."

"You're fucking what?"

"That would be Marcus." She chuckles down the phone. She's *with* Marcus?

"Ask him if he had anything to do with Axel's nightclub closing down. Rumor has it someone ran him out of town," I say.

I hear her relay the question.

"Tell him not to be such a fucking coward and call Alice," Marcus says with his customary French tact.

"Tell Marcus to go stick a baguette up his fancy French ass!"

Laughing, Tilly repeats what I said.

"How is she?" I ask, casually.

There's a pause. "Are you genuinely interested?" says Tilly. "Because if you're not just leave her the fuck alone."

My throat closes up. Oh God, tears are trickling down my cheeks.

"Marcus tells me you were fucking horrible to her," Tilly says.

"Mmm . . . yeah . . . I was pretty bad."

She sighs. "And who's this Vanessa woman you're seeing now?"

I laugh and sit up. "Vanessa's my brother's van. The van Alice drove me from Queensland to the wedding in. Stupid bloody name."

"Well, isn't it about time you found yourself another van and a good reason to go on another road-trip?" says Tilly. "Maybe this time in Europe?"

43

ALICE

"I think you should go to one of their concerts and say hello," says Twister over the phone. This is the sort of useful life tips I get from Twister these days. She's phoned me expressly to inform me that RiffRaff is on tour in the UK. Like life isn't painful enough without knowing Guy is somewhere in the country.

"No thanks. I can't think of anything worse."

"Liar," says Twister.

Honestly, I would do *anything* to be a fly on the wall at one of their concerts, but compete with all those squealing female fans not to mention this new woman, Vanessa. Ugh. No thanks.

"They're playing in York on 1st May," she says.

"I'm working in the pub that day," I say. "I got your old job back."

We laugh.

"How can you know you'll be working, then? It's more than a month away."

"I'll make sure I am."

"God, why do you have to be so stubborn? You know you want to see him."

"Oh, shut up. Anyway, he has a new woman."

The line goes quiet. "You know that Vanessa song was about you."

"Shut up. How was it about me?"

"Perhaps you should go and find out. Anyway, he hasn't got a new woman . . . yet. What are you so scared of, Malice? It's only a concert. Is it because you're still harboring feelings for Guy, by any chance, and you think they might not be reciprocated?"

"God, no!" I say a little too quickly. "He's a complete . . . complete . . ." I can't think of the appropriate word. "Tart!"

"Hmmm, I don't know where you got that idea from. He really isn't."

"What about those photos of him with all those women, including you?" I've been doing my research.

"Last time I checked, it was not a crime to take a woman on a date or have female friends. Besides, the photo of me was kind of deliberate. I was trying to throw the scent off me and Marcus being an item because the press is always all over his ass like a rash . . . Not that Marcus has a rash on his ass. He has a delectable ass—"

"Twister!"

"Sorry. Too much?"

"Way too much."

"Well, I suspect you may still be hung up on our Guy and vice versa."

"Oh, be quiet! That's ridiculous. I was never hung up on him. We barely tolerated one another. He's probably forgotten who I am."

She laughs. "You're such a chump. Every time I speak to Guy, he asks after you. The pair of you are your own worst enemies."

My heart patters thinking about Guy asking after me. He's probably just being polite, but still, it makes me feel a bit better.

"So how is France treating you?" I ask.

"Surprisingly well. I've some news, actually."

Oh God, please don't tell me she's pregnant again.

"Marcus and I got engaged," she says.

I nearly drop the phone. "What? Are you kidding?" I'm over the moon for her. "That's . . . that's . . ." It's freaking amazing! "Congratulations! Wow! Mum and Dad will be—"

"—shocked? I know it's fast and they'll say I'm too young, but when you know, you know. He's the one and only Marcus Sauvage."

"Because grumpy sweaty bastards are all the go?"

"He's very sweet when you get to know him," she laughs.

"Sweet is about the last word I'd use to describe Marcus, but I look forward to getting to know him better. You'd better tell Mum and Dad quick sharp because I'm not sure I can hold on to news like this for long."

I'm helping Mum arrange the daffodils in church for the Easter service when Dad puts an arm around my shoulders.

"What is it now?" I say, stifling a groan.

"I have a small favor to ask." He maneuvers me back up the aisle toward the altar.

Oh. No. I can already guess. I know that look on his face.

"Seriously, Dad?"

"Poor Gladys has slipped on the ice and bruised her coccyx." Gladys is his regular church organist. "Please, could you play today? God will bless you for your service to the community."

Inwardly I groan, outwardly I sigh. "Sure, I can't think of anything I'd like to do better." Other than maybe slip on the ice and shatter my coccyx. "However, I have a shift at the pub at lunchtime." Not to mention the chocolate cream eggs I have waiting for me back at home. This is what my life has become. Twister is being hand fed gourmet cuisine and I comfort myself by inventing new ways to eat my chocolate cream eggs.

"I know, which is why I've already talked to Bernie," Dad says. Bernie being the landlord of the Mucky Duck. "He says he can do without you until midday, which means you've plenty of time to play the organ for our Easter Sunday service before starting at the pub. No need to stay for sherry."

The sherry after Sunday service is the best bit about my Sundays. I do not want to play the bloody church organ, but it looks like I've no choice. Not really. Because Dad is a brick and also the last person I'd ever want to let down. "Don't blame me if I'm a bit rusty. I haven't played for ages."

Dad raises his bushy eyebrows.

"Okay, fine, I'm making excuses. I would love to play the organ, but it'll cost you another cream egg."

"Done," he says, beaming.

"Out of interest, how long does it take to mend a broken coccyx?" I ask as he pushes me toward the winding staircase up to the organ gallery.

He smiles. "Not broken, just bruised, so hopefully not too long."

"You'd better ask the congregation to pray for her bum," I say.

"Absolutely, I will." Chuckling, he takes out his little black notebook and scribbles *Gladys's bum*.

Tempted though I am to play a funeral dirge, I start with the *March Jubilant*. I'm not feeling remotely jubilant, but at least playing the organ takes my mind off other things. With my back to the rest of the church and the congregation, I vaguely listen to Dad's welcome speech.

Welcome to St. John's church, everyone, the place where miracles happen and lives are changed. I can't help but smile at Dad's unswerving optimism. *I'm Reverend Havoc and I believe that everyone who walks through those doors comes here for a divine purpose even if they are not aware of that themselves. It's wonderful to see several new faces in our congregation and before we sing the first hymn, I'd like you to take a moment to welcome everyone to the family of our church.*

I take that as my cue to start playing again.

My mind wanders, as it often does, during one of Dad's services. You can't fault him for enthusiasm and effort.

Once the service is done, I take my time putting on my coat and hat and gloves, not really wanting to be caught up in polite conversation on the church porch step where nosy neighbors will no doubt be asking what I'm doing back here already and where's *the other one* and when am I going to Oxford? The more I think about university, the less appealing that option seems. There are the student debts that Harry is always going on about. If I'm going to get that much in debt, it needs to be for something I'm really passionate about, otherwise what is the point? More than anything, I still want to travel. I have started to put money aside again for that exact purpose, though plans are a little hazy at the moment.

I trudge up the road past home to the pub.

My shift is uneventful, as I suspected it would be, but when I get home, Mum has a wicked grin on her face.

"You got a special delivery," she says, eyes wide. "It's in the kitchen."

I can't help being a tad excited. This is Little Pickering, where nothing exciting ever happens after all, so I'm surprised I didn't hear about the arrival of my 'special delivery' at the pub.

"Dad's gone to bed. He was too tired to wait up." She looks ridiculously excited.

I go into the kitchen and there sitting on the table is an enormous Easter egg. One of those hand-crafted ones. It's even got my name on it. Well, hallelujah there is a God after all and he's sending me chocolate. *Eat me,* the message on the egg reads.

Mum is beaming and bouncing on her toes, her hands clasped in barely restrained excitement. "Well. Go on then. Who's it from?"

"Twister and Marcus, I imagine." I check it all over, but there's nothing else to give me a clue.

"Aren't you going to open it?" says Mum.

"Mum! It's late. I'm exhausted. You always say I shouldn't eat at this time of night, especially chocolate!"

"There are always exceptions to the rules. This is not one of those times!"

"I'm not sure," I say.

"What's there to not be sure about? It's chocolate. It's Easter. This is a sign. It's time to resurrect yourself and hatch open this egg."

I can't help laughing. Mum is such a romantic. "Fine." For the first time in weeks, a frisson of excitement runs through me as I carefully open the clear cellophane wrapping and inhale the glorious smell of chocolate. I'm already salivating.

Mum hands me her kitchen mallet.

I crack open the egg and peer inside. "It's hollow, but there's something in there." I turn it upside down and give it a shake. A piece of paper wafts onto the kitchen table. I pick it up and turn it over. "Oh, it's a ticket to RiffRaff's concert in York."

"You don't want to be mixing with the riffraff," says Mum. Then she sees my face. "Oh, evidently you do!"

I take another photo and text Twister,

THANK YOU!

She texts back seconds later.

Nothing to do with me. Sweet dreams, sis!

44

ALICE

1 st April

I'm beginning to think that trying to keep any sort of journal is a game for fools. But 1st April is a day for fools—fools like me.

RiffRaff's tour has been a sellout success. They've already played in London, Leeds, Manchester, Newcastle and Edinburgh. York is their final concert, but I still can't decide whether to go or not. I mean, am I just asking for heartache? Making myself a laughingstock? And wishing my way to hell . . .

But if I can't believe anything is possible, where does it leave me? I really want to believe . . .

. . .

I don't sleep a wink all night. I'm desperate to go to the concert; I don't want to go. I'm dying to see him, just one more time; I'm terrified he'll spot me in the crowd. There will be hundreds of people; I'll stay at the back. The argument in my head goes back and forth like a tennis match. I'm knackered but also buzzing the next morning because I've finally come to the conclusion I can go because Guy will never know. No one need know. It can be my own secret guilty pleasure.

"I'm going to stay with Gemma," I tell mum. Gemma is one of my old schoolmates.

"I thought she'd joined the army," she says.

"Err, that's right. But she's in Catterick. There's a military, um, ball on or something."

"Oh, well then, you must go to a ball." Mum laughs.

"It's not illegal," I say.

"It's not you either. You hate big events. And crowds. And dressing up."

"Yeah, well, people change."

Her eyes narrow. "Do what you want, my love. It's your life."

"Exactly!" I say. "Can you give me a lift to York?"

The Boiler Room describes itself as, "Once a powerhouse of the Industrial Revolution, now a crucible for musical talent." I'm not familiar with this part of York and I don't know what I was expecting, but certainly not this red brick, crenellated warehouse. It's quirky and more than a little impressive.

Inside, the structure is immense, the ceilings high and raftered, the noise overwhelming. Strangely it reminds me of a church. I'm in absolutely no danger of being spotted by anyone. Several hundred other people have arrived before me, and I kind of wish I'd brought binoculars. The warm-up act is already playing, and I try to blend in with the crowd while also feeling I stick out like a sore thumb in my winter coat, woolly hat and mittens. Of course, it's not long before I'm peeling off layers.

When RiffRaff is finally announced, my heart sets off at a gallop, and there they are, little more than stick figures up on stage: Brum, Fin, Scooter and last on, Guy. The audience goes bananas, and I can't help grinning like the proverbial Cheshire Cat. Gawd. *I've sung with these lads!* I want to shout. They are awesome. All of them. Not just Guy, who is looking, I have to admit, every inch the superstar even though he's dressed simply in jeans and a gray t-shirt.

"Good evening, York!" shouts Guy, and the audience, including me, erupts again. "It's cool to be here. A lot cooler than Australia, to be honest, especially as I forgot to pack a sweater." There is laughter. When he talks into the microphone, my stomach spasms and my knees almost buckle. How could I have forgotten the rich bass lick of his voice? He's the human equivalent of sticky toffee pudding.

Off the bat, they start with one of their new songs, not just covers. It's so-oh great, I'm almost bursting with pride.

"I've dedicated this next song to the love of my life."

Oh. My mouth goes dry. Talk about a change of heart. *What the hell I am putting myself through this torture for?*

"And although I'm not a petrol head, this song is special to me. It's about a van . . . a van called Vanessa. Sorry, really terrible pun." More laughter. He shields his eyes and looks into the crowd. "This particular van holds a special place in my heart for a lot of reasons." He looks behind him at the lads in the band. "All of them private."

I stand on tiptoes, trying to get a better view. He holds up his hand—no longer broken—and the crowd hushes.

"I've not finished. See, she's a looker this van. Cute as a button and draws the eye, if you know what I mean . . . admittedly, sometimes more eyes than I like." More muffled laughter from the room. "Sometimes, especially when it's raining, this van can be a little unreliable. Sometimes her steering is stiff and a little out of whack, to say the least." There are guffaws. "Occasionally, I have to tell you, I want to kick her . . . *tires*"—he grins cheekily and someone yells, *You can kick my tires any day!*—"and my God, this van guzzles fuel like you would not believe . . ." He pauses. Hangs his head. Looks up again. Grins. "But fuck, I love that van." He makes a heart sign on with his hands on his chest, and my own heart flies up to the rafters above us somewhere. "If only this van were mine."

Oh.

My.

Heart.

He starts singing,

> *If you were mine,*
> *Vanessa*
> *A million miles*
> *would never be enough*

I can't stop smiling. I can't believe it's not a song about some random woman called Vanessa. It's a song about us and our van! Well, technically not *our* van, but you know, close enough.

> *And when we're on the road and the going is tough*
> *Remind me if I forgot to mention*
> *You're a heart-rousing ride*
> *and a journey to love.*
> *I will take the road with you*
> *Wherever you lead me*
> *To heaven or hell*
> *You know very well*
> *I open my veins and you bleed me*

> *Ah ah ah*
> *Vanessa*
> *Ah ah if only you were mine*
> *Vanessa*

.   .   .

I need to get a closer look. I scoot down the left-hand side of the room, squeezing through the crowd. People object at first. But for some reason, perhaps one look at my determined expression and gritted teeth, they let me through.

> *A thousand miles to hell and back*
> *Drive me wherever's your pleasure*
> *And when you're missing home, my love*
> *Remind me always to treasure*
> *Home is here with you by my side*
> *I'm gunning to ride*
> *my sweet kookie van, oh oh oh Vanessa*
> *Gonna follow you forever*
>
> *Ah ah ah*
> *My Vanessa*
> *As long as I'm with you, I'm home.*

The closer to the front I get, the more I'm jostled. I try not to think about the fact I'm getting squashed and will possibly implode at any moment.

> *A thousand miles later and there's no looking back*
> *I've lost my heart to the drive of my life, yeah*
> *When it's rough and I'm still not enough*
> *Give me strife, but oh, my life*
> *Stay with me*
> *Vanessa*
> *Ah ah ah*

"Ah, ah ahhh!" I'm struggling to breathe.

> *I won't fall in love, I'd sooner dive right in*
> *Into love with you my driver,*
> *You're the queen of the road*
> *My home, my abode*
> *You make me feel alive, yeah*
> *Take me in, take my soul, take me lost, part or whole*
> *You'll always be my*
> *Vanessa*

I'm crushed up against the metal barrier of the mosh pit. Guy's only a few feet away, but *still* he doesn't look at me.

"Guy!"

> *You're my queen of the road*
> *Forever queen in my heart*

"Guy!" I scream again and again until I'm hoarse. Unfortunately, I'm not the only woman screaming.

> *If only you were mine*
> *Ah ah ah*
> *Less is more with Vanessa*

"Guy!" I yell with the last of my breath.

> *Stay with me*
> *Ah ah ah*
> *Less is most*
> *To Vanessa*

Finally, he turns in my direction . . .

> *Drive me insane*
> *I'll still be your man*
> *Ah ah ah . . .*

"Alice?"

Unable to hold his gaze, I feel shrink-wrapped, struggling for air. Guy's face and the stage are lost in a churning sea of arms and legs and black waves until blissfully it all ceases.

When I'm finally washed up ashore, I am literally flying through the air on my back, looking up at the rafters of an old building.

Am I dead? Is this my soul floating to heaven? Although it seems to be drifting sideways rather than upward. And am I being manhandled? What the hell is going on?

Noise rushes in. There's suddenly an ocean of people on every side, a cacophony around me and incandescent lights overhead. My stomach swoops as I drop. Expecting to hit concrete, instead I'm caught in somebody's arms.

A burly security guard carries me away from the chaos. In a quiet back room, he lays me down on a couch.

"How're you feeling?" he asks, wiping his brow.

Embarrassed. Disappointed. Frustrated. And my head is spinning.

I struggle to sit up. "I'm . . . I'm . . ."

"You'd best stay put," says the man. "Here, drink this." He hands me a plastic cup of water.

"Ta." I gulp thirstily.

I'm in a waiting room of sorts: photos of bands and singers on the wall. Empty beer cans on the table. Jackets flung over the back of chairs. Oh God. A *green* room. "Did I faint?"

The man chuckles. "Aye, lass, you did. You temporarily brought the whole show to a standstill. The lads were very concerned."

"Oh, I'm fine now, cheers. It was just the noise and heat and whatnot. I'm not used to it." Well, this couldn't be more awkward. I take another slurp of water. "I think I should probably make myself scarce."

He folds his arms. "What? No. You should stay here. Don't you want to meet the band?"

"I . . . uh . . . I already met them."

His eyes narrow. "You're that lass in the video, aren't you? The one they used to sing with. The opera girl."

The opera girl? Now, I want to crawl under the couch. "No, that was my twin," I say. "Honestly, I should probably get going."

I get to my feet, trying to ignore the fact that the room shifts with me, sliding off-kilter, fading to black.

I put out an arm and grab hold of the nearest thing. The man. Or at least I think it's the man until a voice in my ear says, "I got you."

I'm laid on the couch again. My eyes flutter open and the world slowly comes back into focus. Is it really him? Guy? "Guy?" I sit up.

Oh dear God. He's not smiling, and I've interrupted his gig. "I'm so sorry," I croak. "You shouldn't be here."

"*I* shouldn't be here? RiffRaff is the main event tonight this evening," says Guy, a smile tilting his lips.

Oh heavens, he's *my* main event.

The bouncer seems to have evaporated and I kind of wish I could do the same because all of sudden, I don't know what to say. "I meant you should be up on stage."

"So should you," he says, quietly. Setting one knee on the couch beside me, he cups my face in both hands, so I have no choice but to look at him.

"I'm glad your hand is fixed," I mumble.

He smiles. "So am I. First time I've had both hands on you, Kook. You got my ticket?"

I nod.

"Corny, but . . ." He frowns. "Have you come here to wreak more havoc on me or what?"

"No," I rasp. "I never meant to cause any problems. I never meant what I said at the wedding—"

"Because I don't mind if you do, so long as you stay."

I think my heart misses a beat or two. Am I hearing things correctly?

"Stay here and rest. We can talk after the show. I, er, really should get back for now."

"Yes! That's what I was trying to say. What are you even doing back here?"

He leans forward and kisses me. It is such a simple kiss. A soft kiss. A no-demands kiss. And sufficient for me to feel faint again. "This. I have my priorities . . . and I couldn't wait. Don't. Go. Anywhere."

I don't think I'm capable.

"Promise me." He kisses my forehead and I close my eyes. I'm in heaven.

"Alice?"

"I'm not going anywhere," I say. Not without him. "Promise."

45

GUY

Attempting to walk in a straight line when adrenaline and alcohol blast around my system is damn near impossible. I'm high, not so much because of the gig, but because Alice actually came. She's here! After the way I spoke to her at my brother's wedding, and she ghosted me, I never thought I would see her again. I don't deserve her. And seeing her again confirms everything.

I.

Love.

Alice.

Havoc.

My heart is in Havoc.

My cravings are real.

The sight of her bright-eyed happiness and somewhat bewildered expression makes me want to bundle her into my arms and ravish her with kisses. I am disgustingly, undeniably, dopily strung up on love.

I bite my lip just to stop the confession spilling from my lips. Containing all these pent-up thoughts and feelings is torture, bloody torture, but I'm also terrified of scaring her off. She refused the offer of a cab back to the hotel the band is staying in, so I asked if she wanted to go for a walk.

And we are walking. And it's bloody Arctic.

At the moment, we are headed up a cobbled street called the Shambles (appropriate considering how I'm feeling) toward York Minster, which is all lit up like me on the inside—lit up and full of hope. The scene brings back all the best memories of New Year's Eve: the gun-smoke smell of fireworks; Alice by my side; the anticipation of everything to come. *Only this time, please God, don't let me fuck it up by calling her the wrong name.*

But I need to explain about Tina. I don't want any secrets between us.

"Alice, I need to tell you about Tina O' Sullivan."

She stops walking. "Do we seriously have to go there? I'd rather not know."

I grab her hand. "You need to hear this. I'll keep it brief because I fucking hate talking about it as well."

She scrunches up her face.

"Before he died, my dad was having an affair with Tina. I caught them at it. A couple of days later, I had this blazing row with Dad and he . . ." Oh God, it kills me facing up to the reality of what I did. The grief I caused my family. "He had a massive heart attack. I'm the cause of my father's death."

"No!" Alice shakes her head. She takes my face between her hands. "No, that's not true. You can't possibly blame yourself for that."

Dammit, I have tears in my eyes. "I do. I threatened to tell Mum about him and Tina and he . . . he collapsed."

"Oh, Guy. That's not your fault." She wraps her arms around me and rests her head on my chest.

"At the wedding, I tried to talk to Tina about what she'd done and she . . . she even fucking tried it on with me!" Shaking my head to try to dispel the image, I unlock Alice's arms and step away.

"But that's terrible! You shouldn't have had to deal with all that yourself. I wish I'd known." Alice looks upset.

"It's still no excuse for all the shitty, miserable untrue things I said to you at the wedding, but I was screwed up. After your song, I thought you were flirting with Marcus and I saw red . . ." I shake my head, and try to get a handle on my breathing.

"I saw you and Tina too," says Alice. "I'm so sorry. I jumped to conclusions and presumed the worst. I thought you were using me as a decoy, and you and Tina were . . ."

A choked gasp escapes me. "You seriously thought I could ever get involved with that woman? I despise her. She's the reason I haven't let anyone get close to me in years. She's the reason I never visit my family because she's always hanging around. And now her daughter has married my brother!"

Alice folds her arms around her middle.

Fuck. This is not how our conversation is meant to go. This feels like my last chance to straighten this out, but the words are coming out all wrong. I sound angry. I am angry. But not with Alice. I don't want to go back to Australia without her. I hate that she has zero faith in me. Yet.

I stuff my beanie back on my head and shove my hands deep in my pockets, feeling numb. Fuck, I would quite like to slither between the cracks in the cobblestones. I am determined to make this right, but I guess warts and all is not such an attractive proposition.

"I'm so sorry I sang that song for Twister and blurted out everything about Tina at the wedding," says Alice.

"Yeah, that sucked, but—"

"You had every reason to be angry. You must hate me too. For the IT game. For everything I got so wrong."

I don't deny it.

A whimper escapes her, and before I know it, she's walking away.

"Alice, wait!" I shout, but she starts running.

God, dammit!

I chase after her, catch her and swing her around. Tears are streaming down her cheeks. I kiss them. "I don't hate you. God, I could never hate you. Stop crying. You'll freeze your eyelashes together."

A muffled laugh.

I take her hands and gently pull them away from her face. "Hey, you weren't the only one that got things wrong. I did too. Perhaps that means we're made for one another."

A sob escapes her. "No, you were perfect." Tears well in her eyes.

"Perfect? Making you my slave?"

"I misjudged you. I was meant to be there to help you, but I—"

I press a finger to her lips. "I don't care about any of that. I *believe* it's possible for us to start again. I believe in us." For a moment she resists, but then she's kissing me with a ferocity that's impossible to misinterpret.

The minster bells start ringing and I swear to God, it starts softly snowing. A smile curves my lips as I deepen my kiss. Oh, sweet heaven. This is bliss. The sweet taste of her. I'm ready to take her into York Minster and marry her right now . . .

"So, Alice," I say, going down on one knee. "I have a serious question to ask."

She looks startled. There is a halo of light behind her and for a split second, I'm worried she really might be an angel, until she says,

"Please don't ask me to marry you. My parents would die if they thought both their daughters were getting married this year."

I laugh. She is too perfect for words, but perhaps now isn't the best moment to ask her to marry me, although it was on the tip of my tongue. It can wait. I don't want to scare her off when I've only just got back to her again.

I scratch my neck. "Not quite, but I do have another proposal for you. How would you feel about . . . and you can say no . . . there's absolutely no pressure . . . but—"

"I would love to come on tour with you and the band!" she gushes.

Told you. She is perfection. Alice is the steeple on the tallest building. The light in the dark. The oasis in a desert.

"I have one major problem though, Guy," she says.

Oh fuck. There's that steely glint in her eyes she sometimes gets.

"You," she says.

I swallow. "Me?"

"Yup, you and your unofficial band rules." She grabs me by the lapels of my jacket and tugs me to my feet.

The heat in her eyes. The love in my bones. I would burn any rule book for her. "What rules are we talking about?" I rasp.

She stands on tiptoes and I have to bend my knees so we are eye to eye. "The one which unofficially states members of the band are not allowed to have relations with one another."

I smile. And I think my chest just expanded a foot. "You'd better not be hitting on Brum, Fin or Scooter any time soon."

She laughs. "I have no idea why I missed you so much," she murmurs.

"Fuck, Alice. I've missed you more than my hand." I squint. She laughs. "Fuck. That sounded all wrong, but, put it this way, Kook, I missed you so much it drove me crazy. I even bought a van."

Her eyes go wide. "You bought a van?"

I shrug. "Yeah, do you want to see her?"

"Do I!"

"You probably won't like her. She's kind of small. Not at all reliable. Probably refuse even to shift in this weather. But I had a bit of a crush on her. Brought her over from Australia in fact." We round the corner.

Alice squeals. "Shut! Up! You bought your brother's van?!"

I nod. "Xanthe found her too quirky and unpredictable, but that's exactly what I love about her."

Grabbing my lapels, she pulls me in for the kiss of all kisses. I am drunk on snowflakes and moonshine and Alice's lips.

"I think I like you," she whispers into my mouth.

I groan. Fuck, I love this woman. More than any van. "Only *like*?" I grumble.

She presses her lips together in a way that makes me want to tease them open. "Give me time, Guy Balcombe," she says, "and I could come to like you a fair bit . . . if you play your cards right."

"What about chess? I prefer my chances. And you still owe me a game." I grin.

"Only if you let me beat you," she says, racing toward Vanessa.

My smirk morphs into a filthy grin as I catch her, wrap my arms around her and press her against the van. Our breath mingles in a cloud of longing. "You can do whatever the hell you want with me, Alice Havoc," I say. "I am at your disposal. Your slave for life."

"First things first, then," she says, grinning cheekily. "Get in the bloody van!"

THE END

Want to read an epilogue? Want to read Twister's story in France? It's coming soon, but subscribe to Anna's Foxtrot newsletter to get extra excerpts and be the first to hear her news.

Find her links in the 'About the Author' section.

Have you read the prequel, Alice in Wanderlust?

GLOSSARY

One of my early readers requested a glossary to help explain some of the French words and the vernacular of Northern English that I've used in this story. If they're unfamiliar to you too, hopefully these will help you to navigate your way!

<u>Northern British English</u>

Aye — yes

Butty (most often a chip butty) — sandwich

Ey, up — hold on.

Bleeding' heck! — see above

Champion and *magic* — similar to saying brilliant/fantastic

Chuffin' hell -—mild Northern expletive like damned hell

Luv and *duck* - love, dear (expression of endearment)

Mum — Mom

Muggins — an idiot

Nowt — nothing

Wazzock — a stupid or annoying person or both!

<u>French</u>

Ça suffit — That's enough.

If you find any more expressions that I've unwittingly slipped into the story that you'd like explained, please feel free to email me: annafoxkirk@gmail.com

ACKNOWLEDGMENTS

Reader warning—there will be a lot of shameless exclamation marks in this section!!!

First of all, I'd like to acknowledge my writing friends, especially my Writers' Clink and the Saturday Ladies Bridge Club. You ladies all do an amazing job, picking me up when I'm down and keeping me sane when I'm losing my head. I love and appreciate you all! I'm also a member of the fabulous Romance Writers Australia—what a brilliant group of mostly women and what a great font of knowledge! The best decision I ever made was joining this group.

A big shout out to my anonymous beta readers in America for their early feedback on Alice and the Impossible Game, but especial thanks to my incredible writing buddies, Heidi Catherine and Danielle Blythe, without whom I'd be in a whole world of pain! You two are my pillars and I cannot thank you enough for helping to shape this book. Late to the scene, but oh-so appreciated, I also want to mention the eagle-eyed and gymtastic (no that's not a spelling error) multi-tasking editor, Helen Jones Hazlewood, for her essential help with copy and line edits. You're a star. Thank you for stepping in at the eleventh hour. I'm so grateful to know you've got my back . . . and also that you're not reading this section and correcting its proliferation of !!!!!!!!!!!

A massive thank you to my readers and foxtrotting fans! You're the bee's knees and the dog's bollocks (that's a term of endearment not an insult, in case you were wondering)! Please continue to spread the word and let everyone know if you enjoy my books!

Last but not least, I would be amiss not to shout about my fabulous Babs friends! You know who you are. You lot literally keep me afloat! I've never felt so buoyed and well-supported. Thanks for your encouragement and for listening to me bang on about my book ideas! I'm truly grateful.

And finally, a massive thank you and *I love you* to my husband, kids and family. You may not always be the most avid of readers, but if these books get any spicier, that's probably no bad thing! Please bear in mind, this writing malarkey is all a figment of my imagination — you are the real deal!

ABOUT THE AUTHOR

Anna Foxkirk is an award-winning author of romcom, fantasy and historical fiction. Her first novella, *Alice in Wanderlust*, was published in November 2020, and in the same year she was voted Favorite Debut Romance Author of 2020 by the Australian Romance Readers Association.

The best way to hear her latest news is through her Foxtrot newsletter where she shares not only what she's up to, but also other author interviews and some exciting giveaways.

Join Anna here: https://annafoxkirk.substack.com

If you'd like to check out her website, here's that link:

https://www.annafoxkirk.com

You'll also find Anna on Instagram:

https://www.instagram.com/annafoxkirk/

And Facebook:

https://www.facebook.com/anna.foxkirk.10/

And last, but not least, TikTok:

https://www.tiktok.com/@annafoxkirk

A final note from Anna...

Dear reader,

REVIEWS make a world of difference!

I really hope you enjoyed *Alice and the Impossible Game*. If you did and would like to make my 'happy ever after', please leave me a short review or a star rating wherever you are able. It doesn't need to be long, but your feedback is invaluable to me as an author and helps other readers find my fiction. Please spread the word!

Before you go, let me wish you all the very best for the year ahead. I hope you read what you love and love what you read!

Warm wishes,

Anna